NO SIN UNPUNISHED

A FAITH MCCLELLAN NOVEL

LYNDEE WALKER

SEVERN RIVER PUBLISHING

Severn River Publishing
www.SevernRiverBooks.com

ISBN: 978-1-64875-465-4 (Paperback)

ALSO BY LYNDEE WALKER

The Faith McClellan Series

Fear No Truth

Leave No Stone

No Sin Unpunished

Nowhere to Hide

No Love Lost

Tell No Lies

The Nichelle Clarke Series

Front Page Fatality

Buried Leads

Small Town Spin

Devil in the Deadline

Cover Shot

Lethal Lifestyles

Deadly Politics

Hidden Victims

To find out more about LynDee Walker and her books, visit

severnriverbooks.com/authors/lyndee-walker

For Chris: the best third musketeer, friend, and brother-in-law, I could've ever wished for, with more thanks than I have words to express for your wit, advice, and encouragement—plus eternal gratitude for hitting a marriage home run of your own and giving me a new sister I truly adore.

"Though hand join in hand, the wicked shall not be unpunished: but the seed of the righteous shall be delivered."

—Proverbs 11:21

PROLOGUE

Fire is nature's most perfect monster. It hunts. It devours. It terrifies.

It cleanses. It reveals.

And it can be controlled by those who understand it.

Scooping a final, careful shovel of goo into the last tank, he screwed the lid into place and tightened it with the vise.

The sharp scent permeated everything in the room, enough to curl a person's nose hairs if they weren't used to it.

Foam sheets stacked neatly in one corner. Glass and steel chemical containers sat squat in three piles a few feet away. An industrial cake mixer stood nearly as tall as he did next to the workbench. He'd built a good workshop. Then he'd built a good product.

He glanced at the TV screen.

"This Greek warrior led the Myrmidons against the Trojans," Alex Trebek read as the text appeared on-screen.

"Who was Achilles?" He flipped to the local news and weather.

Months of planning, maneuvering, and rearranging had gone into this moment, and the gods blessed him.

He raised the nozzle over the cast iron sink and squeezed lightly, a smile playing at the corners of his lips when a perfect fan sprayed from the end, flames springing to life on contact with the metal.

Snatching a smaller canister from the counter, he smothered his experiment with thick white foam.

Hoses: Working. Suits: Check. Tanks: Full.

The weather radar from the local news station flashed across the TV screen. Bands of green, red, and yellow blanketed the outlined counties of the Hill Country where a storm stalled overhead.

The alarm on his phone beeped.

He pulled on one shiny suit, then another. Settled fat headphones over his ears.

Clicked an app on his screen and waited for the blue dot to appear.

The locator spun for two full minutes; tiny beads of sweat popped on his forehead.

No. No no no.

All the planning would be for shit if this piece didn't work.

There. It flashed up. Bobbed around. Moved in a small circle.

He counted to sixty, blotting his forehead with a crisp linen handkerchief, before he gathered his tools.

Every last thing was in place.

Go time.

1

―――――――

"Tell me again who I'm supposed to be?" Graham Hardin kept his eyes on the road and both hands on the wheel, holding my truck steady against strong southern winds. The storm kicked up around us. Lightning split the dark horizon from the low clouds to the ground as he veered right onto the exit ramp for Central.

"You're the muscle." I checked my tight bun and black-rimmed rectangular glasses again in the mirror, then poked the bicep bulging out of his tight, short-sleeved polo. "You just flex and look intimidating."

"And you're the brains. It's not even a lie when you get right down to it. Easiest undercover ever."

"We both bring equal parts kick-ass and brilliance to this deal." I closed the mirror and flipped the visor up. "But they're expecting a hacker and her bodyguard."

"I could do private security someday," he mused. "No uniforms. Better hours. Nice hotels."

"Have fun." I rolled my eyes back far enough to see my hairline. "Given a choice between the kind of people who generally need hired guns and your average murderer, I'll stick with my criminal brand of crazy, thanks."

"Point taken."

"It's been fun working with you on this," I said. "Shall we lay a trap?"

The truck rolled to a stop at a light as thunder rumbled to our east.

"We do have good bait. Though it's going to suck when you have to go back to your world during the day." His hand closed over mine. "Thanks for your help. We wouldn't be here without you."

"Bonus: no corpses," I said. "I can't even remember the last time I went such a long stretch without working a homicide. The lack of dead people is a welcome difference."

I returned the pressure Graham put on my fingers. Four months in, it still made my arm tingle all the way to my elbow when he held my hand. And thanks to Jimmy Sewell's preference for dealing with women, this credit card fraud case had given us eight weeks of working long hours together every day, yet we weren't tired of each other.

It was nice.

I watched the lightning flash, still a few miles off. "Let's get done and get out before that gets here?"

Graham parked in a deserted dirt and gravel lot. "Ten-four. The weather guy said something about hail. In October?"

"Texas thunderstorms don't play by the rules." I gave his hand a last squeeze before I hopped out of the truck and reached behind the seat for a black briefcase I'd carefully packed with ten thousand blank credit cards.

A guy like Jimmy Sewell didn't travel without heavily armed security detail. He had to think he had the upper hand when we walked in, so Graham and I came alone to this quiet, industrial pocket of the North Austin suburbs. A support team of Travis County deputies, plus the Rangers' bank fraud lieutenant and two of our tactical officers, camped with vehicles and weapons in another warehouse three blocks away.

I touched the tiny bone-conduction speaker behind my left ear, glued in place and tucked under my hair. On cue, I heard Manny Gonzalez's deep baritone, ringing through to my cochlear nerve. "You're good to go, McClellan. We've got you on the GPS and the infrared. We'll hear if you need help."

Warm wind gusted ahead of another lightning strike. I stepped in front of Graham and crossed quickly to the door, small tendrils of my hair escaping the bun and tickling my face.

Graham wrestled the heavy steel door open against the wind and held it for me.

The space was cavernous, a single bare bulb lighting it from ten feet over our heads. A smooth concrete floor sent every click of my gray pumps reverberating off the tall metal walls.

"Miss Richardson." The voice echoed flat and cold, almost like the words came from a computer. But what Sewell lacked in social skills, he made up for in sheer brainpower. The dossier we'd compiled on this guy after weeks of weeding through layers of snitches and low-level numbers runners would have stunned the admissions board at any Ivy League university. Perfect scores on every standardized test known by an acronym. An IQ of 165. But Jimmy didn't want to go to college. He didn't people well and had little interest in anything but making money. During the past sixteen months, he'd amassed just shy of twenty million dollars through half a dozen different forms of bank fraud, from old-fashioned check forgery to sophisticated computer hacks. Now he wanted access to credit cards—but faking them is a specialized skill set, so he needed help.

"Mr. Sewell." I answered in the general direction of the shadows. "Thank you for agreeing to be here. I'm glad you understand that with a transaction so large, I wasn't comfortable dealing online."

I stepped to the edge of the bright circle directly under the light, my eyes scanning for Sewell. Five-eight, a hundred and thirty pounds, and a fan of skinny jeans, oversized hoodies, and Gucci sneakers—it wouldn't be hard for him to blend into the darkness.

Feet shuffled. My eyes went to the other side of the circle.

A mountain of muscle encased in denim and black leather emerged from the shadows to stand at attention three feet from me. Sewell's body man had to be six-five, his thighs as big around as my waist, the lines of the quadriceps visible through his leather pants.

The cool metal of my Sig pressing into the small of my back reassured me enough to curve my lips up into a cool half-smile.

"You're not Mr. Sewell," I quipped.

Muscles shook his head, just twice. Extended one arm, hand open for the case I held in front of me.

I swung my arm, shifting it behind my knees. "Mr. Sewell."

"I'm not sure I've ever been so sought after. Not by anyone who lacks a badge, anyway."

He was farther away than I thought, the light glinting off the gleaming gold tips of his tennis shoes before I could see his face.

Well. Half his face. The top was obscured by oversized Ray-Ban Aviators I could only see myself in.

I felt the air move as Graham stepped closer to my back.

"Who's your friend?" Sewell's voice grew high and tight.

"Just an associate who will make sure I walk back out of here with no extra holes." I tipped my head toward Muscles's Glock 9mm. "Same idea, I imagine."

Sewell folded skinny arms hidden in miles of cotton sweatshirt. "So let's see them."

Without a table or chair in sight, I knelt and laid the case on the floor, keeping one hand on the handle as I clicked the locks open.

Muscles stepped forward, eyeing Graham. Sewell rummaged through a stack in the center of the case and grabbed a blue card from somewhere near the bottom. He reached for his back pocket. My free hand went behind me when his did, and I knew without looking that Graham's was on his sidearm.

Sewell produced a cell phone with a credit card reader sticking out of it.

I blew a slow breath out through my nose.

"Quality control." His long, thin fingers jabbed the card into the port sticking out of the phone.

I watched the screen. It would work. He thought they were counterfeit, of course. But when I'd managed to land a face-to-face with the brains behind the fastest-growing fraud operation in the southwest, the three biggest banks in Texas agreed to provide me with the cards and dummy accounts we needed to lay a trap.

Sewell was a big fish.

I'd baited my hook carefully over the course of several weeks.

Time to start cranking the reel.

A green checkmark flashed on Sewell's screen as the first sheets of rain pounded the metal roof over our heads.

The smile his lips stretched into when he raised his head made the hairs on my arm spring to attention. It looked unnatural. I had to concentrate to keep myself from grimacing in return.

I snapped the case closed and stood.

His eyes raked from my windblown hair to my sensible pumps. "You're smart. And you're not, like, old."

He was still more than a year from buying a legal drink, so that was supposed to be a compliment. "Age has nothing to do with ability," I replied.

"Exactly. How'd you get into the business?" He turned the card in his hand over, holding it up to the light. "These are good. Like, really good."

"I heard you only deal with the best. I came to impress." I kept one hand on the case and stuck out the other. "Are we in business together?"

He started to stretch his hand out, then pulled it back, his eyes going to Graham. "You didn't answer my question."

I held his gaze. Archie always said my shitty lying ability was a curse in this job. I wasn't sure I'd ever had quite this kind of test, but here went nothing. "I worked for a bank."

Graham's hand landed on the small of my back where Sewell and his goon couldn't see it. I didn't hear a trace of tremor in my voice–the words came out even and easy. Almost nonchalant. Thank God. We'd practiced them enough in the past week.

"In the card printing division and then in accounts receivable," I continued. "I paid attention."

"Me too. I worked in a bank part-time. In high school." There went the smile again. Shudder. "No better way to learn the lay of the land than from the inside. Greedy motherfuckers, bankers. It didn't take me long to decide it was their turn to feel some of the pain they put other people through."

I nodded along as he spoke, keeping my eyes on my reflection in the shades so I didn't have to look at the smile. "Not like they should miss it," I said.

He pulled the sunglasses down to cover the middle of his face, pale eyes blinking as the pupils shrank even in the dim light. "I'm never wrong about people, Miss Richardson," he said. "Kind of fucked up when you think about it, because for the most part, I don't like people. But I get how they tick. And we're going to get along well, you and me."

His eyes flicked to Graham before he settled the sunglasses back in place. "She has nothing to fear here, my man."

Muscles relaxed his pose and took a step back without Sewell even looking his way.

"So we're in business then?"

Sewell raised the phone and touched the screen a few times. "You're paid in full."

I pulled out the burner Droid I'd been using to talk to him and opened an app. Yep. One million dollars, transferred in bits of data in less than a blink.

"It's been a pleasure." I put my hand out and stared into the sunglasses.

Sewell's palm was cold but damp. "I will be in touch." He picked up the case and turned for the door.

"That's an ambitious start for a new enterprise," I said. "You have plans for them already, I assume?"

Sewell's Gucci sneaker stopped in midair, his head swiveling to me. "Looking to cut around me?"

Shit. No, I just wanted him on the recording saying he was going to sell them. But I got greedy and now I needed to talk my way out of it.

Muscles turned back and brought his tree trunk arms up to fold over his chest. Graham positioned himself between me and them.

I raised both hands. "Not even a little bit," I said. "Just making conversation. My curiosity gets the best of me now and then, and yours is the biggest order I've ever had. Just wondering if my little cards are part of something big."

I didn't even process the words before they rolled off my tongue, but Sewell's smoothing brow above the coppery rims of his shades said he bought every one.

"I don't do small, Miss Richardson." He resumed his stride. "I'll be in touch."

We lagged and let them leave before we did, Graham and I both tense and silent until we got back to the truck and several blocks away.

We couldn't go to the mobile command center because if we were being followed, we'd get people—maybe ourselves—killed. Couldn't go home for the same reason.

Graham wove through Austin's never-ending rush hour traffic, expertly jumping off and on 35, rain pelting the windshield in sheets so thick it was hard to see more than the tail lights in front of us unless we were coasting under a bridge. Thunder rumbled. I reached for the temperature controls and cranked the knob to the red zone to stop my shivering. "He took the bait."

Graham kept both hands on the wheel and both eyes on the road. "Nice work, McClellan."

"Nice work yourself, there, Hardin. So. Now we wait. Food?"

"Exactly what I was thinking."

I pulled my phone out and checked the signal as we slid into the right lane between a farm truck and a Tesla. Not that I expected the hits to start coming in tonight. Surely it would take Sewell a hot minute to disburse that many cards. But after weeks of working this case, studying his ever-growing criminal machine, I was itching to see what the hell he was up to here.

Graham held the wheel steady when the truck hydroplaned onto the exit ramp. I didn't even flinch. Graham was a smart man, a great driver, and a meticulous cop. When I was with him, I felt the safest I had in decades.

He stopped at a little postwar ranch house long ago converted to a Tex-Mex mecca, and before I'd settled into the just-distressed-enough, brown leather booth bench in the corner opposite the door, he'd ordered my margarita—on the rocks, not frozen, because October—not because he needed to be macho, but because he knew me. I always order the same drink depending on the time of year, and things between us had gotten just that easy. It was the double Jack and Coke he requested for himself instead of his usual Corona with lime that sent my left eyebrow up.

"You okay?"

He sat down across from me and mumbled a thank you to the server who put chips and salsa between us on the table. "I am more okay than I've been in a long time. You know, when you left the SO to move to the DPS, it put me in a bigger funk than I could even admit to myself for a long time. These last six months have given me my game back, Faith. We are such an incredible team, me and you—"

He stopped talking when the server returned, setting our drinks on the table before she pulled out a pad and pen. "Do y'all know what you want to eat yet?"

Graham's chin dropped to his chest, a short breath huffing out. I opened my menu with my free hand. "Maybe just a couple of minutes?"

She disappeared. Graham downed half his drink.

What the hell?

I caught his eyes as he put the glass back on the table. "What's up?"

I had to concentrate to hear his words and not Archie's. My oldest friend, mentor, father figure—Archie Baxter held a lot of titles and did a lot of things, and being damned good at reading people just about topped the list. Three days ago, he'd turned to me at a stoplight on the way to the bank to pick up the cards and drummed his fingers on the steering wheel. "Hardin's going to propose, Faith. Do you know what you're going to say?"

When I could make my vocal cords work, I'd laughed. Graham Hardin wasn't looking to get married. We'd only been together for a few months. It was crazy.

I'd have been a thousand percent sure of that if the idea had come out of anyone but Archie.

"You love him. I can see it. You don't want to hurt him. So you need to have an answer ready. That's not the kind of moment you can take to pause and consider all the ramifications. A quick answer is vital."

The light changed, Archie put his foot on the gas, and neither of us said another word about it. I'd done my best to forget the whole idea.

Marriage.

Jesus. What a big, sticky mess that would be.

We were happy. I wanted with everything in me for both of us to stay that way.

But now Graham was sitting here gulping whiskey and talking about what a great team we were, and I could feel heat rising in my cheeks as my heart rate picked up.

He couldn't ask me that.

"You like the fajitas here, right?" I spit the words a little too fast. "I wonder if they'll do the combo with steak and veggies on separate plates?"

"Sure, that sounds great. You can have all my rice, too." He let go of my hand and scooped salsa onto a chip.

The rest of his drink and half the chips later, he hadn't spoken again and I was officially out of random things to blurt out for him to nod at.

I've never been happier to see a plate of food in my life.

Watching him pick at what I knew was just about his favorite dish, I sighed. "Graham, listen," I began. "I don't—"

My phone bleated.

He leaned forward in his seat reflexively.

"Surely not." I pulled it out. "I'll be damned."

"Already?" Graham stood and slid into the booth next to me.

"No rest for the wicked, I guess?"

"We're the good guys, baby."

My lips tipped up at the slip the same way they always did. When we were at work he was careful to avoid endearments, but he'd tossed that one out a few times in the past few weeks and I liked hearing it. It was a little weird, maybe, finding our footing in an intimate setting and marking the lines between work and home, but I thought we'd done a good job of it.

I just didn't want Graham thinking we were somewhere we weren't. And the case was like a distraction sent straight from the heavens. I touched the gold star on my sister's charm bracelet, never far from my wrist, and whispered a thank you.

I clicked the app the cyber guys had put on my phone. One card, swiped seventy minutes ago for a dollar, and again just now for a little more than three hundred.

I clicked the transaction history.

PBJM Inc.

PO Box address.

"It's Sewell, but what's he up to?" I tapped one fingernail on the edge of the screen.

Graham tried to scroll past the bottom of the address.

"There's nothing else there," I said.

He pulled his phone out and touched the screen a few times before he reached for mine.

"He's got to be playing around with it," I said. "You don't think he suspected anything was off?"

My impulsive question at the end of the transaction replayed in my head on a fast forward loop.

"This is an LLC registered to an address in Goliad County that appears to be in a...trailer park." Graham put his phone down and met my raised eyebrows with a pair of his own.

"I'm telling you, it's a test. Twenty bucks says he's got goons watching this for so much as a drive-by from a patrol car. He's a smart kid. And I shouldn't have tested my limits asking what he was planning to do with the cards."

"We're smarter." Graham touched the screen again, putting the phone to his ear. "And you were pretty fucking amazing in there. That steroid factory he had with him was easily three times your size, and I believe with everything in me that if the situation had called for it, you'd have taken him in a fight."

I patted his hand as he sat up straighter and pinched the phone between his head and shoulder. "Hey man, it's Hardin in Travis County," he said. "Good, good, how are things there? I hear that."

I listened to his end of the conversation while I watched my phone for another transaction. A guy like Sewell didn't get where he was, especially at his age, by being stupid or reckless. Nobody's luck is that good.

"Listen, we're working on something big here, and I have an address in your backyard tied to it. I'm not sure right now what this guy is up to, but I need any and all police activity in this area vacated for the rest of tonight and tomorrow. I'll owe you, man."

Graham reeled off the address.

"Thanks, man. Let me know what I can do for you." He hung up. "There. Nothing to see here, Mr. Sewell." Graham flashed a bright white smile.

I leaned in and kissed him. I just meant for it to be a quick peck of thanks, but his arms went around me and pulled me close, and it took less than thirty seconds for us to forget Sewell and Graham's friend in Goliad County and our food.

Losing my thoughts in Graham's kisses was fast becoming a favorite pastime.

It might have been three minutes or three hours by the time we disentangled ourselves and he returned to his side of the table, picking up a fork and building a fajita.

"Quick thinking, Hardin," I said.

"Like I said, we make a good team." He said it so softly I wasn't entirely sure I heard him right. And either way, it made me sad, Archie's prediction ringing in my ears.

When we had paid the check and stood to leave, I stuck my phone back in my pocket and reached for the keys, eyeing the melting ice cubes in the two tall glasses on his side of the table.

"I'm okay," he said.

"I know you are. I also know I'm driving. Let's go, cowboy, it's getting late."

The place had emptied out. Two tables and one guy hunched over the bar were the only people besides us not cleaning up for the night.

Graham followed me into the car without a single grumble, and I had the engine running before he twisted in his seat and grabbed one of my hands between both of his, his face serious.

"Faith, there's something I need—" The last word stuck in his throat, his gray-green eyes going wide as they fixed on something behind me. I turned.

I saw it too, but I didn't believe it. I clambered out of the truck, unable to tell if the cold water pouring from angry clouds or the scene in front of me was to blame for the goosebumps racing up my arms.

"What the fuck?"

I fumbled for my phone. "Texas DPS Ranger Faith McClellan requesting all nearby units and AFD to Cabrerra's off 35 at Clay Street," I barked.

"I'm sorry, did you say AFD?" The dispatcher didn't believe it either.

But my eyes hadn't moved from the climbing wall of orange-red flames.

"Every available ladder and engine they have." I kept my voice steady. "They'll be able to see the fire from the restaurant parking lot."

Graham's hand closed on my shoulder. "But it's raining," he said. "It's been raining for hours."

2

I started running before I ended the call, Graham keeping stride like he hadn't swallowed a drop of whiskey.

The pounding rain stung my face with every step, water sluicing over my already-drenched hair. I made it to the front edge of the cracked concrete sidewalk before the heat stopped me. Almost like a force field, the air felt thicker and way, way too hot. Graham hooked an elbow under my shoulder and held on. I shook my head and shouted, "I'm not going any closer," but his grip didn't relax. Mine wouldn't either if I had the scars covering most of his shoulders and back and the memories of the recovery that went along with them.

"Do you want to go back to the truck?" I asked the question without turning around.

"I'm good here unless it moves this way. But thanks."

The siding was green, the clapboard weathered by half a century of sun and rain. The water poured, but the flames coming through the roof didn't seem to notice, climbing skyward from the front left and rear right corners of the building.

"How is it burning in this weather? Lightning strike?"

Graham pulled me closer, folding his thick arms around my shoulders. "I don't think lightning works differently than any normal fire."

A strong gust pushed the heat wall close enough to produce beads of sweat on my forehead. Graham stepped backward, pulling me with him.

"What's that smell?" I asked.

"Gasoline?" Graham flinched when he said it.

"Not quite." I wrinkled my nose, trying to get another whiff, but the wind had died down and there was zero chance he would let me even a half step closer.

"Burning paint?"

"Or asbestos?" Graham's arms tightened around my shoulders. "AFD is on their way." As the words left his lips, the first sirens reached my ears. And they were gaining fast.

I leaned back into the solid wall of his chest, his heart hammering so hard I could feel it through my shoulder blade.

The sirens drowned out the thunder and the dull roar of the fire, stopping behind us. A tall, middle-aged captain appeared at my elbow as his men fanned out around the perimeter of the burning house.

"McClellan?" His eyes rested on me. "Jerry Fox, Austin Fire."

"Nice to meet you, Captain Fox. What the hell am I seeing here?"

He straightened his helmet and turned to face the flames. "Accelerant for sure. Wet wood doesn't burn without it. What kind, I can't say for sure yet." He put his gloved hands on his hips and looked around. "The storm will save us a perimeter, at least. No matter what this is, it'll burn out eventually."

"What if someone is in there?"

"The building was abandoned ten months ago. Owner died, no will, stuck in a web of red tape," Fox explained. "No danger to life apparent—you two are welcome to head on home."

I glanced around, the goosebumps returning even this close to the heat.

"I'd like to hang out, if you don't mind." Graham's brow didn't even furrow. He was curious, too.

Fox shrugged. "You're welcome to wait in the truck." He pointed to the open door of an engine before he turned for the building and started barking orders.

Graham offered me a hand up. I took it even though I was capable of climbing up on my own. He shut the door behind him. Inside with the door shut it was quiet. Still. "How does an abandoned house catch the kind of fire that burns in the rain?" he asked.

I already had my phone in front of my face, swiping impatiently at the drops of water falling from my nose to the screen. "Working on it," I said without looking up. "But I'm going to guess the answer is with a lot of help."

Maps. Current location. 4207 Clay Street. I highlighted the address and copied it. "I'm wondering who puts this much effort into burning down an abandoned house."

"What are you looking for?"

"Something that makes what I'm seeing make sense. A vacant house, owned by the same couple from the day it was built until she died in it with no heirs last year." I talked as I scrolled through the obituary of Mrs. Thelma Lynn Brady, former owner of the inferno in front of us, on my screen. "Whoever did this must really want the place gone. Why?"

"They like to play with fire? They wanted to see if they could make it burn in the rain? Someone trying to buy the lot off the city? Who knows."

I tapped one finger on the seat. He was probably right. And at least the place was empty.

I surveyed the street. Cars, mostly older models, many with mismatched paint, sat sprinkled along the curbsides. AFD trucks turned sideways made effective traffic barricades. Light spilled from windows onto lawns and porches.

"Where are all the neighbors?" I was talking mostly to myself. "I've never seen a fire, in real life or on TV, where the neighbors didn't come outside to watch the show." A Channel Two truck rolled to a stop ten feet from us. "So why does it seem the press is the only party around here who cares?"

"It's dumping down rain," Graham offered.

"People are nosy by nature." I shook my head, flicking to the last screen on my phone. The one with the apps I'd found on the dark web. Something was off. I could feel it even if I couldn't pinpoint it. "And everyone has an umbrella."

I opened an underground locator app—sort of a yellow pages for subversive activity. Clubs and parties, criminal safe spots, U-houses where people could meet up for dope deals or prostitution: all your illegal location needs in one handy click.

I found and typed in the address, not big on giving whoever created such a directory access to my GPS, and waited.

It took three seconds for a purple pin to load over the house that was burning in front of us.

"It's a U-house." I reached for the door handle, not so sure there was nobody inside anymore.

"A...oh, damn." Graham followed me out of the truck.

The neighbors weren't outside because when the local criminal hub is suddenly burning during a raging storm on a random Thursday night, folks who didn't see anything don't have to worry so much about their home being next.

I sprinted back toward Captain Fox. Waiting for this to burn out might not be an option if we wanted any evidence left of what had happened here and why someone wanted the place destroyed. But how the hell do you stop a fire that isn't fazed by a downpour?

Every drop of rain had one of sweat to match by the time I found Fox screaming into a cell phone thirty feet from the longest intact wall of the house.

"Class B! This rain might as well be my dog pissing kerosene at these flames, so A isn't going to do a damned thing here. We have vapors we need to smother. I need as many trucks with as much Class B foam as we can get our hands on, and I need them now."

He jerked the phone away from his face; I thought he might throw it. "Can I help you?" It came out sharper than he intended from the way his brow scrunched.

"There could be evidence in there," I said. "There might even be people inside." I brandished my phone. "It's not vacant, at least not all the time. I found the address on an underground locator. People meet here for illegal or subversive activities."

Fox's eyelids went down and up in a slow blink. "I can't even put my equipment near this place, this shit is burning so hot. The only place in the county that has the foam we need to put this out is the airport, but planes don't fly out after 11, so there's nobody there. Trying to wake the operations director was a bitch, but I think we're getting somewhere now."

Fox bent his head, going still for maybe half a minute before he cupped both hands around his mouth and bellowed, "Perimeter sweep!"

The firefighters standing around the scene with useless hoses pooled on the ground hustled over. "Keep a safe distance, but everyone move to look for an accessible entry point," Fox instructed. "Possible human life at risk, unknown habitation status."

The firefighters took off in all directions, their shouts rising, audible but unintelligible, as they fanned out around the building.

Fox walked toward the structure and Graham and I followed as close as we dared, my eyes scanning for any safe window or vent.

No dice.

Fox's phone rang before we made it to the corner. He raised it to his ear and grunted a couple of acknowledgments before he hung up. "Foam is on its way. Probably twenty minutes out in the storm even with no traffic."

Twenty minutes might as well have been twenty years to anything inside the burning house.

"Nothing is making it out of there alive or intact." Fox said what I was trying not to think, wiping his brow on his forearm as his crew began to return from their perimeter search, shoulders drooping and heads shaking.

"What could be causing this?" I checked my watch. "It's been under a constant stream of gallons of water for thirty minutes, and it might as well be laughing at us."

I slumped back into Graham's chest and felt his arms go around me, the flames climbing higher, defying the water.

"Could be a lot of things. Chemicals. Alternative fuel. But from the sheer stubbornness of it, my money's on napalm. The foam will help me figure out if I'm right."

My jaw loosened as Graham's grip flexed tighter.

A criminal element the neighbors were scared of pissing off.

Napalm.

What in the actual hell had we stumbled across here?

3

A watched pot never boils, Sugarplum.

I could still hear Granddaddy's voice in my head, reminding me to be patient. Let things come in their own time.

Patience had never been my thing, but I liked to think I'd gotten a bit better at heeding his advice over the years. Watching the horizon for signs of the airport fire trucks Fox had been promised, I learned I hadn't changed much since my days of curling up on the big leather sofa in Granddaddy's family room, flicking sleepy eyes at the soft glow of the Christmas tree while I waited for Santa. Charity had camped out with me until she was fifteen, determined to help me hold on to any vestiges of childhood magic in our crazy world.

But the twenty-three minutes we spent prowling as close as we dared to the little green house were the longest and most frustrating of my thirty-seven years.

Two sections of the roof collapsed, one taking part of an exterior wall with it. I jumped backward both times, away from the waves of heat rolling from the openings. The firefighters shouted and moved ladders and equipment around us, but Fox forbade anyone from going inside an unstable structure, gear be damned.

A Dwayne Johnson lookalike with biceps the size of tires squatted at the front corner of the yard. I felt every hitch of his breath, and this wasn't even my wheelhouse.

Not exactly, anyway.

Firefighters, police officers—we save people. We run toward scary things that other people flee. We put ourselves in harm's way every day to protect and serve our fellow humans.

But there's a difference between heroism and flat-ass suicide. Graham Hardin is the strongest person I know, and his reluctance to get within spitting distance of any section of the house told me all I needed to know about the pain and trauma of burns.

"It has to be a professional hit," Graham said into my ear, keeping his voice low. "If you're right about what this place was used for, this isn't random, and it's not asshole kids being bored."

The hot spots that had been burning since we arrived showed no signs of slowing down. Even my limited understanding of napalm knew that was characteristic of it. The lone Channel Two truck had been joined by one from Eleven, but even on a slow news day, a house fire wasn't enough to draw interest from every media outlet in the city.

I needed to do something besides standing around feeling useless. And Graham had a good point.

"Let's see what we can find out."

Graham's eyebrows went up. "What did you have in mind?"

"There's usually a regular cast of characters around a place like this," I said. "And the neighbors not being outside still bugs me." I started toward a house two down with light spilling from every window.

"You think if they didn't come out to gawk, they're going to open the door for the police?" he asked.

I glanced down, then up with a raised brow. "Seems undercover was handy for more than one thing tonight. I'm not wearing my badge, are you?"

"You do have a point."

I jogged up the steps and pressed the plastic bell button, looking up at the awning over the porch. We'd been standing in the rain for so long the absence of it felt strange.

I counted off thirty seconds and pressed the bell again.

"People don't exactly drop by at nearly eleven o'clock for good reasons, Faith," Graham said.

"But they're up." I pointed at the window.

"Maybe. But they're not answering."

After another full minute of staring at a locked flat panel wood door, I sucked in a deep breath before I plunged back into the storm.

And right into a microphone.

"Terra Peters, WTRV News," she said, her free hand holding an umbrella over perfect hair. "Is that your house?" She pointed to the blaze.

Maybe the undercover clothes would work in our favor for a minute after all. Not my fault she wasn't thorough about doing her job—she'd been on the scene for half an hour. Skye Morrow would've at least checked the county property records.

I shook my head.

She leaned in. Squinted.

Looked up at Graham, then back at me.

"Are you Faith McClellan?"

Fan-goddamn-tastic.

"No comment." I moved to step past her.

She jumped to the side to block me, a smile lighting her face. "No wait, please, I'm a big fan."

Uh.

I glanced at Graham.

"What?" I blurted it before I could stop myself.

"You have the only perfect record of any homicide investigator in the whole state, did you know that?" Her voice went up an octave with excitement.

"I...uh...I never asked anyone."

She looked around. "Oh my God, have I stumbled into a Faith McClellan murder case?" She snapped her fingers at her photographer, who was getting drenched behind her. "Get everything. No idea what might be important here, I'll figure it out in editing."

I held up one hand.

"Hold on. First, I'm not here in an official capacity. Second, we have no information that anyone is dead. Third, stay behind the trucks and don't get in the way." I reached for Graham's sleeve, pivoting to walk around her. "Fourth, and finally—no comment."

"What about the car in the alley?" she asked.

I turned back. "What car?" The fire crew had fanned out all around the building. They didn't say anything about a car.

She pointed. "In the alley around back. There's a black BMW SUV. Kind of sticks out around here."

Graham and I took off without another word. I could hear her yelling at the photographer to keep up behind us, but she was low on my list of concerns at the moment.

We rounded the back corner of the neighboring house and stopped.

"I'll be damned," Graham and I muttered in unison.

Probably fifteen feet from the back of the burning house, a large, late model luxury SUV stuck out in an alley populated with garbage cans, possums, and rust-speckled pickups.

"Why wouldn't the firefighters have mentioned this?"

"Because they're not cops." Graham pointed. "It could be parked at that house or the one next door. And their focus was on hunting an entry point to the building."

Better late than never. At least now I had something to do.

Ducking under the aluminum carport alongside the house next door to the blaze, I pulled out my phone and opened an investigation.

"Ranger, is the owner of the car inside?" Terra called from several paces back.

"Miss Peters, if you follow my career, you know I'm not fond of talking to the press. I appreciate the tip, but for the last time: no comment."

I turned my back on her and typed the license plate number for the BMW into the DPS website.

Between the storm and the dead cell zone, the wheel in the center of the screen spun for a solid three minutes—long enough for Terra to figure out I wasn't going to talk to her and disappear.

Graham hung over my shoulder, watching the screen with me.

"You really think whoever was driving that is in there?"

"Maybe whoever lives there"—I jerked my head toward the house next door—"is doing something that allows them to afford a car like this. But—"

I stopped talking when the result came up.

"Nobody who lives around here is driving a seventy-thousand-dollar car registered to the biggest law firm in the city." Graham blew out a slow breath.

"And anyone skulking around a U-house who arrived in that car would've left when the sirens got close if they could've," I finished the thought for him.

There was someone inside all right. And the hairs standing up on my arms said they weren't coming out alive.

I shoved the phone back into my pocket. The airport trucks had arrived.

Three blinks later the Austin fire guys, all clad in hazmat suits, pulled hoses and shouted orders as a grim-faced Captain Fox warned us to vacate the area. "Trust me, you don't want this stuff on you," he called, pointing before he climbed to the controls of the ladder truck.

We backed to the outer perimeter of the Austin fire trucks, keeping our distance from Terra. At least she was leaving us alone as we asked. Skye would never.

A silver-suited young firefighter tied a hose around his shoulder and started climbing.

I looked away before the ladder lurching made my stomach do the same.

"The foam looks like snow," I said.

"But the chemicals are bad news," Graham said. "I read an article about that not too long ago. A bunch of military firefighters that have to use the stuff on the regular are getting sick. We're better off back here, and I'm glad they have suits."

Whatever was in the stuff, it was working. The flames were already retreating.

"Thank God," I said.

"Anything else from Sewell?" Graham asked.

Pulling my phone out, I checked my notifications. "Nope. Just the one charge. I bet you're right; it was a test."

"We'll get him. You couldn't have laid the trap more perfectly."

My gut said when Fox and his crew could get inside they'd be pulling remains out of there—I just wasn't sure if they were going to find bodies we could identify or ashes nobody would even notice.

It wasn't my case. I'd just happened to see something off and called the fire department. But the longer I stood there, the more convinced I became that something had happened here, and like Terra said—I stick with things until I find answers other people miss.

How could I help Fox and his crew?

Why here? Why tonight? The why is always the most important question in a criminal investigation, and it often gets overlooked in the early stages because it's also the most frustrating to try to answer. Experience has taught me that keeping it in mind while I sort through the details helps me notice the ones that matter.

I turned a slow circle, my eyes probing the darkness blanketing the familiar landscape for an answer. We'd eaten at Cabrerra's my whole life. There was a framed, signed photo of my father with the owner just inside the front door. What was different tonight? Anything?

"Did you hear something?" Graham's voice was soft.

The neighbors might have seen something, but they weren't talking.

What about the customers—and cameras—at the restaurant?

4

I ran for the restaurant's door, checking my watch. Twenty after eleven.

It was locked, but the lights were on. I rattled it in the frame and watched the window.

Not a soul in sight. I raised a fist and banged on the glass, my legs starting to shiver in the cool night air on the restaurant's porch, out of the rain.

Ten seconds. Thirty. Ninety.

Nothing.

"They're probably in the kitchen cleaning up, Faith." Graham hammered the door with one fist.

A pair of men appeared from the bar side of the lobby. We moved back as the bigger one pushed the door open.

"Come on, man, you gotta stand up." The tattooed bartender I'd seen on our way out half-carried a large, rumpled man with hair that would make Don King raise an eyebrow. "If the driver reports you it'll be a PI ticket for you and the cops will be up my ass for over serving you."

On cue, a Toyota SUV turned into the lot, the headlights bouncing off the restaurant's windows.

Graham jogged up two steps to offer a hand on the drunk guy's other side. "Here we go, my man," he said, turning to open the rear passenger door of the SUV with his free hand. He leaned in and strapped a seat belt around captain crazy hair, then shut the door. The front passenger window lowered and an annoyed woman's voice floated from it.

"I don't clean up puke for free."

"His account, ma'am. If he hurls in your car, feel free to add the fee." The bartender flashed a smile.

"This is bullshit," she muttered. "Snotty-nosed kids all day and puking drunks all night." The engine revved as she pulled away.

"Thanks, man." The bartender put out a hand for Graham to shake. "I've never seen anybody get that drunk that fast. I poured him three relatively weak margaritas and you'd think he had a bottle of Cuervo. Not used to it, I guess."

"Some folks have no tolerance for booze," Graham agreed.

The bartender started back up the steps, but I stepped in his way. "Faith McClellan, Texas Rangers," I said.

His face fell before his hands came up. "I didn't know you were a cop, but I was telling the truth," he said. "I didn't give him too much."

I had zero interest in harassing this guy about his observational skills. "I know. I'm wondering if we might be able to ask some questions inside."

He stopped backing away and folded his arms over his chest. "Questions about what? Somebody in trouble?" He looked around. "I heard sirens earlier, what's going on?"

Graham flipped his wallet open and flashed his shield. "Travis County Sheriff's Office. There's a fire in a neighboring house. We'd like to know if anyone saw anything coming or going from here this evening that might help our investigation."

"Like you think someone set a fire?" The guy's entire posture changed the second he saw Graham's badge, his eyes hooding, smile vanishing.

"We can't rule anything out so early in an investigation." I smiled around the words. "Just gathering information. We'd appreciate your cooperation."

I followed him up the steps and took a longer look at him under the lobby lights. Probably early twenties, hipster beard, tight T-shirt showing off full-sleeve tattoos on both arms—one a dragon and one dominated by Darth Vader.

"Can you get me a manager who can pull camera footage and credit card receipts from nine to ten this evening?"

"I heard the sirens, but I didn't go outside to look." His hands went to his hair, fisting around the curls. "I grew up in this neighborhood. It's mostly quiet people who work hard."

"We're trying to help those people. Every minute that passes in an investigation like this makes it harder for us to find the answer." I laid it on extra-thick, skipping over my suspicions about the current use of the house in question. "We need to know who might have seen something they don't even realize they saw, and the faster we can talk to people, the better their memories will be when we get to them. You can help the neighborhood the most right now by helping us do our jobs."

He sniffled in a long, halting breath. Rolled his shoulders back. "I'll go get Marco."

Graham rocked up on the balls of his feet as he watched the guy disappear. "Nice work."

"What the fuck have we walked into here?" I sucked in a deep breath. "Bank fraud is nice, you know? Nobody dies, nothing burns, no talk of substances that are literally against the rules of modern warfare."

"Nobody has told us anyone died in there yet. No assumptions. We'll get the information we need and proceed as necessary."

Tattoos reappeared, a gangly guy with thick dark hair and a crimson button-down on his heels. "Jack said something about a fire?" He put his hand out to shake Graham's, then mine. "Marco Hernandez. I'm the GM here, what can I do for you folks?"

"We need credit card receipts for the past few hours and any surveillance footage your system might have of the back parking lot." I pointed to myself and then Graham. "Faith McClellan, Texas Rangers, and Graham Hardin, TCSO."

His eyes went to the photo of the Governor on the wall behind me when I said my name.

I nodded and he flinched, flashing a too-wide nervous smile and clapping his hands together. "Right away, of course, Officers. Anything we can do to be helpful." He started toward the back of the building and waved for us to follow him. "Was anyone hurt?"

"We're waiting on a report from the fire department at the moment," Graham said.

"I mean, I heard the sirens but I figured it was a medical thing," Marco said. "This neighborhood has a lot of older people, and we get ambulances blaring by almost every day. Jesus." He shook his head, leading us through the kitchen and into a cluttered shoebox of an office. Manila folders and papers teetered in piles on every available surface, including the beige folding chairs on the front side of the desk. Marco bent over the computer and clicked his mouse a few times.

"Our camera on the back of the building gets the parking lot and the dumpsters, but I'm not sure how much of the street it picks up."

He gestured to the screen and stepped back. "That's what I have for you to look at."

"Thank you." I leaned over the monitor, Graham stepping behind me, hovering over my shoulder. "How long have you been here?"

"Since two-thirty."

I clicked the upper right corner of the screen to see if the footage would zoom. I could see the street in the background of the parking lot feed, but it wasn't close enough to make out anything but the outlines of the first house and the street stretching into darkness beyond it.

The closer I tried to bring it, the grainier it got, and the resolution wasn't exactly HD caliber to begin with. I zoomed back out. Better to watch for something and then try to enhance.

"You didn't hear anything unusual at any point this evening? No customers talking about something weird outside, no one coming in asking for help?"

He shook his head. "It was a normal Thursday night. Busy, but not crazy. We had staffed up; the first cold front of the year usually makes people want Mexican food." He tipped his head to one side, his eyes on Graham. "Didn't I see you earlier?"

"We came in for dinner."

Graham and I watched the screen. His hand rested on the small of my back, warm and comforting, but I could tell he was thinking the same thing

I was. We were here when the fire started. Not even two football fields away. What had slipped past us?

I ran the feed forward to nine and played it.

Three groups left the restaurant from cars in the back of the lot. I noted the plate numbers in case we needed to interview them.

One car turned onto the street and stopped at the first house on the right. Someone got out and went inside, leaning on a cane. Nine minutes later another came toward the camera, passing under it on the way to the freeway. The mid-1990s truck I'd seen in the alley. I noted that, too.

"No BMW," Graham said.

I shook my head.

Sixteen minutes of feed later, at nine twenty-seven, a black late model Lincoln passed the camera. Went about halfway down the street.

Hot damn.

I zoomed in on the freeze frame of the car stopping. There were no flames in the photo, but the distance sure looked right for the burning house.

"Now we're getting somewhere," Graham muttered, leaning over my shoulder.

Play. A figure emerged from the back seat, stopped to say something to the driver, and disappeared inside. The more I tried to zoom, the more pixelated and fuzzier the image got. But someone went inside. Someone with a luxury car and a driver, because the Lincoln disappeared a few seconds later.

I watched until the flames emerged, a bright spot in the grainy gray feed. Nobody left the house, at least not from the front.

"Someone was in there," Graham said.

My eyes didn't leave the screen. Flames came first from what looked like the back corner, then from the front windows on the same side, spreading toward the camera, across the front of the house.

"So that dude who went in set the place on fire?" Marco asked.

I didn't think so.

The video was fuzzy, but I imagined napalm would require some sort of heavy-duty container. The figure that exited the Lincoln didn't even carry a briefcase.

"Not unless they stashed the accelerant they used on the property in advance." I drummed my fingers on the edge of the keyboard. "But that leaves a risk. Someone could find it, it could ignite or detonate early, a potential target could see it and run. Either way, nobody would set a fire like this and stay in the building. So if the fire wasn't started from a distance, whoever started the fire went into and out of the house a way we can't see here." I wouldn't have been the first call to the AFD if anyone was alive in there.

I needed someone who might've gotten better eyes on the scene in real time than I could through their low-end surveillance feed.

"Anyone go out there for smoke breaks?" I asked.

Marco held up one index finger. "Xander!" Hustling to the back of the kitchen, he jerked open a large steel door to a walk-in refrigerator. "X, you back here, man?"

No answer.

"I only have one guy on my crew who takes smoke breaks. And he should still be here." He led us through the building back to the lobby calling for the missing kitchen employee.

Graham and I stayed on his heels.

Tattoos stuck his head out of the bathroom when we stopped in the lobby. "He left," he said. "About eight forty-five. He said he didn't feel well and I figured he shouldn't be in the kitchen if he was sick." He looked at Marco. "You were busy. Sorry, I forgot to mention it."

"Anyone else still here?" Graham asked.

Tattoos shook his head. "People are pretty efficient at getting their shit done and getting out of here when we lock the doors."

"You didn't have cause to go outside tonight?" I asked.

He shook his head. "First chilly night of fall and they put margaritas on special with ads on Instagram and Facebook. My arms are tired from shaking drinks and I still haven't had any dinner."

I thanked him, taking the list of credit card charges Marco handed me. Definitely the needle-haystack method of searching for a lead, but good to have if we needed it.

From what we had, it looked like our fire starter came and went quickly, from the far back corner of the house—which might have been the most useful piece of information we had, if it held up.

Because it meant we were likely dealing with someone smart enough to think of everything from napalm to surveillance cameras.

Graham was right: all the signs so far pointed to a professional hit.

5

A half-dozen more reporters and twice that many cops had arrived by the time we got back down the street.

I surveyed the crowd. Recent J-school grads stuck on the night shift, every one. Terra was still there, but no Skye Morrow. Thank God. If this took one more weird turn, her spider-sense would start tingling and she'd be a giant pain in everyone's ass for the foreseeable future. For now, we had a pass. I'd take any little win at this point.

An Austin PD patrolman had a perimeter set up and raised one hand when we got close to the tape. Graham flashed his badge as my eyes landed on a familiar Stetson fifteen yards in front of us.

I stepped forward without my badge and the patrolman's hand came up, but stopped before he caught my arm when Archie's voice boomed. "McClellan! I was getting ready to send out a search party!"

The patrolman stepped aside and Graham and I jogged up the street, my pumps slipping on the wet asphalt every other step.

"What are you doing here?" I checked my watch, stopping in front of Archie. "Isn't it past your bedtime?"

"If you'd stop finding shit for me to do, I might have a weekend every once in a while." His eyes crinkled at the corners with the quick smile. He glanced from me to Graham and back again. "Let's have a talk."

My brow furrowed. The calmer Archie got, the more there usually was for normal people to freak out about. What now?

The slight limp from a bad knee didn't slow Archie's gait, even at the end of a long day. Graham and I had to speed walk to keep up as he led us away from the scene.

Archie stopped out of earshot of anyone else on the scene and pulled out his phone, touching the screen a few times. "Please tell me you disappeared because you were finding out something useful about what happened here tonight."

"Nothing yet, but I'm working on it." I took his phone. "Who is this?" Armani suit, Ray-Ban sunglasses, tall, fit, jet-black goatee to match a thick head of hair only slightly graying around the temples. Good-looking. Distinguished, with an air of almost aristocratic self-possession that came through even in a digital photo. And that was a private jet in the background. My stomach closed around my fajitas.

Graham leaned over my shoulder. "Let me guess. Dead rich guy in there?" He jerked his head back toward the house.

"He would go with the BMW SUV in the alley, but the idea that his presence here bothers Archie makes me nervous," I said.

"It should." Archie tucked the phone back into his pocket. "Right now I'm praying on every candle I've ever lit in my life that my information is wrong. That is Benham Avesta, Iranian Ambassador to Mexico, and nephew of Azari Avesta, head of the Iranian judiciary."

I choked on the *oh, shit* before it even made it out of my throat.

This wasn't just a nightmare.

It was a goddamn international catastrophe.

"Avesta's uncle sent him to Mexico for good reason—he has a checkered history with the law," Archie explained. "But he's also the nephew of a powerful man who never had any sons—a powerful man who raised his nephew after his sister and her husband were killed."

Graham's eyebrows went up. "They thought he'd be less likely to find trouble in Mexico?"

"They thought the trouble he found would be less noticeable in Mexico," I replied.

Archie pointed at me. "Exactly. But he's been here four times in the past eighteen months. His past suggests that's not coincidence, nor is it leisure travel. On his last trip, we got a joint warrant with the DEA to track his cell location when he's on Texas soil. I've been watching it since Monday, and he hasn't strayed from his hotel room for more than a few minutes at a time. Until we got a ping from here tonight. The triangulation isn't perfect, it works off cell towers like the signals we use for 911 calls, so at first I blew it off, thinking he was at Cabrerra's. But then I saw on the news that you were here."

"What time did you get the ping?" I asked, the blurry figure exiting the Town Car on the surveillance video flashing through my thoughts.

Archie checked his phone. "Nine twenty-nine."

That would fit.

I glanced around the scene for Captain Fox.

He called something too muffled by crowd noise and distance for me to hear, and the fireman on the ladder shut off his hose and climbed down. Returning to the truck, he dropped the foam hose and picked up another one from the ground next to an AFD truck, scaling the ladder again.

"I thought water wasn't helpful here."

"It's out," Graham said. "They're rinsing away the foam."

I waved a hand at Archie's cell phone. "I take it the tracker doesn't show that he left?"

"The cell towers don't think his phone left the area, anyway. Not while it was on."

I pulled out my phone and Googled Avesta. On page three of the results, I found four articles from independent news outlets. A garbled Arabic-to-English translation later, I could see why the guy's uncle wanted him quasi-exiled.

"Suspicion of blackmail, close ties to known narcotics traffickers, whispers of espionage—Jesus. This guy has his fingers in everything but buying and selling people," Graham said, reading over my shoulder faster than I could.

"If he's in there..." I sighed, looking up at Archie. "I can probably help."

"Oh, you will," Archie said. "But that's still an 'if' right now. Let's see what Fox and his crew find before we go jumping into solving a problem we may not even have. This technology is far from perfect."

I nodded. Still clad in the hazmat suits, the firefighters were methodically rinsing the building in quadrants. Foam flowed in rivulets down the driveway, collecting behind a long plastic berm. A hazmat team would dispose of it once Fox and his crew had cleared the scene.

When the water started to run clear, Fox pulled off his hood and approached us. "Any better idea what our investigators are looking for?"

"There could be remains inside, but we don't know for certain."

"The building is a total loss. We've done all we can for right now—we'll keep a perimeter around the area until we can get inside, but it's going to have to cool and we'll need a structural inspection. Late tomorrow will be the best we could hope for, but I can't make any promises about getting an inspector here on a Friday evening."

"I have someone I can call if you need." Archie handed Fox a card.

"I will take you up on that." Fox slipped it into his jacket. "I'm a licensed fire investigator, usually just to pitch in when our guys get backlogged, but I admit, this one has me wondering if I'm right about what the hell we just wrestled with. I want to see for myself, and the faster we find out, the better." Fox gave a shrug and walked away.

Archie pointed to the small knot of reporters. "My mission here is to contain the situation. If Avesta is dead, it can't get out before we make an arrest."

True story. International relations are tricky business, and the particularly gruesome murder of the nephew of a powerful and respected Iranian leader—even a nephew nobody liked—could be fodder for a breakdown in already tenuous relations. Retaliation could range from attacks on the Middle Eastern oil infrastructure that keeps American cars and trucks running and fuel prices reasonable to the lives of Americans on foreign soil.

"There are an awful lot of people milling around here with cameras," Graham said. "Do y'all really think we can keep someone from leaking a photo or thirty?"

Archie tipped his head toward the reporters. "They're too far away to see anything, especially from behind those trucks."

Graham pointed to the firefighters. "Every cell phone has a high-resolution camera. I'm not worried about the press getting their own footage, I'm worried about them buying it if there's so much as a breath of scandal attached to this."

Shit. He was right. And scandal was an understatement if Archie's information was valid. A case involving a missing diplomat came built-in with a loudly ticking clock, limited access to information, and zero margin for error.

Just another day at the office.

"So the trick is to not let anyone know," I said like that was any sort of easy. "Not even Fox. Did you tell him why you were here?"

Archie shook his head. "Nothing specific. I can play it a dozen different ways if he thinks to ask."

The Commander was right to send Archie here: he was the best we had at keeping things close and solving complicated murder cases quickly. But if ever there was a murder I was born to work, one tangled up in high-level political sensitivities was it. I knew the world. I knew the conventions, the loyalties, the feuds. I still knew a whole lot of the players, and my last name would carry weight with the ones I didn't.

The firefighters shucked hazmat suits and started rolling up hoses. I paced between Archie and Graham and the back of the nearest fire truck.

"Who owns the house?" Archie asked.

"According to the county, no one. Fox said the owner died without a will or any heirs, and the county has let it sit just as she left it for almost a year while they wade through paperwork."

"The neighbors didn't even come outside while the place was burning. Which I'm pretty sure means they're not talking. I think our fast lane for right now is to see if they find remains Jim can examine."

Graham put an arm around my shoulders. "I still say this was a professional," he said. "Someone with the wherewithal to access napalm when the weather wasn't going to cooperate with a kill-and-burn plan."

"Could be," Archie said. "And if we're working the assumption that Avesta was in there—"

"Which we have to until we know he wasn't in there, at this point," I interjected.

"We need to know more about him," Archie continued, nodding. "I have a contact at the embassy I can call tomorrow."

"And I can see what the internet has to say about any of that."

"Not much, I tried that before I got here," Archie said. "But you're usually better about finding shit online than I am, too, so what do I know?"

"Okay, Mr. 'Contact at the embassy.'" I rolled my eyes. "Is there, like, anywhere on the planet you don't have a friend? Your network beats my computer snooping all day long."

"I said contact, not friend." Archie winked.

Captain Fox strolled over, his shoulders slumped and his face tired.

"We won't be able to get inside until late tomorrow at the earliest." He pointed to where the roof had caved. "There's a matching spot to that one in the back of the opposite side, both places where the accelerant was likely concentrated. We will get samples to test, but I'm not sure what we're going to find in there at this point, folks. If anything."

"Definitely arson, though." I didn't bother to inflect the question mark on the end of the sentence.

"Without a flash of doubt. I assume you folks have no statement from anyone claiming it, nothing online pointing to a perpetrator? Anything I need to be worried about my men coming across inside?"

I looked at Archie. He shook his head, checking his phone to be sure.

"Y'all think there was someone inside?" Fox asked.

I shrugged, wanting that to stay close for the time being. "When you get inside, I'm hoping you'll be able to tell us that."

"Lord, I hope you're wrong. Who the hell could do something like that?"

"Not many people," I said. "Which should help us once we start to get a handle on this."

"We'll try to get a structural engineer out here as quickly as we can, and I'll take a team of arson investigators in there as soon as the engineers give us the green light."

"Is there anything we can do to make your job easier or help you get information faster?" Archie asked. "I'm happy to pull all the strings I have access to, you just say the word."

"Know any construction guys?" Fox flashed a smile. "I want into that back room, but I know rushing in might get me killed. The thing is, the longer it sits there, the more likely it is that the whole damned thing will collapse, and anything we might have been able to find will be lost."

"Kind of makes you wonder if whoever did this wasn't counting on just exactly that," Graham murmured close to my ear.

Construction background went onto my mental list, my fingers practically itching for a whiteboard and a marker.

"As a matter of fact." Archie pecked at his phone screen with one finger and put it to his ear. "Bobby, Archie Baxter here, apologies for the hour, but I need your help." He paused. "Far north end of the county. I'll send you the address. There will be an engineer out here to inspect early afternoon." He held Fox's gaze and got a nod before he continued, "I need you to bring a crew out around three." He paused. "Yes, I do know it's Friday...No, I didn't know the Alabama-Clemson game was on tomorrow night. I have a building that needs to stay standing so we can get into it."

"I don't believe there's a person walking around all of Texas who doesn't owe him a favor or love him enough to do him one anyway," I whispered to Graham.

"At midnight, too." Graham sounded impressed.

Archie tucked the phone back into his hip pocket after he thanked Bobby. "They'll be here. Anything else?"

Captain Fox grinned. "I'll certainly ask if I think of something. Much obliged, sir."

"Let's just catch whoever did this," Archie said. "Quickly and"—his eyes went not subtly to the reporters gathered several yards away—"quietly."

Fox's head bobbed as he waved a tall, lean firefighter over. "Nobody talks to the press. No cell phones near the scene. Information leaks will be met with a fury y'all don't want to see. Spread the word."

"That ought to do it," he said. "The rookies think I'm scary, and my veterans know what a dick I can be when somebody crosses me."

Fox walked off to join his men.

"I hope he's as much of an asshole as he thinks he is when he's mad," Archie said. "That's one problem mitigated."

"And we might not lose the scene before we get a look at it," I said. "Now what?"

"I say we call it a night, it's past this old man's bedtime." He pointed at me. "We need rested brains and fresh eyes on this. Sleep, don't stare at your computer. I'll see y'all tomorrow."

Graham looped an arm around my shoulders and pulled. "I'll make sure she rests." He flashed a smile at Archie and leaned into my ear. "He's right."

I knew that.

I just had too much work to do to want to admit it.

6

He could've sworn on a stack of Bibles that their insides cooked right along with the plaster and cheap flooring and faded furniture.

The horror on their faces melted almost instantly when he pointed his hose and sprayed. They didn't even have time to scream.

He was well versed in the uglier parts of a war, and this was a war—maybe fought with different tactics and on different terms, but only because the situation demanded it.

From the doorway, he could only stand a five count, spraying everything from the ceiling to the floor and watching the polyester curtains and mattress explode into a fireball. He shut the door, heavy and solid. It began to warp and blister almost instantly. Backing through the house, he waved the hose like an eraser, watching the gel splatter over and then eat the evidence.

Target time: In and out in less than two minutes. Two oh five was the top edge of the exposure limit. In the front bedroom, on the same side of the house he'd entered, he opened and jumped from a stiff, heat-warped window.

The gushing rain cooled his everything. He watched steam rise from his arms and feet as he walked, quickly but not notably so, down the side of the house and up the alley before he turned, crossing the road closer to the corner.

Around the camera's eye, into the darkness.

The suits were soft, less rigid, as he peeled them off and tipped his face to the cool rain, before he stuffed them into the hole and replaced the post.

Now the tanks.

Around the cones. Under the tape. Into the pit. The muddy bottom was slick, but he was light on his feet.

The rain made mud. Mud was easy to dig with his hands, and easier still with a fat stalk of rebar he pulled loose. In five minutes, he had a hole wide and deep enough to lay the tanks away. He covered them, walking on the mud he used to tamp it down before he replaced the rebar and left.

Day after tomorrow, the ground would be dry. The concrete truck would back up to the pit. Anything that could trace back to him in any way would be buried. For good.

He tossed a glance back at the climbing flames of his masterpiece, defying the rain. If he was lucky, nobody would notice for a while. If he was the luckiest fucker alive, by the time anyone did they'd call it an accident in a house nobody cared about while he went to the next name on the list.

7

Pinky-peach rays filtered through the blinds, the angle telling me we'd overslept. Blinking, I shifted, my back pressing into Graham's chest and abdomen, his arm curled heavy and comforting around my waist.

I tried to crane my neck to look at him. He slept so hard there was little chance I'd bother him, but I couldn't see his face without turning. Tucked comfortably against him, I relaxed and closed my fingers softly around his hand and let a few tears leak from the corners of my eyes into the pillow. It had been a great summer. Somewhere in the back of my brain, I'd known it wouldn't last. I didn't deserve him.

I swiped at my eyes with my free hand. No time for that today. Or probably any day in the near future. I'd never been good at Charity's philosophy of leaving problems for "future me" to figure out, but I had no choice—we had one disaster on the table and another waiting to happen if we couldn't figure the first one out.

Graham's arm tightened when I stretched and arched my back away from him.

Clock check: eight seventeen. Damn.

"Two more seconds," he mumbled.

"It's after eight, Commander," I said, wriggling onto my back and tipping my face up to kiss his bristly chin. "We are way past late."

Graham groaned as he dragged his eyelids open. "Liar. It cannot be after seven."

"I wish. Come on. Nobody ever solved a murder from the bed." I slid off the edge of the bed and padded in bare feet to the closet.

"It'll be hours yet before anyone can get into that house." Graham propped himself up on one elbow.

I opened my mouth to argue—what, exactly, I wasn't sure, but didn't get any words out before his phone buzzed itself right off his nightstand.

"Hardin." He pressed it between his cheek and shoulder. I yanked on my boots.

"Slow down." Graham's tight voice drew my attention. He reached for the pen and notepad he kept next to the bed.

"Okay. Okay. Yeah, I'll be on my way as soon as I can." He stood, pulling on pants and buckling his belt. "I don't know, man. Let me see what I can do."

He put the phone down and ran a hand over his close-cropped hair. "The address we got on the credit card hit last night..." Graham shook his head.

I swallowed hard, crossing the room to look over his shoulder at the notebook.

Human remains. Probably female. Burned beyond recognition.

"We cleared the decks for whoever did this, Faith." Graham choked on the words, shaking his head.

I wrapped both arms around his middle and squeezed as tight as I could. He couldn't know that. Not yet, anyway. But right then that wasn't what he needed to hear.

"Let's go," I said.

⸻

By the time we were in the truck and headed south, my phone showed two pings on Jimmy Sewell's fake credit cards that now seemed like I'd dropped them off a hundred years ago, and a call from a Dallas number I didn't recognize.

I changed lanes and laid on the gas, wondering about the credit card pings. Someone in cyber ought to be watching for them, too, but the back of my brain wanted to see what Sewell was up to.

Too many geese to chase.

I needed to pick one. The problem was knowing which one was the most likely to go straight to an answer without meandering uselessly. But I also needed to take care of Graham. Right or wrong, I couldn't say for sure, but he felt responsible for the body a couple of kids found outside a trailer park in Goliad this morning.

"The sheriff's office in Goliad has taken down two meth labs in three months, both of them in that same trailer park," Graham said, clicking the radio off. "Which means half the department is buried in paperwork and DA investigators, and the other half is trying to take up the slack. The captain thinks the girl was likely a junkie or a prostitute."

"Which means she's low priority." I said what he didn't want to. Graham was too much of a gentleman to admit to some of the shittier parts of this job, one of which is that when you have finite resources, allocation isn't always fair.

"They'll get to it when they can, but since there are no cameras out there and they pulled all units from the area last night..." He let it trail off. Because they did that on our request.

"We don't know anything yet." I squeezed his hand. "Who are we going to see?"

"Goliad County Justice of the Peace, guy named Cory Whitehead. Probably an old country judge." Graham punched it up on his maps app and clipped his phone to my dashboard. "They have to hold the body there until the Travis County ME's office opens on Monday."

Less populated counties often rely on the nearest big city for forensic help, and sometimes the old country judge is a more important law enforcement persona than the local police, depending on who's who.

"Anything from our financial fraud boy genius this morning?" he asked.

"I got two pings, but I haven't looked at them yet."

Graham plucked my phone from the cupholder and punched the passcode in.

"Should be on the main screen," I said.

He swiped down and clicked. "Two pings. Two different cards." I watched him poke at the screen from the corner of my eye.

"These were both last night," he said. "I thought it was supposed to be instant notification."

"It is," I said.

"Oh wait. No, these are from last night and there are two more here today."

"Same cards or different?" My eyes drifted to the phone screen, and the truck drifted to the bumpy shoulder.

"You drive, I'll read," Graham said as I jerked the wheel back to the left.

"Read faster."

"Keep your eyes on the road."

I was so relieved at the return of our easy banter and affectionate tones, my chest actually felt lighter. Like it was a little easier to breathe, even counting a missing diplomat and possible looming international crisis.

"Um." Graham trailed the last letter out, his thumbs flying over my screen.

I waited. Three beats. Ten. My fingers white-knuckled the wheel. "What?" I was impressed with my volume control, all things considered.

"These ones from last night." He put the phone back into the cupholder. "They're from a square, large amounts, registered to the restaurant address."

"What rest—" I stopped. "No." Now it was my turn to drag the letter out. I followed it with a whistle for good measure. I didn't have to ask if he was sure. The long pause was his methodical triple-checking at work before he said anything. Somehow I kept my eyes on the road and the truck in its lane, autopilot taking over as my thoughts spun forty different directions at once. If I hadn't been so used to it, it might've made me dizzy.

"What the hell are the odds?" Graham mused.

"How much?" I asked.

"Twenty-three five on one and twenty-one on another."

I tapped one finger on the steering wheel. "That's oddly specific. And not what I expected, either. The usual MO for this kind of stuff isn't huge charges that would trigger the bank's computer algorithms. It's nickel and dime theft over a long period."

"But the banks are letting these go through to track them," Graham said.

"But the people who have them aren't supposed to know—" The sentence lurched to a stop. "Shit. Is it possible that he's playing us?"

"Possible...hell, at this point I think what we need to know is if it's likely. You said he was a smart little bastard."

I shook my head, flipping back through every nuance of every interaction I'd had with Sewell.

"I was so careful," I said. "I covered my digital tracks precisely every time. I set up a whole undercover identity traceable online complete with fucking yearbook photos. How could he have possibly figured it out?"

"You think he had the shades on last night because he didn't want you to be able to read him?"

"He wears them all the time. I don't have a single surveillance photo of him where he doesn't have them on. I don't have medical records, but I assumed he had some sort of photosensitivity condition."

"Yearbook photos," Graham said.

"Huh?"

"Do we have his yearbook photos? If he had a condition, we could at least almost safely assume it's congenital given his age."

"So he'd have to be wearing the shades there, too. I don't remember coming across those, but I'll look into it."

"In the meantime, we have to assume this was on purpose," Graham said. "That he knew our play last night when we saw the first ping."

"Sewell is a thief, not a murderer," I said. "You saw him. He'd have trouble overpowering my grandmother's cats."

I could feel Graham's head swivel toward me.

"You said yourself he's going for the big time with this deal."

"He's a weasel." I shook my head harder, my ponytail whipping into my jaw. "He's not a killer. He doesn't have it in him."

"The small mountain who accompanied him to the drop yesterday definitely does."

I tipped my head side to side. It was at least more plausible, though Sewell's muscle had been silent to the point that I hadn't tried to read him. He was menacing by look, for sure, but sometimes guys that looked like that were big old marshmallows, and sometimes they'd snap your neck like a twig as soon as look at you. I hadn't paid enough attention to this one the day before to try to read which one Sewell had along, because I was so focused on making sure I sold my alternate identity well and searching every word Sewell said for clues to what he was up to.

Had I paid attention to the wrong thing?

Twenty-four hours before I wouldn't have thought it possible. Now I wasn't so sure.

"One thing at a time almost sounds like a luxury this morning." I clicked the blinker on for the upcoming exit. "Where were the other pings? The ones from today?"

Graham picked my phone back up. "One in Houston, one in Baton Rouge. Both of them at hotels. Couple thousand each."

"Text Gonzalez and make sure he sees that?" I asked.

We fell silent as miles blurred past the windows, the cornflower sky and endless fields soothing.

Texas is such a study in contrasts—a short drive from a sprawling metropolis, the world rolls into a stretch of land so peaceful and a sky so wide it can make you feel the best kind of alone in the world.

I didn't want to be done with Jimmy Sewell; I'd worked too hard on that case. The thing worrying around the back of my brain right then was how Sewell got the cards out so fast, and where he got his contacts. The first ping had come just hours after I dropped off the briefcase, and out in the middle of nowhere.

Followed hours later by a dead body.

Nothing about either case added up. And the equations grew more complicated with every revelation.

The one thing I knew for sure right then was that I was right about Sewell—he was a thief, not a killer. So the faster we caught the killer, the faster I could get back to the thief.

8

"You want to come in?" I took my phone and tucked it into my pocket as I slid from the truck outside the JP's listed address ninety minutes later, stretching my legs. "I don't mind checking it out alone."

Graham's face softened into a smile. "Thanks for looking out for me, but I'm okay. I made the call. I want to see what happened for myself."

We climbed wide wooden steps to a sprawling ranch-style house and spotted a sign under the wall-mounted mailbox: *C. Whitehead, Precinct 4 JP*. It's not uncommon in rural counties for local justices of the peace to have offices in their homes, but I had to wonder where this one might be housing a corpse until Monday as I rang the doorbell. A green, wood-framed screen door was latched from the inside with an eyelet hook, the burnished walnut door behind it open to the October breeze.

Footsteps fell from the other side. A petite redhead with gorgeous curls and eyes such a bright blue they popped despite the shadows and the screen between us appeared, wiping her hands on a red-and-white striped dish towel.

"Hey there, what can I do for y'all?" Her eyes flicked from my face to my badge and back again.

"We're here to see Justice Whitehead. Apologies for just showing up, but it's urgent. We'll try to be brief."

"I tried to call," Graham said. "I did leave a voicemail."

"Come on in." She opened the screen door, waving us inside. She was older than I'd thought at first, but it was hard to see, just a few faint lines around her makeup-free eyes. Her legs, long and toned with a fading summer tan, looked strong under her denim cut-offs. "I guess you're here about the dead girl?"

Graham and I stepped into the small, linoleum-floored foyer, both of us nodding. "Is the justice here?" I asked.

She flashed a grin. "Corie Lynn Whitehead, nice to meet you."

I gripped her offered hand. "Faith—"

"McClellan," she said. "I know who you are. I don't imagine there are many folks who work around the law in Texas who don't."

Graham coughed to cover a laugh. I shook my head. "I'm flattered, even if you are wrong about that." I landed a teasing elbow to Graham's ribs. "This is Commander Graham Hardin from the Travis County SO."

She shook Graham's hand before her eyes came back to me. "Frank Lonas usually helps out with murders around here. Is he okay?"

"He's fine, as far as I know," I said. "We're not here to help out the locals as much as we're following a trail on another case."

She waved us deeper into the house. "I see. I was just getting ready to conduct a preliminary examination. Her tissues looked pretty badly damaged," she said over her shoulder.

Graham and I exchanged a look. "Is she—" He cleared his throat. "Is she, uh, here?"

Corie pushed a thick white door wide and flipped a light switch, pointing to a box of blue mushroom cap hair bonnets on a hanging glass-and-macramé table just inside possibly the cleanest remains exam lab I'd ever seen—and I'd seen more than my share.

I stopped so short in the doorway, Graham nearly knocked me over when he ran into me.

"I—" It stuck in my throat.

She laughed, her blue eyes dancing when I turned mine to her.

"It's not just you, nobody ever expects it. I had the Uvalde County Commissioners out for a tour last month. They knew why they were coming, and three of them still popped off with some version of 'Holy shit' when I opened the door."

The room was probably half as big as my house, an odd mix of sterile and homey. The macramé table holding the gloves and bonnets had a twin next to a flat steel exam table, the second one home to a face shield with a light, and a gleaming set of silver scalpels and tweezers.

"This is...impressive," I admired, turning back to the hallway that led to her kitchen. And her bedroom, about ten steps past the door where we stood, it looked like.

"Yes, I live here. The dead don't scare me nearly as much as the living, Ranger McClellan."

"Faith. Please."

"Come on in. I'll get set up."

It was easily ten degrees cooler two steps into the room. Graham shut the door behind us and put a hand on my shoulder when she disappeared through a door that looked a lot like it led to a walk-in freezer. I twisted my ponytail up and pulled a bonnet over my head, handing Graham one.

"Did we drive into the twilight zone?" His lips brushed my ear, he leaned so close. "This is weird. Right?"

"Mmm-hmmm," I hummed, fixing a smile in place when Corie reappeared, pushing a gurney with a body bag on it. It was downright bizarre. But I was more curious than horrified. I liked her—earnestness practically seeped from her pores. This place was a story waiting to be discovered.

She opened the bag and transferred the remains to the exam table every bit as carefully as Jim. Practiced. Professional.

"How long have you been here?" I asked.

"Two and a half years." She raised her eyes to mine, white teeth flashing between pink lips. "It's quiet. People are mostly nice."

I'd missed her utter lack of an accent at first. She spoke the way I did. The way my mother had taught Charity and me—not quite the King's English, maybe, but precise. Not giving anything away.

I watched the expert way she handled the tools on her cute little macramé table. "And how long were you a medical examiner?"

She pulled the shield over her head and clicked the bulb on. "Long enough to decide I don't fear the dead, but spending all my time with them was detrimental to my mental health. Having some variety in my days— weddings, misdemeanor charges, even a few criminals now and again—is a welcome balance."

I put my hands in my pockets and rocked up on the balls of my feet. Graham stared at the macramé weave, probably counting threads so he didn't have to look at the corpse on the table.

The woman's limbs were drawn up almost into a fetal position. "Jesus, was she trying to defend herself?" I winced.

"Impossible to tell." Corie gestured to the remains. "She might've been, but it's normal when a body is set on fire for the long muscles in the arms and legs to contract like this. If the remains are left to cook for long enough, these muscles will separate at the end joints, and then the bones will crack. Her flesh is burned, and the muscles drew up, but I see no immediate evidence of separation. So the heat didn't get intense enough to cause that before someone noticed, or the accelerant in question burned out."

Wow. She couldn't do a full postmortem out here. I didn't think. But that was a hell of a start. Having her look over the remains now provided a great opportunity to make sure we caught everything we could.

Corie touched her phone screen a couple of times before snapping new gloves into place.

"Corie Whitehead, Goliad County JP, initial observations Jane Doe number four, October 9, 2020."

She moved carefully, searching for signs of antemortem trauma but obviously trying to avoid altering anything.

"Subject exhibits visual evidence of partial attempted cremation," she said. "Pugilistic posture evident in arms and legs. Hands are detached, but patellas and feet appear intact. Strong possibility of dental evidence recovery."

I reached for Graham's hand and gave it a squeeze, looking around. She didn't have an X-ray machine or even many tools or instruments visible, but her lab was a damn smart idea for cases like this one. It's not often that remains degrade to the point of obscuring evidence terribly quickly, but sometimes the ability to examine them faster allows for homing in on tighter time windows, and in a homicide, that can make the difference between a closed case and one that winds its way past a million dead ends to the basement at Rangers HQ.

"Minimal insect and scavenger activity," Corie intoned. "Clothing fibers melted to dermis in places, disintegrated in others."

I stepped closer, forcing myself to see past the gruesome picture in front of me to the details. The kinds of things I was good at noticing that other people often missed.

The woman's face was charred beyond a reasonable guess at age, and Corie was right, her clothes were burned in an uneven pattern of missing and melted. Her mouth was frozen open in a silent scream, perfectly bonded molars visible under Corie's light.

She pulled a dental impression pad from her table and pressed it first to the victim's bottom teeth, then repeated the process with the top ones.

"That'll get us an ID. Not sure how fast, but I might get lucky." Corie crooked a "come closer" index finger.

I leaned in, holding my breath to avoid the smell as I studied the whispery frayed edges of what had been a gorgeous silk blouse probably this time yesterday. My eyes moved to a skirt molded over her hips. Leather. Probably originally black, but I couldn't say for sure. Shoes. Her feet were the least burned, and I spotted bits of green silk. Open toes. Three-inch stilettos.

My mother had a shoe closet that would make Imelda Marcos sob—those were some variety of big-name designer. I leaned over the table. Not a speck of red sole. Not a logo, either. I could only see bits of tan leather peeking through the charring. But if they hadn't cost more than a thousand dollars, I'd shine Ruth McClellan's entire collection.

Graham cleared his throat, leaning over my shoulder and focusing on the shoes. "What are we looking at?"

"Her clothes. You said your friend told you the local PD said she was a junkie or a prostitute." I stood.

"That's because of where they found her," Corie said. "That trailer park is known for dope dealing and the sex trade. They figure a pissed-off dealer or john dumped her because that would fit the story out there. You see something that says different?"

"This outfit approaches the two-thousand-dollar range. Retail," I countered.

Corie's eyes popped wide behind her face shield. "That's..." She let out a low whistle. "That's too rich for any junkie I've ever seen. Or anybody I've ever met, at least around here." She gave me a more shrewd once-over. "How sure can you be of that?"

I flashed a smile. "I'm sure. I didn't exactly grow up in the 99 percent," I said. "That mulberry silk charmeuse disintegrated everywhere it wasn't touching her because it's thinner than your average Kleenex. And runs about as much per bolt as you'd pay for a decent used car."

"So how did a woman who could afford an outfit that costs more than most people's mortgages end up out there?" she asked. "I guess that's why y'all are here?"

"It would certainly help to know who she is, but this could be any number of things: kidnapping gone wrong, domestic dispute, drug deal gone bad..." I let the sentence trail.

"Of course," Corie said. "We're out of luck on fingerprints—the hands go first in these cases; the tendons detach and they quite literally fall off. But the lab in Austin should be able to get you a dental from these impressions."

"Do you see anything indicating cause of death?" I asked.

"No visible wounds. I try not to disturb too much before they make it to the ME's office. I just don't like seeing evidence lost to time skipping by before the transfer, so when the Travis lab said they couldn't process the intake until Monday, I wanted to have a look. Glad you folks came down, I would've missed the bit about her clothes."

"How many murders do you get out here in a year?" I asked.

"Five, give or take, since I came here," she said. "But no matter which precinct they happen in, everything in the county comes here if there's a reason Travis can't take it right away."

"I'm sure the lab appreciates the help," I said.

"James Prescott in Travis County is as good as you get at making dead folks talk," she said, her tone softening with admiration. "He's the real deal. I'm happy to help him however little I can."

"Jim is incredible," I agreed. "Is there anything you can see that stands out to you as something we could look into before the postmortem can be scheduled?"

Corie shook her head. "Not from what I have here." She tipped her head to one side. "I'd like to turn her on her side and have a look at her back without putting pressure on the flexed arms and legs, but I'm afraid of disturbing tissue."

"Jim would rather we not miss anything, trust me." I stepped to the edge of the table. "I can help lift if you need."

She raised an eyebrow. "You'll need gloves."

I slipped some on and moved to Corie's side, awaiting instruction.

"Slide gently this way and then lift under her hip and thigh and turn her on her side in one move. Don't pull too hard on her skin. On three."

My lips flexed up in a quick smile. I liked her use of personal pronouns, keeping the victim human and real. I did that, but a lot of other folks didn't.

She counted and we turned.

Graham sucked in a sharp breath as Jane Doe settled on her right side, her face pointed at him. He turned away.

Corie was too focused to notice.

The burns extended only to the edges of the victim's clothes and skin.

"She was already lying down when she was set on fire." I didn't realize how relieved I was until I heard it in the words that came out of my mouth.

She had shiny mahogany hair that probably hung halfway down her back when it wasn't tangled into a small bird's nest. No blood meant no head wound, a common cause of death in a heat-of-the-moment murder. The silk blouse was a creamy rose gold color, the skirt a soft, supple black leather that probably felt like a second skin.

"There's a high degree of lividity here—normally I'd say she's been dead at least twelve hours, but sometimes the heat can accelerate that." Corie plucked a magnifier from the little macramé table and leaned in, studying the woman's matted hair before she reached for a pair of tweezers and plucked out several small light green leaves, placing them carefully in a petri dish.

"What is that?" I asked.

She moved one dish to a counter and returned with another one, shrugging her reply before she went back to work, this time pulling a half-dozen shreds of some kind of purple-pink petals free and laying them in the dish. Using the tweezers, she prodded strands of hair apart, but didn't find anything else to remove.

She finished her notes methodically, mentioning the materials in the clothing, the tangled hair, and the lack of posterior burns before she reached to lift the clump of hair away from the back of the victim's neck.

The skin was a mottled purply red, punctuated by a large, egg-shaped lump about halfway between her skull and her shoulders.

"Is that?" I stopped short because I didn't know how to finish the question. It was a hell of a goose egg to have been caused by a blow, but a growth or a tumor didn't seem likely given her clothing and probable social status. Women with means who put this much effort into their appearance would speed to the nearest surgeon and demand an immediate audience over something like that.

Corie used two fingers to prod deliberately before she stood. "I think I have something interesting for you. I don't recognize these flora samples, and I suspect her neck might be broken."

"May I?" I leaned over the dish, peering at the plant bits. "The police report didn't say anything about plants in the field where she was found?"

Corie shook her head. "Trailer park is a generous term for that place. Trust me, nobody out there is landscaping anything. You'd be hard-pressed to find anything underfoot but dirt and scrub brush."

The delicate little leaves and indigo flowers looked exotic. My knowledge of plants was limited to pretending to listen to my mother when she bragged about hers at the garden parties she'd loved so much as First Lady, but I was pretty sure the remnants in that dish were not scrub brush. "These petals are torn, they were probably on the ground wherever she picked them up," I murmured, pulling out my phone to take careful photos of them from several angles.

I spun to face Graham, who looked more relaxed. The fire wasn't the cause of death. And she might not even have been killed where she was found. Maybe the link we thought we'd seen to Sewell and the credit cards and the fire wasn't a link at all.

I couldn't be sure of anything.

Except that we couldn't let this go until we were sure what happened to her.

9

Every killer I've ever hunted thought they were smart enough to get away with it.

None of them has ever been.

By the time Graham and I made it halfway back to Austin, Google had given me the addresses of five plant nurseries within driving distance of the remains discovery site.

Whoever that woman was, however she ended up in that field—whether it had a thing to do with us or not—she deserved justice.

We hit the place closest to the highway first, an inviting lot with neat rows of everything from conifers to lantana.

Picking our way through plants and customers to a hut with a "checkout" placard hanging from the roofline, I kept my eyes wide for the pinkish-purple petals and the tiny, fat, bright green leaves.

The teenager working the register bobbed his head to whatever blared through the Beats headphones covering his ears, flipping through a magazine. I waited for a five count before I stuck one hand between his face and the page he was reading.

He bolted upright in the chair and yanked the headphones off. "Hey, sorry," he said. "What can I help you with?"

His eyes lit on my badge as the last word left his lips. "I, uh, I mean..." His eyes shifted to a greenhouse and back to us. "I'm not sure..."

"Just looking for some information on a certain kind of plant." I smiled. "A legal kind of plant."

"Oh." His shoulders relaxed. "Kim isn't here right now and she knows more than me, but I can try."

I clicked to the photos on my phone and turned the screen to face him. "Any ideas?"

He bit a scabbed-over lower lip as he peered at the screen. "I mean, it'd help if the flower petals were whole. I can't tell a shape, you know? Like did they go through a mower or something?"

I glanced at Graham. "I have no idea," I said. "But that's a good point, thanks."

"No worries. Wish I could be more helpful."

A woman in yoga pants and a tank top walked up behind me with her arms full of mums in five different colors. I peered at the long, skinny petals as we turned to leave, but nothing was the right color.

Two more stops didn't get us anywhere at all—a teenage girl rolled her eyes and said, "Like, I don't get paid enough to like, be a plant expert or something like that, you know." A cigar-chomping, sweaty man at the third place waved a dismissive hand as he told us he didn't sell weird stuff and he had customers to attend to.

By the time we parked at the fourth place on the list, tucked back off a dirt road miles from anything, I turned to Graham and sighed. "My kingdom for a tiny break."

He brushed two fingers over my cheek and kissed the top of my head when my chin dropped to my chest.

"It's early. We'll get there. We always do."

"Still nothing from Archie or Fox."

"I imagine they're going through anything still standing with a magnifying glass and a construction crew before they let anyone in. Give it more time."

I nodded and swung down out of the truck.

A petite blonde with a tan turned from watering a flat of daisies and shaded her eyes with one hand. "Hey there, what can I do for you?" She paused until we'd walked over to her. "Officers?" she added.

"I'm really hoping you can help us identify some bits of plants." I pulled out my phone and loaded the photos. "Though I understand we don't have a whole lot for you to work with."

She put the hose on the ground and brushed her leather-gloved hands off. "May I?"

I handed it to her. She pulled her right glove off and pinched at the screen to zoom in on the petals, her brow furrowing.

"Huh. No, this doesn't bring anything to mind, I'm sorry."

I scrolled to the leaves. "What about this?"

"Hmmm. Some sort of shrub, maybe. That looks kind of like a Boxwood leaf, but not quite. It's too fat and too bright on the top." She shook her head. "It's not often folks can stump me when it comes to plants."

"Is there anyone around here who has a thing for plants that are unusual?" I asked.

"Every bored trophy wife in the Arrington Garden Club. I stopped selling to their president two years ago because she's such a stuck up bi—" She swallowed the back half of the word when our eyes went wide. "She is quite demanding about what she wants."

I pulled a notebook and pen from my hip pocket. "Arrington Garden Club, you said? And who is the president?"

"Bethany Marcil."

I wrote it down. "Thank you for your help, Ms..."

"Zink. Carrie Zink."

"Faith McClellan and Graham Hardin," I introduced. "Enjoy this beautiful weather."

"I hope you find what you're looking for," she said. "Though I would steer clear of Mrs. Marcil if at all possible." She picked up the hose. "Say—have you folks asked Dan Fortwright about those?"

Our blank stares must've been all the answer she needed.

"Oh, you should definitely stop by there. He's our resident exotic plants expert—he's made a fortune off catering to the likes of Bethany and her ilk. Always wanting the newest and best."

I flashed a smile. "Wonderful. Thank you so much for your help."

Back in the truck, I Googled Dan Fortwright.

"Distinctive Landscapes by Dan." I hit the map button on the website.

"Sounds appropriately snotty, anyway." Graham put the truck in reverse. "Still nothing from Archie?"

I shook my head. "You?"

"Nope. It's still relatively early."

"Let's go see if these plants are distinctive, shall we?"

Distinctive Landscapes' home was anything but. I wasn't sure what I'd expected, but a wide clearing on an old farm didn't scream "landscaper to the rich and picky."

We hopped out of the truck in a gravel lot populated with cars that cost more than some houses. A clearing full of pots holding everything from ornamental trees to low crawling ground cover lay to our left, just uphill from a barn that belonged in a painting—the red and white timbers rising against the cornflower sky downright breathtaking.

Graham and I crossed the parking lot, people milling amid Japanese maples, vining hibiscus, and about a dozen other beautiful things I didn't recognize.

That was saying something, given that I'd spent the bulk of my childhood roaming immaculate gardens that Ruth McClellan oversaw with an unforgiving eye. The queen of the Austin garden party, Texas's First Lady loved few things more than having a new prize to show off.

But it seemed specialty landscaping had changed in two decades. We made it about a dozen paces toward seeing how much before a stocky cowboy spotted us as he finished loading four small purple trees into the back of a large BMW SUV.

The same kind of SUV we'd seen the night before, but white.

It didn't stand out in the lot, full on this sunny October Friday. I counted three more BMWs, a Jag, two Cadillac Escalades, and one shiny black King Ranch pickup that had never seen the working side of a farm and probably had the highest price tag of the bunch.

The blouse. The skirt. The shoes.

Our Jane Doe would fit right in here.

What if she'd been killed in her own garden and then dumped in the middle of nowhere?

"Hey there, can I help you folks?"

I couldn't see the guy's eyes for the wide brim of the Stetson sitting low on his forehead. He pulled off leather gloves.

I turned square toward him. I couldn't swear the sunlight didn't glint off my badge—his eyes locked on it and widened in a way that made Graham put a subtle elbow into my upper arm.

"Faith McClellan, Texas Rangers," I said. "This is Graham Hardin, TCSO. If you're Mr. Fortwright, I'm told you're our best hope for identifying some plants."

"Dan Fortwright." His grip was firm, his hand rough but not sweaty. "And you've come to the right place." He knocked the hat brim out of his eyes and turned, spreading his hands. "It's my whole life."

The BMW drove off and a land boat of a Lexus pulled into the spot it vacated.

"Travis!" Dan called.

A lanky young man looked up from where he was pointing out different types of small shrubs and trees to a tall balding guy in a suit.

"You got the whole floor for a few," Dan called, waiting for a thumbs-up before he turned back to us. "All yours, Officer."

I pulled out my phone and tapped the screen, pulling up the photos of the leaves and petals.

"This is all we have to go on, I'm afraid."

He squinted at them.

"Well, this one here is pretty likely a teasel petal." He pointed. "These leaves, they could be a couple of things, we'll need a closer look for the best match."

"A...teasel?" Graham asked. "What on Earth is that?"

Fortwright flashed a grin, white teeth bright against a tan that said the hat didn't keep him out of the sun entirely.

"Dipascus fullonum. It's a European and Asian flowering plant that's not unlike a sunflower. Feeds pollinators by the dozen and looks pretty in bloom. Some folks call them weeds because the native leaves are pointy, but they're a great addition to any garden."

"You have any idea who grows them around here?" I asked.

"McCain's in San Antonio sells those."

We didn't have time to cut all the way over to San Antonio, but we could call.

"But they die in the summer heat here," he added. My face fell. Fortwright pointed to my phone. "May I?" Zooming in on the photo, he nodded. "This isn't from McCain's. It's a special varietal."

"Mr. Fortwright, do you have any idea where we might be able to find this plant?" It sounded like there was at least a chance locating it would narrow the places our victim might have been near the time she died. It might not be our case, but now that I'd seen her, I wanted to know what had happened to her.

"Sure thing. I bred that—I can show you one right here."

He waved for us to follow, leading us past the sales area. Graham and I hurried to fall into step on either side of Dan.

"So how did you get into the plant business?" Graham asked.

"My family's run this land for generations," he said. "Started out a farm, then my great-grandaddy ran moonshine for most of the '20s." He shook his head like he disapproved. The art deco mansion I spied on the hill in the distance said the moonshine had done his great-grandfather well.

"More profitable than vegetables and hay," I quipped.

"For sure," he said. "And then during the Depression the fields fed everyone around here for miles. They hired day laborers to work the crops and just left bushels of fresh food out at the road. There were several shanty towns all through here, and people knew to come here at the end of the day to get fixings for supper. They planted and replanted the land so much trying to keep up that they stripped all the nutrients right out of the soil. By the time the war started and my grandfather went to fight Nazis, you couldn't even grow grass for the cattle to graze on out there. My grand-mother had my father and his brothers to look after, and she took in boarders to make ends meet."

We passed the back end of the barn and kept going down the hill toward the biggest greenhouse I'd ever seen. Longer and wider than the majestic red barn but not as tall, it was hidden from customer view by the topography. We stopped in front of the greenhouse door and Dan pulled a keyring from his hip pocket.

The building in front of me certainly wasn't anyone's definition of run down, but it wouldn't pass a Ruth McClellan inspection—or, I'd wager, fit the kind of image Dan was trying hard to project to his customers these days.

"My grandmother's roses won prizes at every county fair for a decade, so she started growing and selling them to all the young brides buying houses up north of us. After she passed on, my dad was the only Fortwright brother who came back from Vietnam, and he...well." He shrugged. "He managed to hang onto it. Raised a family here. I came home after he died so the state wouldn't take the whole place."

Graham and I exchanged a glance.

"And you found a new niche when the suburbs exploded into exurbs," I said. "Because the size of the houses did, too."

He waved us inside, the air a good ten degrees warmer under the glass.

"I learned a few things about unusual plants overseas. Learned a lot about people, too—folks who have everything love having things their friends don't," he said. "I have to keep logs by address so that neighbors don't wind up with the same plants. But I'm well compensated for my time."

"That's genius." Graham's words rang with admiration as I turned a slow arc at the head of the greenhouse rows. The air folding around us was as warm and thick as a favorite sweater, a musky combination of loamy soil and exotic flowers.

I didn't need to search long for little pinky-purple petals.

I spotted some towering over everything else halfway down the second row and started toward them.

"Good eye," Dan said, close on my heels. "That's teasel."

I stopped in front of the plant, noting the tiny petals protruding from a conical head about a quarter the size of a basketball. The petals Corie Whitehead pulled from the victim's hair weren't torn, they grew in little bits. "How lovely," I said, my fingers going to the large leaves fanning out from a thick stalk. "This looks almost like a sunflower leaf. Related?"

"Those are native to much cooler European climates. They won't grow here without help—so I cross-bred them with sunflower to make them hardier."

"I would say you've found your niche indeed, Mr. Fortwright. Can you help us with the leaves? They certainly didn't come from this guy."

He gestured to the screen. "I think they're a mossy ground cover. Golden moss, maybe?"

He pointed to a far corner of the room. I followed a spotless concrete path to a whole table full of different moss varieties. "This one." I pointed.

"I think so, yes."

The tiny yellow-green leaves rose out of the pot in overlapping waves, tendrils crawling into nearby containers.

"Folks overlook moss as a pest when they're planning a garden, but it's a great addition," Dan said. "It holds water, cuts down on the need for mulch, and adds a bit of Texas history to your landscape."

I raised an eyebrow. "History?"

"Yes, ma'am. Native American women used it to make dresses. Colonists mixed it with mud to make mortar when they were building homes. Hell, modern manufacturing even used it in fabric before there was polyester, because moths don't eat it the way they do wool and cotton."

I bet Dan here was good at trivia games.

"So, why do you need to know about these two?" he asked. "I promised myself I wasn't going to ask, but I can't help it. I love detective shows. This is like my boyhood fantasy come true." He flashed a crooked grin. "With a real live Texas Ranger and everything."

"We're investigating a suspicious death," I said. "You said you keep records of which plants go where. Can we see those?"

"They're up in my office. Long as you promise to disregard the mess in the house. I don't get much company out here, and I'm an old bachelor who never learned to keep a proper house."

I softened my voice just a hair. "I appreciate your help." He was flirting pretty brazenly, and if it would get me a look at his logbook without a warrant, I could play along.

Graham didn't say a word, just raised a brow as I followed Dan past him to the door.

Dan wasn't kidding about the mess.

I'd been in smack houses that looked more presentable. The living room was a hurricane of newspapers, Diet Coke cans interspersed with beer bottles, overflowing ashtrays on every flat surface, the smell of stale smoke thicker in the house than a swinging-door honky-tonk.

He slid a gorgeous mahogany pocket door back into the wall on the opposite side of the hallway and waved us into the office.

Here, the chaos was a bit more controlled. Papers were at least stacked, even if some of the piles were teetering, on the massive polished cherry desk. My eyes went to the carvings, intricate vines and leaves weaving their way in and out of the wood along the perimeter. That had to be an antique.

"What a beautiful piece." I gestured to the desk.

Graham stood at my right shoulder, his hands linked behind his back, shoulders lifted and wide.

Behind the desk, Dan opened the top center drawer and pulled out a thick ledger, spinning it and waving a be-my-guest hand.

I flipped the cover open. His writing was small and neat, letters and numbers crammed against one another. Sections went by streets; each half page was titled with an address. Some had long lists of plants. Some only had one or two, some were marked with asterisks, some not.

I fanned pages with my thumb. There were probably three hundred with writing on them.

"I don't suppose there's an index?" I asked. "Or that you recall selling both of those plants to the same person?"

Dan shook his head before he turned it to cough into a crooked elbow. The sheer volume of stale cigarette butts left me surprised that was the first one we'd heard. And strengthened my resolve to remain an ex-smoker. "I'm afraid not. This is one of our busiest times of the year; even if I did make the sale, the chances I remember anyone who's not a regular customer are slim most of the time anyway. But in the fall or the spring, forget it. But you're welcome to look through; take as long as you please. I'd offer you copies if I had a copier."

"If you trust me to let myself out, you can go on back to your customers." I followed the soft tone with my best dazzle-the-judges pageant smile. "I don't want to keep you from anything important."

I saw Graham's jaw flex out of the corner of my eye, but anyone who didn't know him as well as I did wouldn't have noticed it.

Dan tipped his hat the barest bit, pulling it back down over his forehead before he smiled. "Just let yourself out when you're ready to go."

"Do you have a card I could keep handy?" I kept the smile.

"I don't find much use for such things. In this business word of mouth and happy customers are everything."

I pulled one of mine from my back pocket. "Well then you hold onto mine. My cell number is on the back."

His lips tipped up at the corners as he pulled out a hand-tooled leather wallet with an intricate phoenix emblem on the front flap and tucked the card inside. "I'll do that. I hope you find your answers, Ranger McClellan. And I hope I've been able to help."

"I appreciate your time, Dan."

The front door had barely clicked closed when Graham moved to the bookshelves lining the back wall. "I didn't like the way he looked at you." He said it more to the rows of books than to me, but I heard it all the same.

"I don't care who looks at me how, Hardin." My hands got busy flipping pages of the ledger, snapping a photo of each with my phone. We didn't have time to pore over this right now, but I could look at it later. "Next time I say I'm glad not to be working with corpses, shake me, would you?"

"You know your words didn't make anybody die any more than a butterfly farting in China made it rain last night."

"It's a butterfly flapping its wings, and that's a real thing," I said. "Whether I can wish up trouble by commenting on a lack of it is admittedly debatable. But it doesn't hurt to avoid tempting fate, my granddaddy always said. She can be a real bitch sometimes. Ready?" I had all the images in under ten minutes.

I shut the ledger and turned it back straight on Dan's desk, my eyes falling on an invoice.

"Teasel," I murmured, plucking it from the stack it was poking out of. "Two of them."

The floorboards creaked as Graham moved to stand behind me. "What've you got?"

"Maybe nothing. Maybe a lucky break." I raised the phone and took a shot of the address just as it started ringing.

Archie.

"Hey." I raised the phone to my ear.

"The beams are set," he said by way of hello. "We didn't lose the structure. Fox and his crew are so excited they're taking me in with them. Get your ass back down here."

"Yes, sir."

I tucked the phone back into my pocket and started for the door. "Archie's guy saved what's left of the structure for re-entry. They're going into that back room."

Graham opened the front door and held it for me, raising his brows. "They?"

"Archie said the fire crew was so thankful they're taking him in, too." I stretched up to kiss Graham's cheek. "I'm not expecting you to come in with us."

"Us? Since when are you an arson investigator?"

"Just nosy." I started for the car. "And Fox may tell me to take a hike. But either way, Archie wants us there, and we have more work to do than we have daylight left."

10

We stopped at a barricade on the service road, a uniformed DPS officer waiting to check our IDs. Eyes hidden behind my sunglasses, I scanned the throng of reporters jostling for a spot on a small patch of grass on the other side of the road. Still no Skye.

Excellent.

The trooper took one look at my star and waved us through. The fire engines were gone, replaced with department SUVs, squad cars from three different police agencies, Archie's Crown Vic, and a couple of black sedans I didn't recognize. I stepped out of the truck before Graham even had a chance to cut the engine.

He caught up with me at the back end of one of the black cars.

"US Government plates," I muttered. "Dammit."

"I would think they'd be at least marginally helpful."

"They have thirty protocols and ninety pages of paperwork for every detail," I said. "Depending on who's in there, the more people know what happened here, the less chance we have of keeping it quiet until we have a suspect. And the higher chance we have of starting an international incident that would carry the kind of political ramifications we usually try to avoid involvement in."

"My men won't talk if yours won't, Ranger McClellan." The low, honey-smooth voice came from behind me and I turned, nose-to-tie-tack with a dark-suited agent whose chin had to be close to a foot above the top of my head. I leaned back.

"Ranger McClellan." The guy stuck out one baseball-glove-sized hand. I stepped backward and shook it.

"No disrespect intended, Agent..." I arched a brow.

"Jenkins. ATF, Dallas office."

"ATF?" That was Graham, behind me. "There wasn't a bomb here."

"Commander Graham Hardin, Travis County," I introduced.

We'd have felt an explosion at the restaurant. And it hadn't yet been twenty-four hours, which made me wonder how the Dallas ATF office found out there was anything that might be interesting to their agents here in the first place.

"Lucky for me, bombs aren't the only reason for me to look into a situation." Jenkins clasped his hands behind his back and flashed a tight smile.

I refrained from actually rolling my eyes. "Care to let me in on what brings you here?"

"The accelerant used here could be a matter of federal interest in a case I'm working." Jenkins fixed his attention on me. "I've reached the point of chasing any wild goose that might get me to the bad guy, so here I am. I didn't come here to leak information. Or to compromise your investigation. I'm actually excited about the opportunity to work with you. Nice bonus, and I take my wins where I can find them like most people in our line of work."

Excited to work with me? Now I was curious. I'd assumed Archie told him to watch for me until he said that.

Graham's jaw was the kind of tight that said asking about that now was a lousy idea. I stepped toward the front of the building instead. "The wider perimeter your idea?"

Jenkins frowned. "There were reporters practically on the front porch when I got here. If the aim is to keep this quiet, keeping them out there where they belong is the easiest way to go about it."

I nodded agreement. Archie saw the press as a tool at worst and an ally at best, and as such he tended to give them more leeway than I ever would. Admittedly, I'd have made them stand up the hill on the side of the freeway if left to my own devices. Jenkins's solution was the middle ground, and probably the best general place to hang out.

A white uniform-shirted AFD officer waited at the open front door. "Battalion Chief Kerry Simon," she said, extending one hand to me.

"Faith McClellan, Texas Rangers." I pointed. "Graham Hardin, TCSO."

Jenkins put one hand out. "Cameron Jenkins, ATF. Have you found any viable samples of the accelerant?"

Simon directed her answer to me. "There's not much inside that's not pretty useless, but our investigators are looking for anything that might help you. There's another Ranger in with them at the moment. Would you like to join him?"

Graham put one hand on the small of my back as Jenkins stepped in front of me. "Thank you, Chief Simon."

She raised one hand. "I wasn't talking to you, Agent."

His mouth opened and then closed again three times, his cheeks flushing.

I pulled paper shoe covers from a box near the door and slipped them over my boots, snagging gloves and a mushroom cap, too. "I'll be right back," I told Graham.

He stepped back, waving for Jenkins to join him. The Fed's face said he wanted to pull rank and push his way inside, but it was awfully early in the case to go pissing off a high-ranking local officer. No idea why she didn't want him in there, but I had time to care about that later.

Simon handed me a respirator mask and clipped an oxygen tank to the back of my belt, nodding when I gave her a thumbs up. She stepped aside.

Jesus.

It was nearly impossible to tell what used to occupy this space. Everything was black and shiny-sticky, with ashy particles floating in front of my face.

That used to be a sofa. I stepped closer to the object nearest the door. Graceful lines. Wood trim. It looked like a piece my mother would choose for a sitting room. I squatted, my eyes examining every inch in the dim light. There. Lower back side, nearest the door. A tiny scrap of upholstery that was merely browned instead of charred. Dark blue silk jacquard.

Huh.

I stood, turning a slow circle. The deeper into the building I peered, the less the objects dotting the floor resembled furniture and the more they looked like piles of ashes. Like Fox said, the whole thing started in the back, and spread through the interior to the front. But there were definitely places throughout the space where the house was much more decimated than others.

Picking my way through fallen ceiling fragments and curled, blackened carpet, I heard Archie's voice.

"Captain, I think you're going to want to see this," he called.

I moved toward the sound, my flashlight bouncing off one of the thick metal beams the construction crew had installed every few feet to hold the roof up.

"Arch?" The sound reverberated in my ears, echoey and too loud thanks to the respirator.

Footsteps. "I should've known you'd talk your way back here," he said from a doorway in the back corner.

Captain Fox appeared at my elbow. "You have something, Baxter?"

Archie waved a *follow me.*

I obliged, trailing Fox into an entire charred-almost-beyond-recognition room. We didn't need the flashlights back here, the sun streamed down thanks to the lack of a roof.

"You said that it was clear from the burn pattern that this fire started in the far right corner of that front right room," Archie said. "But..." He pointed at a wall that appeared to be made of cinderblock, streaks of black etched into the first inch or so of the surface in several places.

Fox flinched. He moved closer, watching his step around roof and ceiling debris. "What the hell?"

"And there." Archie pointed to the opposite corner. "What kind of heat would it take to do that?"

"The kind that your average house fire doesn't produce, that's for damned sure," Fox said. "At this point if the chemical analysis doesn't say this was some variety of napalm, I'll scrub every truck in my company with a toothbrush. Those walls would've had to be exposed to heat at somewhere around 1500 degrees or better for hours to scorch like that. It's the only explanation I can think of."

"Does napalm burn that hot?" I asked.

"The kind you make with Styrofoam can burn that hot for a long time if the right accelerant is added as the fuel source."

"You mean like gasoline?"

"No. Gasoline tops out at about 12 or 1300," he said. "But there are fuels that will burn hotter. Diesel, jet fuel, methanol, ethanol...The trick would be getting the chemical ratios right to do something like this. That would mean you're looking for someone who knows their flammable liquids. And their chemistry. The lab should be able to give us the compounds."

The whole structure was a loss, but the places Archie pointed to were clearly more burned than anything around them.

"Why these two places?"

Fox tossed his hands up in the air. "We don't know anything yet, it's too early, and we'll have power records and wiring to examine and samples to test, so I don't want to open a can of worms with you folks without knowing for sure, but...my nephew is a cop and he's all the time telling us that the bad guys who get away do it because a trail goes cold so fast and people don't call the police until it's almost too late a lot of the time."

"That's true," I said.

"So. My guys pulled what we're pretty sure were bodies from this room an hour or so ago," Fox acknowledged. "Two of them—or rather, two of what was left. From under this part of the collapsed roof. I've never seen remains so badly damaged, and I don't know what the lab will be able to tell you, but...I'd guess maybe the wall caught the overflow from whatever was done to them."

Archie and I froze for a five count while that settled.

"Someone. Set. People. On fire." I didn't say it loudly. I didn't even really know why it was any different, thinking that, than the idea that someone set the building on fire with people inside.

"How would you go about something like that?" Archie had processed it and moved into picking it apart way faster than I could. "I mean...wouldn't you think one person would've moved to disarm the attacker while he was setting the other guy on fire? Or at the very least, wouldn't they run?"

I examined the cinderblocks for chips consistent with gunfire as he spoke, wondering if he shot them first. I didn't see any.

"Maybe they tried," Fox posited.

I poked at the floor with a gloved finger, a strange softness, watching fibers disintegrate. "This was a rug. A thick one. Probably expensive."

"Wool doesn't burn nearly as fast as polyester," Fox explained. "The natural fibers take longer to catch and spread than the synthetic ones. It's why what was a seventeen-minute window to control a house fire when I was a rookie is now a four-minute window. The stuff they make furniture out of these days just explodes into a fireball the minute the flames touch it."

The sofa in the front room. Wood and silk, and away from the accelerant. That's why it wasn't ashes.

Fox turned back from the wall with three evidence bags nearly half-full of blackened...something. Thinking about the remains on the way to the morgue, I didn't want to consider what.

"You're getting that to test for accelerant, right?" I thought of Jenkins, frankly surprised he hadn't argued his way inside yet.

"I am."

"If this attack was on people more than the building, they would have it on them, right? Maybe more of it than we'd find in here?"

Archie patted my shoulder as Fox drew out his phone. "Good point. I'll call the morgue."

I looked at Archie. "Jim?" My favorite medical examiner was usually an auto-request for any case Archie had a hand in.

"Is there even anyone else there?" Archie flashed a grim half-smile.

"I'll call, Captain, if that's all right with you," I said. "We have a friend who can help us out with whatever you need. I'll have you top of the list for any reports, of course."

Fox waved a hand. "I don't give a shit about that. If we're right about what might have happened here, let's just do everything we can to catch the bastard responsible for it."

I liked him. More than I could say for the ATF guy outside, though I couldn't pin down why he bothered me.

"I got this, Faith," Archie said. "You go get on the case. The clock is ticking."

"Have you even been to bed?"

"I caught a few hours on the couch in the commander's office."

"You are not twenty-five anymore. Let Captain Fox and his crew do their jobs. Go home. Sleep. Eat. Call me tomorrow morning and I'll meet you at HQ." I put my hand out. "If I'm going to the morgue to see Jim, I can take those by the lab if you'd like, Captain."

He handed them over, his shoulders heaving with a sigh that fogged up the mask on his respirator. "Baxter here says you two are the best in the state at what you do."

"I said we were the best. I didn't say anything about the state," Archie said.

I held Fox's gaze. "We'll find them, sir."

"I have young guys here who have never even seen a fatality in a house fire," he said. "This is going to give them nightmares."

"More incentive to keep the details from them," Archie said.

"Thank you." Fox shook our hands in turn. "Both of you."

I turned to the door, tucking the samples under my shirt and into the waistband of my Wranglers. So much easier than arguing with Jenkins about it outside.

The only thing I'd ever read about napalm involved it being dropped out of planes, because it gave the soldiers distance from their targets. Who could throw liquid death on another human while looking them in the eye?

I knew how Fox felt about his rookies—because I wasn't sure how the hell I was supposed to work the case without sharing such an important detail with Graham, but damned if I could bring myself to even consider the alternative.

11

Jim's white King Ranch F-150 rolled to a stop in the parking lot as I turned in. He stepped down and waited for me to park, shading his eyes as I crossed the parking lot. I'd skirted having Graham tag along by telling him Archie needed a babysitter. He was thankful to have something to do that didn't involve an autopsy, and Archie didn't grumble too much because he knew exactly why I didn't want Graham with me.

"The one Friday I try to get out of here early, McClellan."

"No rest for the weary, right?"

"I'm pretty sure I haven't done anything wicked in at least a few decades, so yeah, I guess." Jim opened the front door and held it for me, waving at the front desk attendant, who was shutting down his computer as we passed. "Baxter's voicemail said burn victims. How bad?"

"I'm not sure anything could've made it out of that building but bones," I said. "Maybe not even all the bones. But you're the expert."

"Jesus." He flipped on the lights in his body room and pulled a gown and gloves from a shelf by the door. Pulling on his gear, he pointed me to the shelf. "Grab one if you're staying. By your presence I'm guessing this isn't your run-of-the-mill fire. Or maybe not run-of-the-mill victims. Which am I dealing with?"

"Both?" I snapped gloves in place. "Where's the fun in simplicity, right?"

"Who's in my cold storage?"

"I don't know."

His eyes narrowed. "Who do you think is in my cold storage?"

"I can't tell you," I said. "That's hard for me to say to you, Jim, but I can't. I need you to trust me. I will explain the minute I can."

"I trust you with the most precious thing in my life, McClellan." He pulled the door to the freezer open. "What am I looking for that will help you?"

His wife was newly in remission from a rare form of cancer, and my ability to wheedle, argue, and bribe a favor out of Chuck McClellan had made that possible. "Accelerant." I winced around the word.

"On the remains?" Over his mask and his wire-rimmed bifocals, Jim's bushy gray brows shot up.

"On the remains."

He waited for me to elaborate for a beat, then shrugged and retrieved the first stretcher. I grabbed the opposite end and helped him line it up with the table.

"You sure you want to hang out?"

"I'm good." I was not. I've seen firsthand evidence of just about every way humans can think to be horrible to one another, but this was a new one on me.

Right then, I was rooting for evidence that these folks had already been dead when the fire started. I wasn't sure it was possible, given everything we'd noted at the scene, but it helped me feel better for the moment.

Jim unzipped the bag and moved the remains to the table without a batted lash or casual comment.

My breath hissed in loud enough for the both of us.

I dissolved from the gasp to a coughing fit, the stench of chemicals tinged with gasoline and the sour bite of scorched hair and flesh mushrooming out to permeate the whole room.

Still vaguely human-shaped, the mass Jim stared down at as he positioned his lights and pulled out tools was missing delineated arms and legs, but I barely noticed the vacancy. The skull held my eyes and refused to let go.

Grayish-black bone was visible above the left eye socket, remnant bits of blackened flesh that verged on ash curling back at the edges and drooping toward the table. The skull was small and misshapen, fractures splitting the parietal bones but sparing the facial ones.

Jim donned a clear face shield and leaned forward, clicking a button on a small, stick-shaped silver voice recorder. "James Prescott, Travis County Medical Examiner. Today is Friday, October 9th, John Doe Male, structure fire, postmortem attended by Faith McClellan, Texas Department of Public Safety, Rangers Division."

He stuck the recorder in his pocket and moved through the examination. "Severe and potentially fatal tissue damage due to burns evident on all visible anterior tissue surfaces. Possible contamination with external fibers, will require further examination."

He clicked the recorder off and pointed. "Do you see what I see here?" His finger hovered over the exposed skull.

"As much as my impending nightmares wish I did not."

"You asked about accelerant on the remains I assume because you have reason to suspect someone set these people on fire?"

"It is one of the theories I'm tracking."

"It's quite possible that if that happened, it started right here."

I swallowed hard. "On his...on his face."

Jim grunted a disgusted agreement.

The central goal of every question I ask when I'm working a murder is finding the person responsible. So who in the name of all that is holy could do this? Setting another human's face on fire, on purpose...even if this damage was postmortem...I was looking for righteous or crazy, and honestly not sure which of the two I'd prefer.

Jim moved to the central torso, sunken and bubbled in places under a charred exterior. "Subject's skeleton exhibits fracturing patterns and missing limb bones consistent with prolonged exposure to intense heat, as well as significant absences of soft abdominal tissues," he said into the recorder.

"How long would the fire have to burn to destroy a person's organs like that?" I asked. The blurry man in the distant surveillance video was dropped off an hour before Graham and I spotted the flames. It had taken almost another hour for Fox and his crew to defeat the fire.

"It depends on a lot of variables, but the thing that really points to the duration and temperature extreme is the fracturing of the bones here." He pointed to the rib cage area. "Either these remains burned for a long time—as in, several hours—or they burned at an intense temperature."

The cinderblocks. "I think intense heat is a safe bet," I said. "That's why the fire captain and the ATF guy are curious about the type of accelerant. Austin Fire mentioned napalm last night. I know different accelerants burn at different temperatures, but I'm not well versed in the specifics of that."

"Modern napalm only burns as hot as the fuel used to make it," Jim said. "The difference is the stickiness of it—because the fuel is thick, it's hard to get it off, and the gel base from the Styrofoam makes it nearly impossible to put out. It even burns in water. I can't tell you what was used, but I can say that if regular gasoline or kerosene did this, it took a whole lot of it, and it burned for hours."

Jim finished his examination, taking scrapings from the area by the skull fracture, the abdomen, and the legs, sealing them in small plastic petri dishes before he moved the remains back to the bag, leaving a fine dusting of ash on the table. When he'd cleaned it up and we'd exchanged the stretchers, he started over with a different body that was indistinguishable from the first, save for a difference in torso length.

"This person would've been quite a bit taller," I said.

Jim went through the same steps he always did, meticulous, not missing a stray fleck of ash.

"This one seems to have started here, across the sternum, and moved out." He noted a crater in the bone where it looked like it had actually burned away.

"A crematorium burns at 1800 degrees and it takes four hours to cremate a body," Jim said. "So this burned at or almost that hot at its highest point, right here"—he pointed to the bone damage—"but not for long enough, and not once the flames spread out from the accelerant. What it did do is make it damned hard to recover any kind of evidence from these remains."

"Of course it did."

Jim clicked off his recorder.

"There may be a better way to find you something you can work with here," he said. "There's just so little I can examine on sight, I'm not able to tell you as much as I usually can."

I arched an eyebrow. "Anything that might help is a fantastic idea."

"I haven't seen remains this badly damaged by fire since the DuGray girl was found. And the way we determined cause of death with her was a head CT that showed the staining on the interior skull. So let's see what technology can tell us about these folks."

A low hum from the machine was the only sound as the images of John Doe number two loaded onto the wide computer monitor in front of us.

The first set of remains had given up no secrets. Even the dentals wouldn't be much help unless we got a lucky hit with the records Archie was trying to find for Avesta—6 for 32 on intact teeth, maybe enough for a partial match. It would help, but it might not be definitive and it would damned sure take time Archie said we didn't have to spare.

So far, there was no clear evidence of antemortem trauma that might point to the victims being dead when the fire was set. Jim said the fractures could mean they'd been beaten, but the patterns looked to him like the bones had broken from the stress of the fire. No visible remodeling meant there was no way to know which theory was correct given the information we had.

Jim scrolled down, sitting up straighter in his chair.

"What?" I leaned forward, looking over his shoulder and getting a whiff of Old Spice.

"That's a foreign body." He pointed to the screen. A wide, bright outline about an eighth of an inch thick, its edges blurred, encircled the victim's knee like a glowing halo.

Jim clicked the mouse to zoom in on the image. It pixelated, the gray of the bone blurring into the white of the other object where they met. Add in a bit of image distortion, and it became downright difficult for me to tell what I was looking at. The same thing happens to me when people want to show me sonogram stills. Everything looks like a gray blob inside a gray blob, but I smile and nod like I can see what they do.

Here, I didn't have to pretend.

"What is that?"

"This machine is a goddamned dinosaur, so I'll have to retrieve it to be certain, but my money's on a knee replacement." He turned with a triumphant smile.

"Hot damn, we've got an ID." I pumped one fist into the air. Artificial joints carry serial numbers. The serial numbers are registered with the FDA. Which meant I wasn't doomed to spend crucial days poring over dentals or begging for help and hoping to hit a DNA profile.

Back in the body room, he arranged the remains on the table, gowned and gloved himself up, and turned the light on before he started the recorder again. "Subject File 20-0001009-2, continued. Physical examination of foreign object detected by CT scan in subject's left patella." He set the recorder on the table and picked up a scalpel, moving to make an incision above the general area that should be occupied by the left knee. The blade met resistance, something I'd never seen in an autopsy. Jim laid his free hand above his target spot and pressed harder.

The whole leg snapped, flakes of ash scattering across the table.

"Sweet cartwheeling Jesus." Jim dropped the scalpel. "There's nothing left except brittle bone. Not just no tissue on the surface, no tissue. No moisture at all. What the hell?"

"That's not normal?" I asked.

He shook his head. "Structure fires don't normally burn hot enough for long enough to burn all of the moisture out of a human body. This"—he waved one hand over the ash—"is like 60 or maybe 70 percent of the way to cremation."

"Holy hell."

"The house is still standing?"

"Not all of it. But parts, yeah."

"So whatever kind of accelerant these poor souls were attacked with, it was controlled, and it burns hotter and longer than most readily available fuel. You said the fire investigator mentioned napalm, but..." Jim pointed to the ashes again, pulling the light down and waving me closer. "This whitish gray? Run-of-the-mill, internet-recipe napalm wouldn't even do that. And the building didn't get the same treatment if it's still standing. So you're looking for—" He blew out a slow breath. "Something I've never seen. Something like napalm, but worse. Napalm's overbearing big brother."

My teeth went to my lip, raking over the skin as I tried to focus. Calm. Clear. I was just trying to get a serial number. To tell whoever was missing this person what had happened to him.

One step at a time.

"You think the implant is still intact?"

"They survive cremation, so yeah." He put the scalpel back on the tray and picked up a bone saw. "But getting to it isn't going to be pretty."

I winced and let my eyes fall shut until the whirring stopped. When I opened them, particles of ash floated above the table, and Jim held a hunk of chrome with pieces of charred person stuck to it.

"Knee replacement." Triumph practically dripped from the words. "Get some gloves and you can clean this up while I finish reviewing the CT scans for anything we might've missed on the first pass."

"I can...what?"

"This is not the time to get squeamish on me, McClellan. The oxidation and adherence of charred tissue need to be cleaned off so we can find the serial number, and the serial number is going to get you an ID a whole lot quicker than hunting down a partial dental on a John Doe skull this badly damaged."

I swallowed hard. Fine. I prided myself on my ability to hold my stomach in the autopsy room, and I'd spent years giving Graham hell about his inability to do the same.

"Put these on." Jim held out a pair of gloves that looked like they'd enable underwater welding.

I pulled them on. My hands slid, sweaty, inside them, though from insulation or nerves, I couldn't say for sure.

Jim waved me toward a counter, where he spread a blue and white sterile pad and laid the artificial joint down, blackened flakes dusting the papery white surface. From an overhead cabinet, he pulled two small brown glass bottles and one big glass jug, putting them down before he pulled a wad of steel wool from a drawer.

"You're going to need a good mask." He pointed to a box as he filled small bowls with sharp-sour-smelling chemicals.

I coughed as I looped one over my ears.

"This one first." Jim dipped the steel wool into the closest bowl. "You must keep the gloves on until you're done with this stuff. It doesn't play nice with your skin."

He wiped gently at the surface of the metal and, like magic, bright streaks of silver appeared through a veil of charred tissue. "Easy going, gentle, you don't want to melt the numbers off. Uncover them, then dip the whole thing in there"—he pointed to the solution in the sink—"and put the gloves in there. Get regular gloves and a paper towel and switch to this." He pointed to the other bowl. "Easy enough?"

I nodded, not wanting to open my mouth with the rancid smell of the acid still coming through my mask.

Jim handed me the scrubbing cloth and disappeared back to the CT room.

I wrapped the end of one index finger gently in the steel wool, the acid warming my finger through the glove, and touched the rounded edge of the implant.

It didn't take much pressure to clean it. Light strokes worked just fine, Which made me wonder what the hell kind of chemical was only a fat layer of polymer away from eating my skin. I squashed the thought and kept going. Jim was right, the trick was to not go too far. Kind of like Magic Erasing pencil marks from a wall without taking the paint off.

I worked my way around, one layer at a time. It got easier as the minutes ticked by to focus on the tediousness of the task instead of what I was actually wiping off.

On the far edge of the outer rim, in the curve toward a rod with a screw held in place by...well. I found the serial number. Better to not think about what was holding the screw in its little hole.

I leaned in, ignoring the stench of the acid, and peered at the etch marks in the metal.

Light stroke by painstaking light stroke, I uncovered each digit.

A muscle in my shoulder seized and I stood up straight, rolling my shoulder backward and holding the metal piece up to rotate it in the glaring overhead light.

5J3KWZ...692YM40B

I couldn't even tell if it was two or three digits I couldn't see in the middle.

"Dammit." I put the implant carefully on the pad Jim had laid out for it and dropped the cloth.

In half a blink, the pad under the steel wool dissolved down to the blue plastic.

I took a step back, my eyes going to my hands, still safe under the crazy gloves. "Holy shit."

I needed a paper towel. The slivery streaks on the steel wool and my own iffy feelings had me afraid to try more acid, at least not until Jim got back. But there was at least one digit in the middle of the string I couldn't make out, and it might be two. The spacing was odd and the imprint was small, so it was hard to say. Stepping to the sink, I dunked the whole thing in the chemical he'd left before I put it back on the other side of the little pad and shucked the gloves into the basin. Grabbing a paper towel, I turned to pull on a pair of latex gloves and dabbed up a bit of the second glass bowl's solution.

I tested it on a corner of the implant. Nothing blew up.

Going to work on the area around the serial number, I managed to polish up the letters and numbers I could see, but didn't make any progress on the part that I couldn't. And the fat-finger gloves and steel wool didn't leave an option for precision.

"Damn," I muttered, wondering if the database could be searched with a missing digit or two. I could at least narrow it down. I put the implant down and stripped off the gloves, tossing them in the garbage before I took a photo of the serial number with my phone.

It started ringing as I snapped the picture.

Graham.

"Hey. Everything okay there?" I put it to my ear.

"Archie went home under serious protest, this guy from the ATF is a douche, and I'm going to eat my boots if I don't get some dinner soon. How're things there?"

"I have newly honed skills in the areas of lab technician and errand girl Friday, but hopefully one or both of those will get us a lead to follow while the trail here is still a little warm. I should be done in just a bit, but feel free to eat without me." I glanced at the remains on the table. "I'm not hungry."

"Got something to work with?" Jim's voice behind me about sent me out of my skin. I fumbled the phone without dropping it and turned. "Graham, I gotta go—I'll call you when I leave here." I clicked off the call and turned to Jim. "I got most of the number. Part of it is missing in the middle, but hopefully this will be enough to narrow the pool."

He adjusted his glasses and peered down. "Looks like you're missing a digit or two. That will get you something, but I'm sorry it's not better. I can have Florence run it down for you, but she won't be back until Monday."

"I'll get on it in the morning, thanks. We're already out of time on this one. You find anything else useful upstairs?"

He shook his head. "I do think there's enough to track down partial dentals on both, but no more magic bullets, I'm afraid." His shoulders dropped with a heavy sigh.

This line of work makes it easy to see lost lives as methodology. It's less a person and more an equation to solve. That's how a lot of folks cope with spending their lives working around death without losing their minds. But this felt different.

Burning humans alive was barbaric, reserved throughout history by civilized society for those thought to be too evil for simple execution, and by the uncivilized for people they viewed as less than human. The reasoning was always wrong, of course—but considering it might help us find an answer to the question hanging heavy between me and Jim right then.

Why?

Because the why of a murder case is often the most direct road to the who.

12

"AFD is confident they have cleared the scene of remains." Archie's eyes were still a touch hollow in the shade of the Stetson brim, but he looked better as he opened the front door at Rangers HQ Saturday morning, gesturing for Graham and me to go inside.

I flipped the light switch, rows of fluorescent bulbs crackling to life overhead. "Just the two we know about, right?"

"Just the two," he said. "The place had a small cellar that wasn't even touched by the flames, but the paint bubbled and peeled from the heat, Fox said. He's working chemical analysis with the feds. NBA-tall guy from the ATF? He said he met you."

I rolled my eyes and Graham scrunched up his face.

"I take it I'm not the only one who doesn't like the feds right now?" Archie flashed a grin as he dropped into the chair behind his desk.

"Even Graham didn't like that guy. And I'm not sure I trust him to uncover his own ass with two hands and a flashlight. But the detectives at AFD are good ones."

"Fox will get us whatever they find." Archie waved a hand. "ATF will do their own thing. They always have." The words were tight. The ATF wasn't anyone's favorite federal agency if they'd been around Texas law enforcement as long as Archie had. The fiasco at Mount Carmel had created some long memories among the guys who'd been there.

He raised his chin in my direction. "What've you got so far? Anything come out of your trip to the morgue?"

The purple-haired desk attendant at the state crime lab had taken the samples from the scene and the morgue with a bored stare and a pop of her bubble gum. "Wait times for results are currently six to twelve business days." I had just nodded. Archie had favors he could call in everywhere.

Hoping one of those favors would get us lab reports by Monday, I turned on the lights in the conference room, went straight to the white board, and picked up a marker. "A whole lot of shit news," I said. "But there're probably some leads in it somewhere."

"Let's have it."

I glanced at Graham. "Some of the stuff from the ME's office is kind of graphic." The words came out hedged.

His mouth softened into a smile. "Looking out for me?"

"I don't want you to have to hear anything you don't want to."

"What I want is to catch this fucker," Graham said. "Anything it takes to get there, I'm all in." A dark look flickered over his face. "Anyone who could do what we saw Thursday night knowing there were people in that building deserves a worse fate than I think I can comfortably come up with."

"Amen to that, son." Archie pointed to me. "Take it away."

"So we know this isn't a simple arson case," I said.

"The ATF guy seems stuck on the paid setup theory, which made me instinctively look for places to blow holes in it," Graham said. "Insurance fraud? A developer who wanted the lot?"

I scrawled HOMICIDE in all caps across the top of the board.

"Manslaughter is the charge for killing people trapped in an arson case," Graham said.

"Except the fire wasn't set from outside," Archie said. "Fox showed us how it burned from the inside out."

"The remains showed signs of having been directly affected by the accelerant," I said. "Particularly on the head and face, for at least one victim. So I think the ATF guy is wrong. While our suspect does seem to know a lot about slipping in and killing people without being noticed, the cold, distant hitman puts a bullet in them both, then sets the house on fire if there's evidence to destroy, and walks out. Our guy didn't do any of that."

I wrote *emotional motive* under homicide. "Setting another person's face on fire suggests a personal hatred. Deep, personal hatred."

Graham's lips disappeared into a thin line.

"I think our advantage over the ATF is recognizing that this might have been a personal act," I said. "And that means we know how to work this case. This is our wheelhouse."

"There's where your psychobabble nonsense comes in handy." Archie smiled as he spoke. "Take away the flashy M.O. and the large-scale destruction, and we're just dealing with a homicide. No matter who the victims were." He paused. "Faith, I know you volunteered to be here, and I appreciate the hell out of that, but I should tell you that your bank fraud case has been transferred back to Gonzalez in that unit and you're officially back on homicide as of this morning."

I knew that was coming. And I didn't mind. I was just flat more useful here. Possible political volatility aside, we were hunting a killer. All the trimmings on this one didn't change the core of the case.

And experience had taught me that at this point in a murder investigation, there was no ruling anything out.

Maybe Jane Doe in Corie Whitehead's homegrown crime lab was tied to the fire victims. Maybe not. Some days, the hardest part of what I do is keeping my mind open to all the possibilities and keeping all the facts straight at the same time.

I wrote the generic name on the right side of the board. "Graham and I caught a call about a body in Goliad this morning that was burned. Discovered just after daybreak in the middle of nowhere outside a trailer park." I turned back to face Archie. "I want to make sure we have a wide enough lens here."

"Aside from the burned part, any reason to think she's related to our other victims?"

"The area was related to a ping we got on one of Sewell's marked cards last night. We got another ping from Cabrerra's. Or—close enough to Cabrerra's that the credit card reader people put it at the restaurant because it's the only business for blocks around?" I thought of that as I was saying it, so it half came out as a question, but I didn't hate the theory.

Archie sat up straighter in his chair. "And you didn't lead with this because why?"

"The whole thing is weird. It's weird to think it's a coincidence, but possibly the only thing weirder is thinking it's not. I just want to keep an eye that way until we have proof one way or another, that's all."

"Good enough. Like we don't have enough to do."

"When has that ever mattered?"

"So your Jane Doe is going to remain a Jane Doe until we hit a dental," Archie said. "Are we even close to identifying any of the other victims?"

"What do we know about the fancy SUV in the alley?" I asked.

"I spoke with a senior partner at the law firm it's registered to yesterday. He claims they have a register for who uses it, and it wasn't checked out on Thursday. They keep it for client transportation. They also have an Escalade, a Porsche, and two black Town Cars, according to the DPS database."

I noted the other models on the board. "So he's saying it was stolen?"

"That's the way I took it, because it gave me a window to impound it." Archie flashed a grin. "I put a rush on a forensic detailing, but it'll be tomorrow before they get to it, and even that required a favor. I'll know as soon as they find anything."

"Anything from the embassy?"

"Not yet. My contact was out on Friday, but should be there Monday."

I brandished my phone. "I did find out one of the victims had a knee replacement. I have most of the serial number. It'll take some fancy computer work to track down the owner, but I can get there with some time."

Archie pointed to his computer. "Get to work. The more we know about who is dead, the easier it'll be to figure out why." He turned to Graham. "You up for helping me trace the last few days of movements of a walking political time bomb?"

"The Iranian guy?" Graham shrugged. "I take it he hasn't turned up anywhere?"

"His phone was recovered after it pinged this morning in a coffee shop garbage can," Archie said. "The fire last night put it on a high alert list, so I got the hit as soon as it came up. But he wasn't there, wasn't visible on their surveillance cameras, which do not cover the trash receptacles, and now we have no way to track anything. So I'd like to see where he's been since we don't know where he is. If he's in Jim's cold storage at the crime lab, we're already behind on the timeline of this case. If he isn't dead, how the hell are we going to find him and figure out who killed these people at the same time? Riding two horses with one ass never goes well."

Graham shot me a look.

I knew what he was thinking. But I wasn't going there yet. Archie would hone in on it if we needed it soon enough.

Because if a member of a powerful family with ties to a hostile foreign government—even a black sheep nephew—had murdered two Americans in a horrifying way that the press would delight in detailing when they had Jim's report, we were already in the outer bands of a shit storm the likes of which even I had a hard time imagining.

13

Since 2012, an international registry created to make tracking patient records easier in the event of a device recall has been a boon to police officers and medical examiners with hard-to-identify remains. If the deceased happened to need medical equipment implanted in them somewhere, they're part of a database.

My problem was that I needed a whole serial number, and I only had part of one. A quick Google image search told me I was missing two digits, not just the one I'd hoped.

So first things first: how many of these things were there with the leading numbers I knew?

I pulled up the database and logged in as a law enforcement professional, starting a new search with the first six digits.

More than four hundred results. And since our search had possible international parameters, I couldn't narrow that to the local area. Yet, anyway.

There was no finding my missing needle in that data haystack without more information. With two missing digits, the number of possible answers grew to too many to do by hand. But a handy merit of my extra degree in forensic computing was that I knew where to find questionable things on the internet. The Jimmy Sewells of the world often do this type of work for extra pocket change. An off-server cruise through the dark web netted me three codebreaking apps designed by and for hackers and safecrackers, and a $160 charge to my Amex and a half hour later, I had all three running different combinations on my phone.

But knowing possibilities was only half the answer. Typing all of them in by hand would take way more time than we had. That was where my more above-board IT skills could work for us.

I grabbed a cord from the drawer, plugged my phone into Archie's computer, and hunched over the keyboard.

The first step? Getting the apps backdoor access to the database site so the computers could talk to each other. I settled headphones into my ears to drown out Archie and Graham's discussion about news sites versus traffic cameras as a starting point for data gathering and put my fingers on the keyboard.

My shoulders were tight and my stomach grumbling about long ago Pop-Tarts by the time I cracked the FDA security. Watching the black screen in front of me turn green, I raised both arms and arched my back in a long stretch before I opened the phone's files and started linking.

Once the website started returning possible results, I let out a little whoop and shoved the chair back, jumping to my feet, the earbuds popping loose and clattering to the desk.

Archie looked up. "Got him?"

"Getting there," I said. "The hard part is done. I think." I rapped a fist on the faux wood surface of the battered old gray metal desk. "I'm hoping for a shorter list at the end of this, anyway. How are y'all doing?"

"Benham Avesta landed at DFW International on a flight from Villahermosa on September 25 at five nineteen in the evening," Graham said.

"That was two weeks ago." I turned to Archie. "I thought you said you started tracking his phone six days before the fire?"

He opened an app on his phone. "I got the first notification at seven forty-nine on October first."

"That's not as helpful as I would've hoped."

"I'm sure we have federal bureaucracy to thank. Customs probably reports it to a bean counter who tells ten other people before it gets to the guy who hits the button to send me an alert."

"So are we even sure he's still here? Could he have dumped the phone himself and taken off?"

"According to customs his passport hasn't left the country," Graham said.

I leaned on the back of his chair, laying my hands on his shoulders as I looked at his screen. The customs website had a three-hour lag. "Where's he staying?"

"He was at the Driskill for most of the week," Archie said. "Checked out on Thursday at a few minutes after two."

"He didn't check into another hotel?" I knew the answer before I asked the question.

"He hasn't used a credit card since that day," Archie said.

My mouth popped open into a neat little "O."

Graham stood, nodding to Archie's computer, still returning data. "Is that going to be a while?" he asked.

"It will. How come?"

"Avesta hired a car service rather than renting when he arrived in town. I need more on the car and driver to finish my searches. And it seems the Visa charge here is from our old friend Sergei."

I grabbed my keys. We were going to figure this out. For the first time since I set eyes on the remains on Jim's table the day before, my confidence was high.

One thing at a time. Every box checked. Every lead investigated. Nothing overlooked.

This was why we were good at this job.

"We'll be back, Arch. We have to see a man about a car," I called over my shoulder.

"See a man about some take-out on your way back." He fell into step beside me. "I'm going to the hotel. See if I can get anything out of the staff about what he was doing and who he was seeing while he was there."

Graham and I waved from the truck as Archie locked the door. "You think Sergei will remember us?" I clicked on the radio.

Graham shot me a side eye. "We're good at making an impression."

"This is going to work." I laced my fingers with his.

"Of course it is." He kept his eyes on the road as he merged into traffic.

I wasn't sure he was even talking about the case, but the easy confidence in his tone boosted mine higher. And I could worry about other possibilities later.

Sergei's shop still smelled like fresh grease and stale beer.

Graham and I stepped over a pile of oil-streaked mechanics' rags on our way in through a massive bay door and made a beeline for the glass-enclosed office in the middle of the far left wall.

Sergei bent over an open laptop at five p.m. on a gorgeous Saturday. He hadn't liked us last time we were here, and I needed his help. I didn't have time to get a warrant for the business records I wanted to see, which meant he needed to like me today. The badass act from last time wouldn't do. I cleared my throat and tapped on the glass as I stopped in the doorway, flashing a smile.

"Texas Rangers." Sergei's eyes popped wide when he looked up. He shut the computer and stood in one jerky motion. "I only thought the regular police will come when you call."

Graham and I shot each other a sideways glance so quick Sergei didn't notice it.

"What can we help you with?" I kept my tone even, my lips curving automatically into my long-practiced *you can trust me; I will help* smile.

Sergei threw his hands up. "Three of my cars. Three of my guys. LoJacks don't work. Cell phones don't work. Just missing, all day now."

Oh. Well then.

A thousand questions clamored to be first out of my lips, but my face stayed flat. Calm.

"Have you tried contacting the clients who hired those cars?"

"Only one." Sergei plucked a thin yellow sales slip from a tray on his desk and shook it at me. "Only one customer. Three cars. All stretch. I only have four of these, and he wants three for the same night. I say, 'No problem, I can take care of this.' I cancel a woman who hired for her kid's coming home celebration. She leaves terrible comments on the internet about my company. And now I am out three cars? Three guys?" He buried his head in his hands, fingers tightening around unruly tufts of salt-and-pepper hair.

The hairs on my arms stood up at the idea that "one client" who was important enough to get Sergei to cancel another reservation had orchestrated the whole thing. But I couldn't get ahead of the story, either. The first rule of questioning a witness is to let them ramble, rather than lead them toward what you want them to talk about. It's an entirely different skill set than interrogating a suspect.

Just the next thing.

"Can we get the name of the customer?" I asked.

Sergei began pacing. "Beau O'Brien."

Oh hell. I didn't let my face fall, but it took work.

"He is bigshot here. Beau O'Brien gets what he wants." Sergei threw up his hands, his agitation thickening his accent. "Being on his shit list no is good."

Boy was that an understatement.

I pulled a slow, deep breath through my nose.

"Where did the cars go?" I asked.

"Local fare. O'Brien said is confidential. No address. Back by two, he said."

And Beau O'Brien had the kind of pull it took to get someone like Sergei to agree to that.

"You said you had a LoJack on the vehicles," Graham said. "Where's the last location it returned?"

Sergei paced back to his desk and punched a few keys on the computer. "A parking lot downtown. Thirty minutes after they left here."

"But you've checked that location and they aren't there." I said it because I had to. Every box checked, every rock lifted. Law enforcement will teach a person not to assume anything faster than a rattlesnake will teach one boots are a necessity on a ranch, not a fashion statement.

Sergei's lips pursed in a clear what-kind-of-idiot-do-you-think-I-am look.

"I have to ask," I said.

"They are not there," he said. "They are not at home. This is not like them."

"Can we get a name and address for each missing driver and the plates on the three cars, please?"

"Of course." He sat heavily in the chair and printed three sheets of paper.

I took them with a tight smile. "We'll figure out what's going on here, Sergei. You have my word."

"You will get my cars back? Find my guys? Howie, he's been driving for me since he was nineteen. He is family…" His face crumpled and then smoothed so fast I couldn't swear to what I saw, except his nostrils flaring with a deep breath.

I put a hand out for him to shake. He gripped mine with both of his. "I thank you, Ranger." His eyes went to Graham. "Officer."

I turned for the door. Graham landed an inconspicuous what-are-you-doing elbow to my ribs.

Patience, partner. Two steps. Turn. Half-wattage smile, eyes wide. No big deal. "Hey, Sergei, were there any other high rollers around lately? The kind of people O'Brien would call important?"

He wobbled one hand side to side. "I'm not so sure he is important as he thinks, but there was an Arab, slick, throwing around money." He paged through papers on his desk. "Benham Avesta. Stretch for seven days, last day six days ago."

"Do people often rent a limo for that long?" I asked. I knew the answer.

"Only when they have the big ego," Sergei snorted.

Yep. He knew his market, Sergei.

"Did he have the same driver the whole time?"

Sergei's head bobbed. "Howie. He's my best with the arrogant ones. Knows how to make them feel important, big enough to not have to take their bullshit." He paused. "You don't think…"

I scrunched up my nose for effect as I shook my head. "I'm sure everything is fine. But could we get a list of the places he went? Do you have those records?"

"Sure sure." He went back to the computer and printed two more pages, walking over to hand them to Graham. "Thank you."

"I'll be in touch." I passed him a card. "My cell is on the back. Call me if you think of anything I should know or if you hear from them."

We passed an APD patrol unit pulling into the parking lot on our way out.

"Nice work. And good timing." Graham tipped his head toward the Austin cops. "So where'd our friend go before Archie knew he was here?"

I stared so hard at the papers in my hand I don't know how I didn't burn a hole right through them.

"Faith?"

I looked up, not even seeing what was on the other side of the windshield.

"He went to see my father."

14

"Family is simple. They just love you no matter what."

I could hear the words like my Granny still sat next to me. Hand to God, I could nearly smell her hyacinth perfume.

She believed that with every fiber of her being the day she patted my fifteen-year-old head, wiped my tears, and told me I was wrong about the Governor being disappointed in my declaration that I was going to be a Texas Ranger someday. She believed it still as she took her last breath, her tiny, cold fingers knotted from arthritis and cradled in my hands.

Granny didn't know her only son as well as she liked to think.

My relationship with former Texas Governor Chuck McClellan was more complicated than the wall-sized quadratic equations that once put men on the moon. It certainly wasn't about to get me any special favors. Chuck McClellan was good at showing a smiling face to the world, but behind closed doors he was a vindictive bastard with a controlling streak that bordered on a God complex. Asking him for help would suck. Actually finding a way to get it might be the biggest psychological coup of my career.

"Hey." Graham's deep voice was soft. I loved him so much my heart hurt for knowing he didn't need to say another word.

"Damn Chuck McClellan to the darkest, hottest pit in hell."

I didn't mean to say it out loud. I held a deep breath for a ten count and blew it out in a *whoosh*. Looked at the clock. Two fifteen on Saturday. They'd be drinking already.

Fan-goddamn-tastic.

"1836 Bluebonnet Hills Lane." I wove my hands together in my lap and stared at Graham's, his long fingers gripping the steering wheel. I'd watched him throw everything from a 90-mile-an-hour fastball to a nose-pulverizing left hook with those hands. I didn't even have to try to make goosebumps pop up thinking about how they felt on my skin.

And I was fifteen minutes from taking one of them in mine and leading him into the lions' den.

I couldn't do it. Nope.

My bullshit baggage was my problem. I didn't know a soul more embarrassed of their family than I was of mine, and while I recognized the irony of the sentiment, thinking about it just pissed me off.

What must it be like to actually feel pride in one's heritage, instead of smiling politely when people fawned over the Governor's "accomplishments?" Not that my personal feelings stopped me from occasionally dropping his name when I wanted to get something out of a witness. I put a hand on Graham's knee. "Stop by the office on the way back. Order some lunch. I'll be gone a couple of hours." At least.

Graham's shoulders flexed under his shirt, his whole body going rigid. "Why would I do that?"

"You don't understand what I'm trying to save you from," I began.

He kept driving, shaking his head. "Your mother is intimidating as all hell, but I have met her, and I walked away with no damage."

"You surprised her when she wasn't on her own turf," I said. "You have no idea what you're asking me to do."

"Faith, sooner or later, I'm going to have to meet your father."

I focused on my hands and stayed quiet. Graham turned into a Target parking lot and slammed the truck into park. His hands stayed on the wheel, and except for his breathing, I couldn't have sworn he was still in the car.

The silence stretched and spread, wide and heavy, thickening the air. I cracked a window. I didn't knowingly lead people I cared about into my personal nonsense. I didn't have friends who weren't Archie and Graham—

and they stayed away easy enough. Graham had never been the type to be impressed by my political pedigree or want to meet my father, and Archie had done his time in the Governor's presence. Seen him for the toxin that he was.

"I'm not, am I? You don't intend for that to ever happen." Graham's words were sharp and sad at the same time, the combination slicing my resolve to ribbons. Tears welled and spilled over before I could blink them back. Dammit. I swiped at my cheeks with the back of one hand.

He put the car in gear without looking at me. "Nice to know where I stand."

But he didn't know anything.

And I couldn't tell him. I'd tried a dozen times in the past few weeks, and every time the words stuck in my throat. Graham Hardin was everything that was good and pure in my world.

My father poisoned everything he touched. Hell, some things he barely looked at before they withered and died.

I love my job, but there's nothing like spending your days seeing the worst of what mankind has to offer society to make a person believe humanity is just fundamentally flawed. Graham was my proof that I was wrong.

I wasn't sure how, but I knew in my bones that Chuck McClellan would find a way to poison that, too.

Graham parked the truck in front of Rangers HQ and practically flew out the door, slamming it behind him while I sat in the passenger seat, fresh tears edging closer to spilling over. Archie was back from the Driskill, so at least he wouldn't be sitting in there alone.

He disappeared into the building and I scooted to the driver's seat and flipped down the sun visor. No fear. Ruth McClellan could smell tears like I could smell bullshit—and giving her the upper hand was a mistake I avoided at all costs.

Graham reappeared in the doorway with Archie's keys in his hand, pausing to look at me before he pressed the button to unlock the car.

I backed up and sped out of the lot.

All costs.

Even the ones that were way too damn high for me to handle.

"JR wouldn't have lasted a blue half hour in the governor's mansion," Chuck McClellan was fond of saying when visitors noticed that the front of the house was a dead ringer for Southfork Ranch from *Dallas*.

I gave my name at the gate and then sat in the driveway, staring at the wide double front doors, chewing my right index fingernail down to a painful nub.

Everything about the man was a study in manipulation. Those who noticed and commented on the house were belittled for thinking Chuck McClellan would stoop to building something as beneath him as a TV replica. First time visitors who said nothing were dismissed as "Yankees"— still an insult, and a hefty one to the Governor—their allegiance to Whataburger, Shiner Bock, and fresh flour tortillas called into question before they'd made it to the front door.

My father built a house with the sole mission of establishing himself in a position of dominance over anyone who visited before they'd even been invited inside.

I chase murderers for a living. At times, it's dangerous work. I have stared down the business end of more guns than I care to count without so much as a quick breath or a pounding heart.

Walking into that house?

Terrified me.

I had started on my left index fingernail by the time the front door opened.

"*Mija!*" Erma tucked a bright white kitchen towel into her equally white apron and raised a hand to shade her eyes as she stepped down two of the wide porch risers.

"They're making you work on weekends now, too?" I kept my voice low as I crossed the double wide embossed stone circle drive with both arms outstretched.

She waved a hand. "Party last night. She let me go home and sleep for a few hours, anyway. I'm finishing up. Besides, done any earlier and I would've missed you, my girl." She stretched on tiptoe to wrap her soft arms around my neck, and I returned the embrace.

I don't hug, as a general rule. Erma was special. Besides Archie, she was the only living, breathing relic of my childhood left. The only person who knew my family, knew my story, and loved me anyway. I breathed deep, her woodsy patchouli perfume still blending with Pine-Sol, bleach, and oil soap into the most comforting smell I'd ever known. Two deep breaths and I was back in the mansion on a kitchen stool, scrubbing my hands so my mother wouldn't smell or see the butter residue from the cookie Erma slipped me with my after-school SlimFast shake. Ruth McClellan always had her eye on the next crown, and there was always a pageant around the corner I needed to diet for if I so much as dared a glance at a dessert.

"I miss seeing you," Erma said, stepping back to take both my hands in hers and give me a once-over. "Always so skinny, *mija*. But you look good. That star...*es perfecto*."

"It took me long enough." I squeezed her hands. "I miss you too. We should get lunch one day. Catch up. I want to hear how everyone is doing. Is Jaime still working horses?"

"He'll be happiest if he dies in a paddock."

Her husband was one of the best handlers in the state. Not that he'd ever been recognized for it or paid what he was worth. It was damned unfair, the way the system was set up for one group of people to use and profit off of another. Money and power make the world go round, and they do it hand in hand, mostly regardless of talent. Nobody knew that better than I did—and I had been appalled for years at how many of the people in my parents' circle not only didn't care, but delighted in and exploited it. Sometimes murderers aren't the only folks who can show humanity at its worst.

I pulled a card from my back pocket and passed it to her. "Please call me. I spend more time around Austin lately, and I would love to see you. Away from here."

She tucked the card into her apron even as she shook her head. "Mrs. McClellan would never approve of you socializing with the help, *mija*."

"I am thirty-seven years old and can socialize with whoever I choose. And I choose differently than she does." I arched one eyebrow as I spoke, tucking my lips into my best impression of Ruth McClellan's tight, disapproving almost-sneer.

Erma laughed. "I should get back inside. They're waiting for you in the den."

I linked my fingers with hers as we walked up the steps and through the cavernous doors. "Call me," I said.

She scuttled to the kitchen without a word or a nod.

I squared my shoulders and resisted the urge to rest a hand on the butt of my Sig as I stared at the embossed cherry doors to the Governor's den.

It's an unfortunate truth that a lot of the things that make me damned good at my job run in my blood. I have a rare ability to read people quickly. I have a scary specific memory and a knack for noticing small details in scenes and people that others miss. Graham often called me a human lie detector when we worked together at the sheriff's office. All those things make the routine cases easy—it takes an extraordinary offender to skate through my defenses. And even then, I haven't completely missed one yet.

Because of the Governor. The difference between me and Chuck McClellan was that I used these abilities to help people.

I didn't need to control people the way he did, but I was damned good at running a room. Making sure I had a handle on the situation around me. I'd spent years studying multiple psych disciplines so that I almost always knew what everyone would do before they did it. It took a lot for people to surprise me.

Except here.

In these rooms, I couldn't control shit. And I knew it. The Governor and Ruth were made for each other—they circled prey and pounced from multiple directions like emotional hyenas. Every time I thought I had them pegged, they twisted a different way.

Hoping I was quick enough to dodge, I slid the pocket door to my left and stepped onto a plush Oriental rug.

"Faith." He didn't look up from the book in his lap. "I wasn't expecting a visit this week. Do you need something? Money?"

"Chuck!" My mother was curled on a plush scarlet chaise in the corner, the only piece of furniture in the room not upholstered in rich brown leather. She grabbed a thick crystal highball glass from the marble side table, downing half of the amber liquid in it before she stood, still glaring at the Governor. "No daughter of mine would stoop to slithering in here looking for a handout." She spit the words like they offended her.

I kept my hands folded behind my back and my lips pressed tight together until the Governor raised his eyes, sliding his reading glasses down the bridge of his nose.

My father is the only human I've ever met who can look down on a person when they're standing over him. I laced and unlaced my fingers behind my back.

"She didn't drop in because she enjoys our company, Ruth."

I let the silence stand for two beats. My mother finished her drink, her face a blank Botox-devoted mask of indifference.

"This is an official visit." I stepped forward, nodding to the long unoccupied sofa opposite the Governor. "May I?"

"Of course." He closed his book and laid it on the glass table between two shoebox-sized, ornate wooden puzzle boxes. I knew it was a doorstopper political history tome without looking—he didn't read anything else.

"Why on Earth could you be coming to see us on official Rangers business?" he asked, just as Ruth blurted, "Is everything okay? Lieutenant Baxter isn't..." She let it trail.

I shook my head, surprised she remembered Archie's name. "He's fine. Working ninety-hour weeks as always." I returned my attention to my father. "I'm trying to locate someone, and I have information that he was here not too long ago. I need to know why."

"The Texas Rangers want to know why we're entertaining guests in our private home? Has crime around here taken a nosedive I'm not privy to?"

"Benham Avesta." I ignored his trademark condescension so easily I barely noticed it. "He arrived in town on September 27, and after he checked into his hotel, the first thing he did was come here."

"Mr. Avesta is a businessman. We have some mutual acquaintances. We had people over for dinner. I thought he might like to join us when I heard he would be in town. Nothing suspect about it, I'm afraid."

It was so ingrained in the Governor to dodge questions that I wasn't sure I could trust myself to know if he was hiding something or just being difficult for difficulty's sake.

Deep breath. He wasn't my father, he was a hostile witness. Not that there was a significant difference in dealing with the two.

But thinking of him as a witness made me realize he did not have all the power in this situation.

I sat back, sinking into the cushions and relaxing my pose. "Of course there wasn't. I didn't intend to imply that there might have been. I'd like to speak with him myself, and I'm wondering if you know how to get in touch with him."

The Governor stretched one arm down the back of the couch, matching my faux ease. He didn't miss a trick, Chuck McClellan. "You think I have contact information you can't find? The Rangers aren't what they once were, I suppose."

What I wanted to know was what the hell they'd been talking about, but that might even exceed my considerable interrogation skills.

Talking to the Governor was like playing chess with Bobby Fischer. He calculated every comment with the speed of ten supercomputers, and was used to winning at every turn. He wouldn't lie to me, because I was there in an official capacity, and an arrest would be an image problem. But he still didn't look at me and see a capable officer of the law. He saw pigtails and frilly dresses and bright eyes easily dimmed by a harsh or condescending comment. An easy target, not a worthy foe. So the trick here was to use that confidence against him.

I let my gaze fall. "When the sort of people who get dinner invitations from you don't want to be found, it presents a bit of a challenge," I said. Just the right balance of patting his ego and stung feelings in my tone.

"Why would he not want to be found?" Ruth stood and crossed to the opposite end of the sofa where I sat. "Do you think he's hiding something?"

If I didn't know her, the alarm coating the words would've made me think she was asking because she wanted the Governor to help me. But no. What she wanted was to make damned sure he hadn't invited someone into her home who was about to be associated with so much as a whisper of something that might embarrass her.

Image was more important to those two than air. A threat to it was about the only thing that would crack their thickly cemented alliance.

"I don't know anything for sure until I speak to him." Not even that he was in fact still breathing.

"Chuck, tell her how to find this person." Ruth's voice was flat. Not a request, a command.

The Governor glanced between the two of us and raised two fingers to his chin before he inclined his head ever so slightly my way and reached for his phone.

It was as close to proud of me as I'd ever seen him look.

He read off a cell number. I noted it. "Thank you, I'll try that." Since Avesta's phone was currently in evidence at my office, that wasn't exactly helpful. But it did tell me that my father knew Avesta in more than just passing. And I had Chuck McClellan feeling like I'd just beaten him at his own game in his own house. I also had my mother talking.

I turned to her.

"What did you serve for dinner?"

I kept my eyes on her, but I felt the Governor's narrow. He understood exactly what I was up to before the whole question was out of my mouth, but I knew he wouldn't dare interrupt our conversation to derail it.

The woman next to me had never been a confidant, a cookie baking queen, or a warm place to land, but she was a shelter from the Governor's worst. Because she was the only person he was afraid to cross.

"A wonderful bacon-wrapped filet Sam Johnson cut special for us, roasted asparagus, a feta and candied pecan tossed salad, and lobster tails."

I widened my eyes, licking my lips slightly. "Oooh. That salad with Erma's special dressing? Sounds divine."

"There's nothing better." The utter assurance drifting out of her mouth with the words would have convinced a polygraph she made the dressing herself.

"Dessert? Wine?"

"Homemade dulce de leche ice cream and a Pedernales Cellars cabernet."

"Still the best hostess in my jurisdiction."

I raised my eyes to hers and saw the icy blue ever so slightly surrounded by white.

"Thank you," she said.

Checkmate, Governor.

"I take it the business part of the evening was good?" I turned back to the Governor.

"Time will tell."

"I'm sure you'll land on your feet." I stood. "I would appreciate it if you'd let Mr. Avesta know I'd like to speak with him if you hear from him again."

"I can't make any promises about my memory, but I might."

He was pissed that I'd gotten as much information as I had.

Ruth let her hand drop back to her lap. "It was nice to see you, Faith."

I made it back to the truck without anybody noticing my shaking hands.

It still took me three tries to hit Graham's name on my speed dial.

15

"Slow down." Archie wasn't yelling at me, he was just trying to be heard over my borderline-shrill volume.

I sucked in a slow breath. "Sorry."

"Graham said you went to the ranch." Archie's voice was so dry the Sahara would be jealous. "Why am I not surprised that our VIP possible victim knew Chuck?"

"Because if a powerful guy is into anything shady, there's a good chance of that?"

"And the more powerful they are, the more shade they tend to find."

True story.

"The thing about people like your father is that they excel at covering their asses." Archie's voice dropped, a sad sort of anger adding a gravelly quality I wasn't accustomed to. "Trust me, Faith, you're wasting your time. Chuck McClellan doesn't tip his hand unless he wants to, and then it's about control and misdirection. Nothing about that man is genuine."

I stopped at a flashing red light, my eyes going unfocused on the empty road across the intersection. He was right. But he didn't often talk to me about the Governor. And Archie never said what he actually thought of my father. I didn't quite know how to reply.

"But that's the thing," I said. "I got something. Maybe something thin, maybe even too thin to go anywhere if I can't shake anything else loose, but I have some ideas."

"Trust me, if you got him to say anything incriminating, by tomorrow morning his lawyers will have a paper trail refuting any involvement on his part."

"All I got *him* to say was that Avesta was there for dinner. Which I knew from the car service, and he knew I knew that." I took a left and merged onto 35 North.

"If he was being cagey, he's hiding something," Graham said into the speaker phone.

"Maybe. I wish I could tell if his refusal to talk was about him hiding something, like normal people, or if it was just his way of messing with me."

"Is that why you didn't want me there?" Graham's question was halting. "I've heard enough about your parents, you don't need to be worried about being embarrassed."

"I appreciate that," I said. I was worried about so much more than simple embarrassment. He had no idea what he was asking. But this wasn't the time for that conversation. "I may not be more than a stalemate match for the Governor, but he wasn't the only person in the room. Here's what I know—whatever Avesta was there to talk about, it was with a small group of VIPs. And something she heard them say frightened my mother."

Archie took that with genuine surprise. "Ruth McClellan isn't afraid of anything."

"Exactly. But she was afraid of this. I didn't even know the Botox would let her eyes open that wide. And she squeezed my hand like she was trying to pop my fingers off. She's been there and done that with almost every kind of ridiculous bullshit the Governor has ever gotten into, because she likes being close to power. She never says a word."

"She just retreats from the situation if she doesn't care for it."

Huh. Archie was right, though I'd never thought of it quite that way.

I filed that away for later. "Right. So finding out what's bothering her is the next step."

"You think she's going to tell you?"

"I don't know why she wouldn't, otherwise why risk signaling me in front of the Governor? He doesn't seek out fights with Ruth, but he's not an easy man to live with when he loses his temper."

I almost wanted to swallow the back end of that sentence as it was coming out of my mouth. Too late now.

"She served filet and lobster, which means there were no more than five people at the table including the two of them, and they were people she was trying to impress." I just kept talking, hoping the case would steal Graham's attention from my fucked-up family. "The list of people they care about impressing is painfully short. So we have a place to start."

"Good work, Faith. Come on back to the office and we'll get on it. Graham got you some spring rolls and soup."

My stomach grumbled at the mention of food. "Be there in ten."

Empty white paper cartons littered the big polished mahogany table in the main conference room. Archie, Graham, and I bent over keyboards for the fifth hour in a row.

"This one is a car service out of Waco." Graham sat back in the chair. "That's weird. What kind of visiting dignitary goes to Waco?"

"The kind whose wife watches a lot of HGTV?" Archie asked.

Graham snickered.

I kept my eyes on the traffic cam footage on the left-hand side of my screen, looking for a car at the flashing light nearest my parents' ranch. I'd spotted a dozen so far, but cross referencing with the camera at the end of their driveway, only one had gone to their place. I couldn't see the whole plate numbers from the hacked feed of their camera—it was low-res and grainy, not intended for the web, but it let me find cars headed that way on the state cameras and spot them turning into the Governor's drive. He'd fire his security chief if he knew I was able to get into the camera system at all. I was hoping I'd spy a vehicle registered to someone I knew, and knew well enough to get them to talk to me about something my father didn't want anyone to know about.

That was the second guest at the dinner party Avesta had attended who arrived in a hired car. Didn't necessarily mean they were both from out of town, but it was too early to tell.

"Let's keep going and see what else we find. There's room at the table for one more guest before my mother would've changed the menu to fish or chicken." The Governor just didn't pay enough attention to some details of what went on in his house to know my question about the menu had been more pointed than conversational.

"What?" Graham's brow furrowed. I took a moment to admire how adorable he was.

"Ruth McClellan only serves steak and lobster when there are five or fewer people at the table. Even both of my grandparents joining us for dinner when I was growing up was cause to have something less expensive, like chicken or fish."

Graham shook his head. "You half grew up in the governor's mansion. It's not like she was paying the grocery bill."

"She took being a good steward of taxpayer money very seriously. Once, when the Governor was in Washington at a summit, she got upset at the cost of feeding my sister and me and sent Erma to the market to get ten cans of Spam and five pounds of scrapple. It was all she let us eat for a week. Charity passed out at gymnastics because she starved herself."

"And someone else I know became a vegetarian at the end of that week, if I recall correctly." Archie's blue eyes twinkled as he grinned at me across the table.

"I still can't even stand the smell of eggs because I wouldn't eat the spam without them." I shuddered.

"Hey, what's wrong with Spam?" Graham asked. "I mean, it's not good for you, but we ate it growing up. I liked it on sandwiches with mustard."

"Little different when it's a punishment and you were raised on rare steak and caviar so your parents could show you off at dinner parties," Archie said. "Faith and Charity weren't allowed to eat bread, either, so no sandwiches for them."

"Not allowed?" Graham swung his eyes back to me. "You love bread."

"Carbs make you fat, Faith Lorraine." I sat up ramrod straight in the chair and looked down my nose, pulling off a pretty good impersonation of

Ruth's flat face and cool, condescending tone. "Judges don't vote for husky pageant contestants."

Graham opened his mouth and closed it again several times before he just returned his gaze to his screen.

"That's about what there is to say, yeah," Archie said.

I turned a grateful smile on him. "You always had gum and lollipops for me."

"I was happy to be able to help you have a little bit of normal."

"I'm up to six forty-one on this video and we still have room for one more at dinner."

"Anyone coming after that would be late for cocktails," Archie said.

"Drinks at six thirty, dinner at seven sharp. God help someone who arrived after seven." I laughed, glancing at Graham to make sure he wasn't offended or completely weirded out, which worried me in equal measures.

He muttered, "Jesus, no wonder she doesn't talk to them," almost too low for me to hear, which made me think I wasn't supposed to. I let it go.

I clicked play again, writing down the plate numbers on a sleek black Jaguar and a long white Lincoln Town Car.

Back to the Governor's camera.

Six forty-six: the white Town Car turned into the drive at the ranch.

"Got it. TRL164." I closed the computer and stood, pacing.

Graham was going to say...

"Car service." He looked up. "This one's located in San Antonio. Why would there be three out of town guests for the same dinner, all of them in hired cars from different companies in different cities?"

"We don't know that they're all from out of town, we only know one of them was, and he's the one who got there first." I spun to look at Archie.

"Governor McClellan uses car services when he doesn't want anyone to be able to trace where he's going," Archie said, his lips disappearing into a thin line. "There were certain friends he would visit only in hired cars, once upon a time."

"So who was going to dinner that he didn't want anyone to know about?" I checked the clock. Quarter past ten.

"I've got the company names, but the offices are all closed by now."

Graham shut his computer and stood, stretching his arms up and back. "Let's call it a day?"

Archie was slow getting out of the chair, careful with his knee in a way that made the worry line between my brows deepen. "I thought you'd never ask." He waved to the table. "Leave it. We can't call a car service on Sunday, nobody in the back office who can help us will be there. Let's touch base tomorrow if there's anything new, otherwise, we'll get the passenger lists and go looking for them on Monday. And hopefully we'll know more about Avesta and any other possibilities for his whereabouts by then, too."

Archie's computer beeped as he moved to close it. He raised both hands and stepped back. "Why is it mad?"

"It's done." I pounced, my fingers flying over the keyboard.

"I don't think I've ever identified a body this way," Archie said. "What exactly does 'done' mean?"

I touched keys. "Well, there were almost thirteen hundred possible combinations in the serial number for the computer to search. This list tells us who made the implants that matched any of those possibilities. The company will have records about which medical facility purchased each one, and from the doctor, we'll be able to get the name of the owners. And then we can figure out which one of them is missing."

I clicked to load the results into a spreadsheet and sorted it by the first letter of the manufacturer name. "Looks like there are only three companies here, twenty-seven possible hits. It'll take some work, but that's a hell of a lot better than nearly four hundred I got from trying the partial device identifier."

I saved the file to Archie's laptop and emailed it to myself and Graham.

"Looks like we're working the phones for all kinds of stuff Monday," Archie said.

We locked up and said goodnight in the parking lot. Graham drove us halfway back to his apartment before he spoke.

"I think I'm starting to get why you don't want me to meet your parents," he began.

No he didn't. God I hoped he didn't. But I couldn't say that.

"I can handle more than you think I can," he insisted.

I put a gentle hand on his knee. "Hardin, you're one of the strongest people I've ever met. This isn't about you. It's them." *It's me.* But I couldn't say that either.

He blew out a slow breath and didn't say anything else, turning into the lot at the apartment and parking my truck in the guest spot for his place.

We were halfway across the parking lot before I spotted the black SUV with the engine running, parked under a tree in the far front corner. I paused, laying one hand on Graham's arm and using the other to unclip the safety on my holster.

Graham turned just as the SUV flashed its headlights.

"What the hell?" He stepped in front of me.

The rear passenger door of the vehicle opened, and my fingers closed around the butt of my Sig.

16

Ruth McClellan stepped into the light. I refastened the safety strap and sagged back against Graham.

"Jesus," I muttered, waving her over.

"I guess she is scared."

"We have phones in our pockets," I said as she approached. "You could've called me."

She snorted. "The accountants read every line of my cell bill. He knows every time I try."

I wasn't sure why it gave me pause that the Governor spied on her the same way he had Charity and me, but I stopped short.

"Staring is rude, Faith." The snipped words didn't make it past her lips before she was shaking her head. "Then again so is showing up at someone's home without being invited." She turned to Graham, a small rueful smile tipping the corners of her lips up the barest bit. "Please forgive me, Commander Hardin. I needed to see my daughter."

"You're always welcome here, Mrs. McClellan." Graham's voice was tight, but it wasn't nerves, it was irritation. "Please, come inside." He gestured for her to walk ahead of us to the door.

I kept my eyes on my mother. I didn't bother asking how she knew I'd be here. They knew everything.

She stood aside for Graham to open the door for her, thanked him, and then strode into the living room.

"Something about that dinner party bothered you," I said. "Who was there and what are they up to?"

Her broad shoulders rose with a deep, hitching breath.

Holy hell. She really was freaked out.

"I don't know." She finally perched on the edge of a leather armchair.

I rounded the edge of the sofa and sat opposite her. "I'm sorry?"

Nothing happened in that house without Ruth McClellan's knowledge and approval.

Or at least, I'd always thought that was how it worked.

"I wasn't allowed to be in there. Your father requested the menu and told me to go out or stay upstairs. 'Business matters, peach. You needn't worry your pretty head.'" She deepened her voice in an impression of the Governor that was so dead on it was almost unsettling.

The couch shifted as Graham sat next to me, but it might as well have been tectonic plates moving. Hand to God, the room swam in front of my eyes for half a beat. I thought that was just something women gasped about in old movies, mostly because back then it was men who wrote the lines, until right then.

"Mrs. McClellan, did you leave the house that night?"

I leaned into Graham's shoulder. He always knew when I needed a minute. It was one of the things I had always loved about working with him.

Ruth shook her head. "I did not."

"Why?" The word was small. Graham said it softly. It filled the whole room.

I couldn't even blink, my eyes on Ruth's as a single tear welled, spilling over her lashes and trailing through her makeup.

"I thought he was bringing a woman to my house." She stuck her chin out, sitting up straighter in the chair. So one thing was a constant in my world: Ruth McClellan was never a victim. She was always in charge of what happened in her life, one way or another.

I swallowed hard. "I'm sorry," I said.

It sounded trite. Inadequate. But I had nothing else to offer.

I don't know why it had never occurred to me that he cheated. Why wouldn't he? If there was a type of man who did that, the Governor checked every box on the list. Hell, even Archie thought I knew. His comment about the hired cars earlier didn't go unnoticed.

Ruth flicked at the tear like she was swatting a mosquito. "Don't be. I've had a very nice life, and I knew what I was getting into when I married him. But he's always at least tried to hide it. I think it's part of the thrill, feeling like he's getting away with something." She rolled her eyes. "Or maybe he just likes thinking I'm stupid. Either way, I wasn't having his whore in my house. There's only so far my patience will stretch."

She spoke casually, like she was talking about him losing a little too much at a roulette table in Vegas.

"There's just one, then?" My voice sounded far away to my own ears, all sensation in every limb fading. I hadn't felt that way in years—not since the week after Charity died.

"These days he can't keep up with more than one. You can only take so many of those blue pills, you know."

Ew. I didn't want to know that. But she was talking to me like a witness, and I needed to listen like a detective. People told me their secrets every day. I didn't judge.

This wasn't my family. It was a case. I kept my face blank.

"She's younger than me. She's younger than you, actually. Former pageant queen. Your psychobabble nonsense would probably say she has a daddy complex. But whatever her motivation, she's not coming into my house."

I reached for a notebook. Not that this wouldn't fuel my nightmares for months. But it tied the conversation more to work and less to personal issues. And I needed the tether.

"Do you know her name?" There. I didn't want to know that for myself, for damned sure. But for the case, I had to ask.

"Trinity Meadows. Sounds like a stripper, doesn't it?" The haughty cocktail of ice and superiority in her tone almost covered the hurt.

I swallowed a laugh. Graham snorted next to me.

I noted that. "Did you see anyone come or go from the house that night?"

"The bell chimed four times. All the voices inside were male."

Four chimes meant I hadn't watched the video footage for long enough.

"How long did they stay?"

"One left relatively early, probably right after they ate, maybe even before they were finished."

I put a star by that on the page.

"Did you hear anything unusual that might indicate why?"

"Chuck was angry," she said. "Then the door slammed."

"You couldn't hear what he was mad about?" I had to ask, but unless she'd managed to slip into the room, I knew the answer. They built that house to guard secrets. Solid wood doors and layers of insulation in the walls and floors meant only shouting breached the barriers, and even then, she wouldn't have been able to make out words.

"I left the bedroom door cracked, but I still couldn't hear. They must have still been in the dining room, or the study."

"Did the other men have an accent of any sort?"

She shook her head. "Not that I managed to make out, but I can't say for absolute sure."

"Do you know when everyone else left?"

"Late. I fell asleep a little before two and the door hadn't opened again. But they weren't there in the morning." She twisted her hands together in her lap.

Ruth McClellan didn't fidget. It was a sign of weakness.

"Faith." Her voice was softer than I'd ever heard it. Halting, even.

I gripped the pen so tightly the plastic bit into my fingers, holding my tongue. Patience. Let her talk.

"Why did you come to the ranch asking questions about this?" Again with the hand-wringing.

I let two beats pass, my face somber. She knew. Even if she didn't quite know what the Governor was up to here, she knew why I had been there to ask about it.

"We have reason to believe one of the guests at the dinner might've been murdered. We are waiting for a positive ID." Two more beats. "You're afraid of something. If you tell us what it is, we may be able to help you."

It was so much more than I'd ever asked of any witness. Ruth McClellan valued nothing more than her image, her pride. Anything that might tarnish either wasn't open for discussion—even with her daughter. I knew that. But maybe a dose of fear would tip that scale the other direction.

She didn't blink for more than a minute, tilting her head to one side as she held my gaze. I almost felt like Charity and I were back in her bedroom, cross-legged and knee to knee on her big four poster bed, playing chicken. I nearly always won. Maybe the streak would hold.

Graham shifted on the sofa next to me, and I could tell he wanted to try his expert hand at getting her to talk. I landed a quick, soft elbow to his arm. *I got this.*

"He's in over his head," she finally said, her voice cracking on the last word. "I don't know how or why, I swear, but...he's afraid of something. Something that has nothing to do with you or Baxter or the Rangers. I've never seen him like this. And when you showed up at the house today...I know you chase murderers. I know why you chase murderers, and I know how good at it you are." She stood, collecting her pocketbook and crossing the room to look down at us. "Catch this one, Faith. Before you have to bury us, too." She flicked her cool blue eyes to Graham. "Take care of my daughter, young man."

She swept from the room and the door clicked shut behind us.

"Holy shit," Graham said.

I stood. Paced to the window, watched her hired car turn out of the lot, and strode to the kitchen before I turned back.

The Governor wasn't just a possible witness. He was a potential victim.

17

"Five people at the table including the Governor." I took a bite of my oatmeal and waved the spoon at Graham. "All men. At least most told to come in hired cars. One of them possibly murdered in a horrifying manner less than two weeks later."

"Your dad is into something shady." Graham's voice was flat, declarative. "Are we good to keep working this thing?"

"Good as in, allowed to under department policy?" I stabbed a chunk of strawberry with the end of the spoon. "No. Good as in, am I walking away from the investigation? I am not."

"There's a reason departments have policies on conflicts of interest." Graham's half-hooded stare said he was worried about me getting myself hurt.

"But the reason doesn't apply here. If it was your mother in danger, then sure. We'd need to find someone else. But I don't have a normal relationship with my parents. I don't want them to die a cruel and painful death, but that's also true of any random person I pass on the street. I won't let it cloud my judgment or make me choose rash or unwise avenues of pursuit. Any more than normal, anyway."

He sipped his coffee. "I trust you. But is Baxter going to trust you?"

I didn't know.

We did have to tell Archie about my mother's midnight visit, so I'd just have to hope for the best. "Of course he is." I wish I had as much confidence in the idea as came through in my words.

Graham ignored it, picking up his toast.

Before he could say anything else, my cell phone rang. Dallas number, no name.

"McClellan."

"Ranger, Ray Jenkins, ATF. I need to meet you in the next thirty minutes."

I bit back a "charm isn't your strong suit, is it?" and leaned back in my chair. "Good morning to you, too, Agent Jenkins."

Graham rolled his eyes so hard the green totally disappeared. I covered my mouth to stifle a snort.

"It's urgent," Jenkins said.

"May I ask what's so urgent that you need to see me before noon on a Sunday?"

"Not over the phone." His condescension gave way to a tightness that made my pulse pick up speed.

"Fine. There's a coffeehouse called Lola's in Tarrytown. I'll be there in twenty minutes."

He hung up without another word.

Graham set his coffee mug back on the table. "What the hell was that about?"

"I have no idea. Said he couldn't talk on the phone. He wants to see me." I shrugged. "I'd like to know what he knows. And why he's here. I won't be gone long." Not only did Jenkins not ask for Graham, I knew Graham had no interest in going.

"I'll meet you at the office when I'm done with him. See when kickoff is today and put the chili on so we know when we need to be home." I leaned across the table and kissed him.

"It's not chili when there's no meat in it. It's bean soup. Spicy Minestrone, maybe." His gorgeous eyes crinkled at the corners as he smiled, brushing three fingers across my cheek. "Be careful. I don't like that guy."

"He's a pompous dick, he's not dangerous," I said. "And if anyone knows how to handle a pompous, big-headed jerk, it's me."

"I suppose your dad has to come in handy for something."

For the first time, I gave a fleeting thought to taking him to the ranch. I couldn't, not in real life. But man it'd be fun to watch Graham go toe to toe with the Governor. Hardin had a way of commanding respect without bravado that would turn Chuck army green with envy. And the look on his face said he wouldn't suffer the Governor's bullshit for half a second. Which was exactly why I couldn't let that happen.

Nineteen minutes and the world's fastest shower and makeup later, I turned into the parking lot at Lola's and spotted Jenkins standing at the rear of his government issue Crown Vic.

He waved and stepped to the door of the truck, pulling it open for me. All I could see was my reflection in his mirrored aviators. He didn't return my smile.

"They have the best espresso in the city," I said.

"I don't drink coffee. Chemical enhancement of bodily functions is detrimental to health." He shut the truck door and turned to follow me into the cafe.

"They have water, too."

He pulled the shades down the bridge of his nose and surveyed the shop. "There." He pointed to a cozy corner in the back. Two armchairs. No nearby tables or seating. Away from the counter and the bathrooms. Except the chairs were occupied.

"We could sit outside, too." I pointed to the empty patio.

He shook his head, dismissing me in the direction of the counter as he strode for the corner.

I asked for a coffee with two sugars. The barista didn't look at me, her eyes on Jenkins, who was flashing his badge and ordering the folks in the armchairs to vacate. A muscular young man wearing a T-shirt so tight a single flex of a bicep probably would've split a seam stood, his stony face saying he didn't appreciate the interruption. His friend jumped out of her chair and led him away as I crossed the room.

I stood over Jenkins, sipping my coffee. He looked way more ridiculous than badass wearing the shades inside, but made no move to take them off. "This is a matter of security. Maybe of life and death. Have a seat."

My temper flared at the flat, declarative tone. I pinched my lips together and perched on the edge of the other chair.

"A tanker truck of aviation fuel was stolen from a hangar at DFW International five days ago. We suspect terrorist involvement."

The high temperatures. Near cremation state of the bodies. Foam that had to come from the airport.

It fit. But I hadn't considered it seriously because jet fuel isn't exactly something a person can buy at the corner Exxon.

"And you think it ended up here."

"Some of it, yes. But the fire investigators will know that soon enough, and I don't give a tiny rat's ass about your murders except for what they might tell me about the location of the tank. It's the rest of it that I'm concerned about. There's enough fuel in that truck to burn all of the Hill Country to the ground."

"I dropped samples at the lab Friday night myself, so hopefully we'll have the type of accelerant identified by mid-week."

"The fire department is welcome to run their tests. I can tell you from the scene that no garden-variety accelerant was the cause of your fire. Which means odds are, when you find your murderer, I'll find my truck. So." He paused, sliding the shades down the bridge of his nose. "I know the Rangers don't take kindly to the feds butting in, but I'd like to work with you. Many hands, and all that. Let's get this fucker before anyone else dies, shall we?"

I held his gaze without moving or speaking for three beats.

He was arrogant. He flouted rules.

I could identify on some levels. But I liked to think I wasn't a jerk about it.

Graham didn't like him at all. He wouldn't be thrilled.

Still, we didn't have to like the guy for him to be helpful—and right then, I needed all the help I could get.

I stuck out one hand. "Let's go catch ourselves a killer."

18

Policework can be all-consuming if you let it, especially when a clock might be ticking on someone else's life. Graham and I had a nice little Sunday routine going for the fall—he made vegetarian chili from Erma's recipe, and we ate it with Fritos and cheese and watched the Cowboys game. He didn't even mind when I jumped up and yelled, a habit I'd picked up from my granddaddy, mostly because it annoyed the fire out of my mother.

I waved goodbye to Jenkins in the coffeehouse parking lot.

"This is all strictly confidential, no matter what your reporter friend asks you," he said by way of goodbye.

"Reporter...friend?"

"The woman with the short platinum hair at Channel Two?"

"Skye?" I spit the word so incredulously I choked on it. Coughing, I shook my head. "Skye Morrow is not my friend."

"Huh. I must've heard wrong."

"I have no idea who would think such a thing, but let me just assure you, you did in fact hear wrong."

"I'll bring my file to Rangers HQ tomorrow if you'll have a copy of yours ready for me."

"I will get you what I have, most of which would fit on a Post-it. See you tomorrow."

Graham's whole apartment smelled of spices and peppers when I opened the door, and I could hear Troy Aikman and Joe Buck talking on the television about offensive strategy and injuries.

"How's Agent Personality?" he called from the kitchen.

"He wants to work with us?" My voice went up at the end like I was asking a question even though it was already a done deal.

Graham appeared in the doorway wielding a big wooden spoon.

I scrunched my nose and lifted the corners of my lips into a pained smile. "He knows what kind of fuel the killer used. Someone swiped a tanker truck from a hangar at DFW on Tuesday night."

The spoon dropped to his side. "Damn."

"He's meeting us in the morning. Figures if we find the killer we'll find his missing truck and the rest of the fuel. He seems much less concerned about what was already done with it than what might be."

"He's probably not wrong." Graham sighed.

"More incentive to get it wrapped up quickly, right?" I put as much brightness into each syllable as I could.

He turned back for the kitchen. "Nobody in our starting lineup is injured today. I think that might be all the miracle we can ask for this week."

"Let's hope we're overdue for a double helping." I plucked a Frito from a bowl on the counter. "Tomorrow is going to be busy."

He stirred the chili bubbling in the crockpot, letting a heavy whiff of vegetables and spices out when he lifted the lid.

I stretched onto my tiptoes for a kiss and turned for the couch. "Kickoff is coming up."

He gestured to the sofa. "After you."

I plopped into the deep, soft leather cushions as my phone buzzed in my pocket.

"No phones on Sundays," Graham protested, settling beside me.

"This isn't a normal Sunday," I said.

"What's that like?" He tapped one finger lightly on the end of my nose.

I didn't move, my eyes fixed on the screen.

"What?" Graham leaned in, clicking the mute button on the remote.

"A credit card ping." Jimmy Sewell felt a thousand light years away.

"I thought Archie said they transferred the case to Gonzalez."

"I guess I'm still in the loop for now?"

"Who's he selling them to?"

I tapped one finger on the corner of the phone. Why did this look familiar?

Wait.

I touched the photos icon on my home screen.

There.

Damn.

I stood, pointing to the remote. "Set it to record and come on."

"What now?" He got up.

"Computer based charge. Shipping address used is the same one on the nursery receipt. The one listing the funky purple plant Corie Whitehead found on that woman's remains."

Graham swept an arm in the direction of the door as he picked up the cable remote. "Like we needed shit to get any weirder."

I called Corie's cell number from the truck while Graham drove.

"Whitehead," she said by way of hello.

"It's Faith McClellan," I said. "Wondering if you have the equipment necessary there to get a sample of something that might show the type of accelerant used in this case."

"I have tissue and fabric samples," she said. "But I can't analyze them. You're at the mercy of the state lab for that."

Archie and Jim knew people who could speed that up. Good enough.

"What do you think is unusual about it?" she asked. "I mean, the pattern is a pretty clear spatter dump, I assumed from a gas can, but you wouldn't be asking if you didn't think it was something more exotic."

"Covering every base," I explained.

"Sure." The single syllable said my lying skills hadn't improved.

I tapped a finger on my knee. Generally, the more people who know what trail I'm following in a case, the more chances something gets compromised. So I'm good at keeping stuff to myself. But she was smart, and I needed her to share information with me. That only worked if it was a two-way street.

"I'm looking for jet fuel."

"That's not easy to come by," she said.

"It is not. I'm not at liberty to share more." I paused.

"Well, I'm not sure how it figures in, but I was able to get a match from the dental impression and the recent missing persons list—her name was Bethany Marcil."

"Bethan—"

Oh, shit.

"The garden club president."

"I'm sorry?" Corie asked.

"Never mind," I said into the phone. "How sure are you on your ID?"

"I'm sure. Last seen a week ago, on Sunday evening. So she was missing a few days. The thing I can't figure is the dump location. Right outside that trailer park, someone wanted her found by leaving her there. But why go to the trouble of burning the corpse, especially with something as hard to get ahold of as aviation fuel if you're right, just to leave it in such an obvious place?"

Huh. It was a hell of a good question.

The bodies on Jim's table flashed through my head.

They wanted her found.

But whoever set the house fire, under cover of darkness and rain, did not want those victims found. Those men were supposed to cremate inside the house.

I wasn't sure why I hadn't thought in those terms before, but once the thought was there, I couldn't shake it. It was late—Graham and I practically closed down the restaurant. The neighbors who hadn't long since gone to bed were the sort who knew to keep their noses out of whatever was going on at that house.

The fuel was sprayed directly on the victims.

Jim said they were already "half cremated."

We fucked up the plan by spotting the flames.

And the plan was way more careful than I'd thought.

"Will you drop those samples at the lab tomorrow? And can you send me the splatter pattern you're talking about?" I asked.

"Sure thing," she said. "Text me your email address."

I thanked her and ended the call, clicking her number to send the email address.

My head hit the headrest with a *thunk* as Graham exited the freeway.

I had nothing but my gut saying the woman in Corie Whitehead's odd little makeshift lab was related to any of this. And I might be wrong. I picked up my phone and Googled Bethany Marcil.

She had a fucking Wikipedia page. Great. Former model, she married a computer chip millionaire forty years her senior seven years ago. He'd been dead for two years, no kids, and Bethany was the epitome of the society widow, from the photos on the first page of the image results.

I clicked the family link. Both parents dead, no children or siblings.

No one had yet tipped off the press. And her identity wouldn't go in the police record until Jim confirmed it. Which gave us a head start.

I found her address just as we drove into her neighborhood.

So why would the same killer want her found and try to burn two other people to unidentifiable ash?

"What are you into over there? What'd the home medical examiner JP lady say?" Graham asked, turning the truck onto a tree-lined street full of the kind of homes that belonged to people my parents called friends.

"The dead woman is the garden club president," I said. "The one that woman at the second nursery told us was so awful?"

"So probably no shortage of enemies."

"Probably. But also, I think we messed up his plan." Something else tickled the back of my brain, but trying to grab hold of it just made it more nebulous, so I let it go for the moment. "I think our killer meant for the two victims in the Clay Street house to burn to ash and never be found."

"But then someone kills this Marcil woman and sets the remains on fire. But she wasn't burned nearly like the others."

"And then why would that same killer dump the body in such an obvious place?" Graham eased his foot onto the brake, the truck rolling to a stop in front of a stucco and Spanish tile building that looked more like my college dorm than a home.

I shook my head. I didn't have the first damn clue. But between my mother's wide, frightened eyes, my father's shady business deals, and the never-ending chain of oddities surrounding these dead people we had better figure it out.

I met Graham at the front of the truck and started for the front door. The place practically radiated money, and where money lives, power is usually a roommate.

I couldn't start asking questions about the plants or the dead woman. Not if I wanted to get anywhere.

I pressed the ornate, oil-rubbed bronze bell, rehearsing a speech in my head.

Every word of it flew right out my ear when the door swung wide to a petite redhead with perfect makeup and a wide smile, her impossibly turquoise eyes looking up to meet mine before they popped wide, the smile vanishing as her jaw dropped.

"Faith?" she said at the same moment I coughed out, "Caity?"

Graham's head swiveled between us as her eyes landed on my badge. "Holy Moses, you totally went and became a cop." She teetered a bit on crazy stilettos. She still wore them everywhere—anything to make herself a couple of inches taller.

I blinked twice and found my composure. Waved my hand from her to Graham. "Caitlyn Asher, Commander Graham Hardin. Graham, this is my sister's best friend."

19

"Caitlyn was the best on the bars and the beam." I sipped iced tea and looked around a dark wood and navy shiplap living room that had probably been delivered verbatim from the Magnolia showroom floor.

"And Charity was the best on the floor and the vault. Together, we dominated gymnastics in Texas for half a decade." Caitlyn sounded so matter of fact it didn't even carry a hint of conceit. Not that she didn't have plenty to be proud of.

"Caitlyn was an alternate on the '96 Olympic team," I added.

Her round eyes filled quickly at the mention, long lashes fluttering down to contain the tears. "Charity should've been there," she whispered.

"She would've been proud of you." I cleared my throat and changed the subject before my own tears decided to flow. "How's your family?"

"They are all doing well, thanks." She uncrossed her still-muscular legs and recrossed them in the other direction. "Ashley modeled for a while when she was in college and married a magazine editor. She lives in New York." Her tone said she'd rather have her fingernails pulled out. "Heather's husband is a neurosurgeon at Parkland. They have four boys. Mom and Dad have retired to the farm. And I'm..." She waved her arm in a circle. "I'm here. My husband is an attorney."

She didn't mention kids, and I wasn't about to ask. I had stark memories of doctors telling my mother that the strict dieting and excessive strength training demands of elite gymnastics might cost Charity her ability to have a family. Not that either of them had cared.

"I couldn't help noticing your gardens on the way in. They're breathtaking."

Her face lit like it used to on a gold medal dais. "Thank you! It's my passion." She held out one arm, still deep golden brown just a couple of weeks before Halloween. "That's not sprayed on. I earned it. And the front court is nothing compared to the back." She leaned forward. "Do you want a tour?"

Did I ever. But something in her tone and demeanor said she wanted to show me. So maybe there wasn't anything incriminating. But this was the way to find out. I flashed a smile and stood. "I'd love one."

Graham followed us out to a massive covered flagstone patio with a fireplace I could stand up in on one wall, a pool-table-sized TV on the other, and four fans turning lazily overhead. Looking past three oversized outdoor couches, I found gardens worthy of an admission charge, the mix of floral and woodsy scents twining together on the fall breeze downright intoxicating.

I caught a sharp breath. "Wow."

Caitlyn's smile would've cracked her face if it had been any wider. "Thank you. I think of Charity a lot when I'm out here."

"She would've loved this." I felt myself being pulled to the edge of the patio by something bigger than me. Bigger than this case.

My sister was rarely happier than when she was running through Ruth's grand gardens. True, they resembled a weed patch next to the splendor rolling out in front of me, but so did almost anything else I'd ever seen. "Do you have a landscape design business?" I stepped down to a golf course-worthy pallet of soft grass, past a Japanese maple draping reddish-purple shade over artfully scattered hostas on the end of the nearest bed.

"Oh no," she said. "Jeremiah would never stand for that." Her voice and her eyes dropped.

I kept my voice bright. "How nice to have the flexibility to allow for the choice."

"We are blessed," she said, keeping her eyes on the grass.

I meandered from row to row, bed to bed, and secret hiding place to secret hiding place to secret hiding place. Her work was incredible. I had to remind myself to stop marveling long enough to look for the plant I'd seen on the receipt.

Behind me, Graham agreed. "I'm not sure I've ever seen anything so impressive." Roses. Hydrangeas. Jasmine. Lilacs. Many past their blooming season, but several holding on with bright hues and perfume in the waning days of sunlight and warmth before winter.

Arbors cradled benches tucked into the middles and ends of several rows. "Is that your red wagon?" I asked, pointing to a makeshift planter overflowing with bright red and orange lantana.

Caity grinned. "I improvise a lot. Using things we have lying around and making them fit in is fun."

"Seriously, Caity, you turned a mean Omelianchik back in the day, but it's obvious you've found your calling here."

"It brings me peace," she said. "Soothes the soul."

"Are you in any sort of clubs, or are there photos in magazines?" I asked. "So I can tell my mother."

"Oh no, I don't do this for anyone but Jeremiah and me."

I spied the towering pinky lavender blooms of the teasel in a corner. Consciously slowing my gait, I stopped at three more rows before I wandered toward it. "This is beautiful," I said, brushing my fingers over a sprig. "I don't think my mother has ever had a plant like this. What's it called?"

"A teasel." Caity paused between the words, her speech faltering the barest bit. I let it go by and knelt in front of the bed, pretending to look at the base of the plant.

"It's like an exotic sunflower. How long is the blooming season?" I twisted my neck and looked up at her.

"It flowers in spring and fall and stays green from March to Thanksgiving around here." She shuffled her feet, her eyes darting to an adorable dollhouse of a white and blue gardening shed nestled in the nook of the fence.

My eyes raked the surrounding plants as I stood, pulling out my phone.

"Can you tell me the name again? I don't want to forget before I can tell my mother."

She obliged. "I know rare, flowering, and beautiful fits the first lady well." She pivoted on her sharp heel and pointed. "Over here, there's another I can show you." She headed back toward the house.

I followed, tugging Graham's fingers and tilting my head ever so slightly in the direction of the shed as I passed him on the double-back. He hung back as we moved away, Caity's voice high and her words quick as she strode expertly across the lawn in her teetering heels.

I paused for half a step, my eyes landing on a large gray-green tarp spread over the ground a row behind the teasel.

Caity stopped in front of a vine covered in bright cornflower blue and butter yellow blossoms. I reached for it and she swatted my hand away.

"Thorns. You'll be sorry."

I peered closer and noticed wicked little spikes ringing the vine, almost completely obscured by the leaves. "Thanks. This is lovely. And another I've never seen. What is it?"

"Mine." Her tense smile dissolved into a genuine one. "I bred it, from a morning glory and a yellow clematis vine with a bit of rose thrown in for fragrance."

"Wow." My jaw loosened. Being this good at growing things was impressive enough. But breeding her own hybrid plants? "If you do ever find yourself interested in selling or consulting, you should look my mother up. I'm sure she'd love to talk with you, at any rate." This was the kind of life Ruth McClellan would be proud of. The kind she'd always assumed waited for Charity and me. But a murder had derailed her carefully-constructed plans. In some ways, my sister's death really was the story of my life.

"Thank you for the tour, Caity. It was good to see you." I started back for the house, keeping her attention on me as Graham ducked out of the row with the teasel and caught up.

"You as well, Faith. I'm happy you achieved your dream." Her eyes lost a little light on the last words. She stepped up onto the patio and turned back to us. "Though, come to think of it, you never told me what brought you here."

Damn. Almost home free and she had to go noticing things now.

"A noise complaint." Graham stepped up next to me. "One of the neighbors said there were tools running late into the night a couple of times this week."

"Oh!" Two slow blinks. "I was working on a new bench for the garden in my shed. I didn't realize it was so late. I'm so sorry I bothered anyone." She tipped her head to one side. "Why didn't someone come last night?"

"Our people were tied up working a large accident and a fire." Graham's voice poured smooth. Melodic. While I found it unbearably sexy, I also knew people he was interviewing found it incredibly reassuring. He was kind and had a calming way about him that got people talking.

Was he good enough to get under whatever Caity was hiding?

"Usually in this area these kinds of complaints are easily resolved after the fact without diverting an officer from an emergency."

I could tell by her face she was eating up every word.

"Absolutely. I will be more mindful of the time and courteous of my neighbors from now on." She smiled at me. "Though I can't say I'm sorry this happened. It was good to see you, Faith."

I watched her. Everything about her was more relaxed. I hadn't noticed the tension, but the absence of it was obvious.

We had made her nervous.

"You too, Caity. Thanks for being so agreeable. And do reach out to Ruth and the Governor. You and my mother will have hours of conversation available just about your gardens."

"I will. I bet she doesn't even know she was my inspiration."

"She'd like to hear that, especially once she sees this place." Not that Ruth had a sentimental cell in her body. She'd enjoy taking the credit for something so magnificent, though. And maybe connecting with Ruth's vast network would do Caity some good, as well. There was more than a little lonely around the edges of her pampered housewife facade.

She showed us out, and when we were in the truck and pulling out of the driveway, I turned to Graham. "You were amazing."

"I know."

"What's in the shed?"

"Tools, like she said. Along with a small box of blank credit cards, a half-finished bench, and a tank-powered flamethrower."

20

Owning a flamethrower wasn't probable cause for a warrant.

Blank credit cards would get us one in half a heartbeat, but we'd have to say how we knew they were there, and strictly speaking, the shed was private property and Caity hadn't given Graham permission to go inside. We could probably win that argument with a sympathetic judge if someone were in danger, but we didn't have enough to get there yet.

That didn't mean the things we knew didn't put Caitlyn on my suspect list. For something, anyway. And that was a damned uncomfortable thing to sit with. I've cleared hundreds of cases over the years, and never so much as run across a victim or defendant I'd set eyes on before.

Now in one teeming hot mess of an investigation, my father had surfaced as a potential target and my sister's best friend as a suspect?

"It's almost like the universe wants me off this case," I said, half to myself.

"Nobody would fault you," Graham agreed.

"The commander told Archie to bring me in. Politics. Discretion. Nobody knows the entanglements there better than I do." I sighed. "I know I can keep my impartiality, Graham. I mean, Caity and Charity were friends, but I don't owe her anything. And if she murdered that woman in

Corie Whitehead's drawer and burned her with a flamethrower, I will lead the marshals over there to serve her warrant and pick her ass up myself."

"Who are you trying to convince, exactly? I know you. Nothing is more important than solving the case."

I patted his knee and smiled. "Almost nothing."

"I've moved up in the world."

I landed a light fist on his bicep.

The corners of his eyes crinkled. "So what do we know about this woman?"

"The plant, the one Corie Whitehead found bits of on Bethany Marcil, was kind of hastily chopped up at the bottom," I said. "Given the way the rest of that garden looked, I can't imagine that was purposeful."

"Chopped up how?"

"Like there used to be more of the blooms. Several fresh cuts, right at or above the ground."

"Maybe it broke in the storm," he said.

"True. Or those blooms were dead."

"Or the dead garden club lady fell into it," Graham said. "Nice, slipping the question about the club in."

"Now we need a way to find out if she was lying. No assumptions. We work the case. We only know the facts."

"Who are you talking to? I taught you that."

"I know. I also know how tempting it is to hop from A to B when the gap between is only a teeny one. Hell, I half want to storm back over there. But that wouldn't be a smart move."

"Not with a lawyer husband and the kind of political connections they must have, no."

I leaned my head against the seat. Caitlyn had always been the most likely of Charity's teammates to skip out on curfew or sneak candy bars. She liked bad boys in high school, and drank and smoked weed regularly when she wasn't competing.

She hadn't ever appreciated Charity letting her kid sister tag after them, but Charity had the kind of intrinsic self-confidence that allowed her to give zero fucks what Caity liked. People who moved in Charity McClellan's world were damned lucky to do so, and free to exit if they didn't realize it.

That wasn't even me romanticizing my sister's memory. It was just true. Charity was special. She wasn't big-headed about it, but she knew it in a way that allowed her a rare brand of class, grace, and kindness.

I swallowed hard and focused on Caitlyn. If she hadn't had a change of heart when my sister died, hadn't tried to become everything Charity knew she could be, it was a short stretch to imagine she married an unscrupulous lawyer who wasn't nice to her, and got into breaking the law herself. But there's a big difference between eating a Snickers or smoking a joint and murdering another human. The problem was, she'd met Graham. She'd seen our badges.

So she wasn't going to tell us a damned thing, no matter how nicely I asked.

"Chili and football?" Graham asked, parking outside his apartment.

"Sounds like heaven." I hopped out of the truck and followed him inside. Sometimes, taking a break from the case is the best option for figuring it out.

Putting sheets on the bed five hours later, I got it. So abruptly I dropped my corner.

"What?" Graham lifted his side and shook it out again.

"The servants." I grabbed back onto mine, letting it drift over the mattress before I bent to tuck it under. "I should've thought of it before. People like the Governor and Caitlyn don't see them. It's like they're furniture—they perform a function, but they aren't regarded as thinking or feeling human beings who might understand things they see and hear."

"That's." He paused. "That's, uh, pretty shitty."

"Absolutely. But it's also the key to this case. If Erma was serving dinner for that little get-together, I know she heard something."

"Will she get fired for telling us?"

"I won't let that happen." I slid between the sheets and folded my arms behind my head. "But more importantly, there's less than no chance Caitlyn doesn't have a small army of gardeners, and if there's something going on in that house or in that shed—they're where we might find out."

Graham settled next to me. "She said she did the gardens and earned her tan."

"She might plant things. She might even prune things. I will eat a whole side of beef in your next pot of chili if Caitlyn cuts grass or pulls weeds."

Graham rolled on his side and propped up on one elbow, leaning to close his lips over mine.

The servants and Caitlyn and my parents and the dead people all fell quiet in my head. I had a way forward.

And it would wait until morning.

"There are nineteen landscape companies within a ten-mile radius of Caitlyn Wexley's house." Archie tapped a pen on the edge of the table. "By the time you find the one she contracts and get someone to talk to you about an account that big—assuming it's a large enough company to have an address—whoever stole Agent Sunglasses' fuel truck could burn down half the state."

"I might get lucky," I countered.

"Or you might waste time we don't have to waste. I remember that girl. I didn't like her, and I'm sure she's up to no good, but you said yourself, whatever's going on there is probably connected to a case you're no longer a part of—whether or not you have a personal history with the suspect notwithstanding. Take all this to Gonzalez and let him do his job. He's on Jimmy Sewell now."

"You don't think it's even a little weird that this Jane Doe was burned, too?"

"Sure I do. But I don't have room for it on my plate right now and neither do you." Archie sighed. "Look, Faith, this job can often be about triaging the unthinkable. You have had the relative luxury of working one case at a time, sticking with your methods until you get the answer. But sometimes you have to hand off one terrible thing to another officer because your particular talents are needed on another terrible thing. This is one of those times."

"You know as well as I do that a case changing hands mid-investigation is the surest way for it to end up downstairs in the cold files."

"With a murder, sure. Lost evidence and interpretations, fading memories, cooling trails. But this Sewell thing is theft. And it's too big to go cold. Those bankers want their money. Gonzalez has led the fraud unit for three years. He will get this guy."

I opened my mouth to argue that Gonzalez knew shit about working homicide but Archie raised one hand. "I know, he's not a murder guy. But if you're right and this woman was both a member of high society and murdered because of something to do with Jimmy Sewell, Gonzalez will find out what happened. He's a good cop. I need all your attention on this case."

His voice dropped and so did his eyes.

"What are you not telling me?" I leaned forward. I could argue with him about the Sewell case later. Archie wasn't easily rattled, but something was bothering him.

He pulled a large plastic baggie from the top drawer of his desk, a piece of white paper inside. "This arrived this morning. It was in a leather folder in the front seat of the BMW SUV we impounded from the alley behind the Clay Street fire scene."

A black-and-white printout—or maybe a photocopy—of a photo of my father surrounded by three of his closest elected cabinet members, all of them smiling for the camera.

"My mother showed up at Graham's late Saturday. She says he's in over his head, but she swears she doesn't know how or with what."

He leaned forward in the chair. "Is she okay?"

"She's scared. Scared enough to admit he's doing shady shit and ask for my help. So no."

I tapped the photo. "What would one of our presumed victims want with this, though? I mean, assuming the SUV was left by someone who was inside the house and not by the murderer. Surely driving that car into the alley would've attracted attention of some sort."

"You'd think. And I don't have the first damned clue. But I thought you should know." He sat back. "Listen, I got permission for you to stay on the case if you want, but the commander has agreed to let you step out if you need to."

"You know better than that," I said. "The Governor might deserve this person's anger for all I know, but a murder with ties to my father isn't something I have it in me to step away from. Anything else in the car?"

"A GPS tracker, the commercial kind you can buy online, in the glove compartment. Law office claims it's not theirs."

"Interesting." I pulled out a pad and noted that.

Willing my heart rate to slow, I stood. It was early. We were still the only people in the building—Graham had a staff meeting at the sheriff's office and he'd gone in early to start calling the car services who'd sent drivers to my father's dinner party.

Archie and I had planned to look for Caitlyn's landscapers, but he was right—we didn't have time to sort through so many on a theory. There were more pressing things to worry about today.

I grabbed a peppermint from the star-shaped crystal dish on the corner of Archie's desk and popped it into my mouth, pointing to the photo again. "Prints?"

He shook his head. "It's clean."

Of course it was. "So now what?"

"You said Hardin was chasing leads at the car services this morning. I think that's our immediate focus. Who was at the dinner party your mother told you about? That might give us an idea of what we're dealing with."

The servants.

I reached for the photo, counting.

Five men, including the Governor.

I tapped a finger on it.

My phone buzzed in my pocket before I could finish the thought. I pulled it out and clicked the text from Graham.

Guess what?

I couldn't even begin to.

Probably right. Those cars we tracked to the dinner party? All rented by the same person.

No shit. My jaw slackened. *Now I have a guess: Beau O'Brien.*

Your brain is sexy, you know it?

I clicked the *haha* tag.

You're my hero, as usual. See you in a bit.

Clicking the phone icon, I found Erma's name in the contacts. She was off on Mondays.

She picked up on the third ring.

"Can we get that coffee this morning?" I asked.

"Of course, *mija*," she said. "I drop Javi at school at eight thirty. Meet you after?"

She sounded so happy to see me I felt a couple of pangs as I touched the end button. I wouldn't let him fire her. If I had it my way, he'd never know she'd talked with me.

"You guys check out the drivers, see what you turn up," I told Archie, putting another peppermint in my mouth and snapping a photo of the printed image with my phone. "I'm going to see if any of these guys were at that dinner party."

His brow furrowed.

"I won't let her get in trouble. You know as well as I do they wouldn't ever imagine that she'd talk to anyone. Even me."

"There's a reason they think that. Just don't get your hopes up," he said. "She loves you, but your parents have always taken good care of her family, Faith. There's a loyalty there that runs deep."

"Then she wants them to stay alive," I said. "I love her, too, Arch. I won't let him find out where I got anything she tells me."

If I could get her to tell me anything.

21

The kayak sat undisturbed, a black plastic paddle nestled under the seat, supplies in the nose. Vaulting himself from the chilly water to the shelf, he slid it onto the smooth, black-glass surface of the lake and checked his watch. Two minutes eleven seconds.

He was late.

He pulled the paddle smoothly through the water, hunching his shoulders and ducking his head at the mouth of the cove. The water was receding after the rain, but still high.

No moon tonight—the water was flat, still, and dark, the cloak of night keeping the mission safe. Hidden.

Eighty-seven strokes, the only noise the rustling of his suits as he rowed, and he could reach the base of the dock. Time check: three minutes thirty-eight seconds. He stowed the paddle, grabbed the footer, and pulled the kayak up as close as he could get to the dock. Turning the small vessel, he pulled a length of soft cord from under his feet and looped it around the dock support, tying it off with a bowline knot. Nestled between the looming white bow of the yacht and the dock, the little kayak would disappear in a few minutes.

The location was a stroke of luck. Fate smiles on the righteous.

He scaled the ladder slowly, peeking over the end of the dock and scanning the marina. Still and silent, save for the gentle lapping of the water against the hulls of the boats.

Phase two was a go.

He reset the timer on his wrist as he stepped onto the wood planks and slipped sideways a few paces, vaulting again. His feet connected with the turf on the boat's deck, soft and silent as a prowling cat. Twelve seconds to jimmy the flimsy lock on the sliding glass door from the deck to the living room, where a TV flickered a black-and-white movie, washing the room in a ghostly glow.

Through the kitchen to the fourth door on the right.

Two minutes forty-one seconds.

He paused, listening.

Behind the door, his target snorted and snuffled like he was turning up truffles in the forest. He smiled at the pig image. Fitting.

Backing up, he raised one foot and plowed it into the door. It splintered, pieces flying everywhere including the round king-size bed.

The snoring halted on a long, ripping snort, the target bolting upright under the crisp linen duvet. The room was dark, but he'd always been able to see well in the dark. Eyes like an owl, speed like a hawk.

Three minutes twenty-five seconds.

He moved closer, the cream linen of the bedclothes puddling around a waist that had seen too many rich meals and stiff drinks, making it hard to tell the difference between fabric and skin.

No matter.

"Wha—"

He pointed the wand. Pulled the trigger. Sprayed half-liquid death straight into his flopping mouth. Fire leapt to life, making the man on the bed a fire-breathing bastard for three ticks, sausage fingers decked in fat gold rings flying to his melting cheeks.

The flames swallowed the screams.

He pulled the trigger again. Gel flew. Landed. Ignited.

Flames fed.

The bed took thirty-one seconds. The walls another twenty-eight.

Time was running out. The heat crept in, the suits going soft, air scarce.

Counting down in his head, he sprayed the floor as he retreated. His calculations were right. He'd been over them a dozen times.

The heat would ignite the fuel tanks under his feet in fifteen, fourteen, thirteen...

He ripped the wand from the backpack and tossed it into the flames on his way to the starboard rail. Two rungs.

Ten seconds.

He dove, his ankle catching on the edge of the railing, wrenching his foot back a hundred and eighty degrees. The shock of the water was muted through the suit, still a welcome relief from the heat with a bonus numbing effect for the throbbing foot.

Stretching out into a perfect sidestroke, he kicked hard, pulling with his gloved hands.

Eight. Seven. Six.

He swam like salvation was on the opposite shore.

One step closer, anyway.

He felt the explosion, the energy pushing him forward even as he dove down to avoid rogue debris.

Dragging himself, panting, from the water to the shore, he looked back for just three seconds, at Lake Travis burning.

The suits were heavy regardless of the water. He shed them as he walked, the cool predawn air welcome through his dry clothes. Both suits barely fit stuffed into the backpack. Not breaking stride, only dragging his throbbing foot slightly, he dropped the backpack into a waiting hole, kicking loamy sand and gravel back level before he knelt to spread it flat into the surrounding road with his bare hands. Careful to avoid dragging the foot too much, he started up the hill to the car.

Daylight approached, and so did sirens—so many, so loud, that he didn't hear the high whine of the engine until it was too late to get out of sight. Leaping to the shoulder, he kept his posture easy and his pace steady as the headlights passed. They veered left at the car and rolled on without faltering.

Phase two accomplished.

22

I had enough time to stop by the senate office building at the capitol before meeting up with Erma.

The security guard who'd been at this post since I was just out of pigtails stood up and grinned as he waved me through the checkpoint. "You grew up, Miss McClellan."

"Yet you don't look a day older, Mike. How did that happen?"

"Clean living and good genes, I guess. Is this an official visit?"

I stepped toward the elevators. "Just popping in on an old acquaintance."

"Have a good one, Miss."

"You too."

The cavernous marble hallways were eerily silent, the usual bustle of state government at work not yet awake for the day. But there was one office that was always occupied by seven.

On the fifth floor, just outside the majority leader's plush double-door digs, I found Beau O'Brien drinking coffee and reading the *Statesman* as the Channel Two morning show played on a TV in the corner.

"Some things never change," I said, stepping into the office and shutting the door behind me.

"Faith!" He dropped the paper and stood, grasping my hands and kissing both my cheeks. "To what do I owe this spectacular start to my week?"

I took the high-backed leather chair across from his. "You've been a frequent customer at quite a few Hill Country car services, Beau."

He leaned back in his chair, one corner of his mouth curling up. "I take care of everything from speeches to favors to transportation these days," he said. "Downsizing even extends to the political arena, I'm afraid."

Bullshit. Secretaries book regular transportation, and staff members can be designated drivers for lawmakers when necessary.

I smiled and nodded like he was actually pulling one over on me. Men like Beau enjoy feeling smart.

"I do understand being overworked," I said. "The thing is, these cars you rented have ended up smack in the middle of a case I'm working."

"I can't imagine why." His tone said he knew exactly why, he just wanted to know how much I knew.

All right then.

"Three cars and three drivers disappeared Friday night from one service, and at least two cars rented by you in other cities went to my parents' ranch two Fridays back. Who was in them?"

"Now Faith. Discretion is the biggest part of my job description."

"Then you should've used a different name." The words slid through the smile, my teeth clenched.

He leaned forward in the seat. "The cars and drivers from Friday are all just fine. The drivers are probably better than fine, actually."

"The owner of the service would like them all back," I said.

"They'll be back. On Thursday."

"You only reserved the vehicles through two a.m. Saturday."

"Change of plans."

I sighed. "Beau."

He did the same. "Faith."

"People are dead." I let the words fall flat. "I'm sure you already know that. But I need to know why. And I need to stop other people from joining them."

"That sounds like a you problem." He held my gaze without blinking.

"Just tell me who went to the dinner party at the ranch."

"That, I actually cannot do, because I don't know. I booked the cars. Pickup was in a parking lot, and I wasn't told who would be there."

"Did my father tell you to arrange for the cars?"

"What do you think?"

I closed my eyes for a slow blink and took a deep breath. He was trying to get under my skin. The trick was to refuse to let him until I got under his.

"You owe me, O'Brien."

"I owe you shit, McClellan." He mimicked my low tone.

"You owe my sister."

Pain flashed, brief but true, across his face.

"There's nothing in my life I wouldn't give to have Charity back for just one day," he said. "How dare you come in here with questions and throw her—"

I raised one hand. "How dare I? How dare *you*. Setting up backdoor meetings, rewarding power plays to get a seat at the most conniving, insidious table in Texas politics? Making a name for yourself by hurting and blackmailing people? Charity wouldn't spit on you if you were on fire in the middle of main street. You've let power and money tempt you into becoming everything you two wanted to change about Texas government."

He deflated. I've never seen all the fight go out of a person at once, but Beau's whole power-hungry persona collapsed in on itself right in front of me. He leaned his head on one hand.

"You know how this works, Faith," he said. "Secrets are currency in this world. You stay around long enough, you start to hear a few. You share them with the right people—or better yet, sometimes, the wrong people—and before long you're a kind of broker for them. Without even knowing how it happened."

The words were all directed at the leather blotter in his desk, and I couldn't gauge the sincerity in his flat tone.

"It'd be a shame for a few of your secrets to make it to the wrong person," I said. "Especially if the wrong person happened to be, say, Skye Morrow."

I had no idea what secrets Beau might have that Skye would care about. But the way his head snapped up said he didn't know that. Not for sure. And we knew a lot of the same people and went back a long time.

"Son of a goddamn fucking bitch," he muttered.

Sitting back, he let his head fall against the chair.

I waited.

"They're in Mexico."

"All three of them? Why?"

"All I know is that I was told to rent the cars and tell them where to go."

"Told by who?"

He shook his head.

"Beau." I waved my arm. "Look at where you are. You're in the right-hand seat to the second most powerful man in the state."

"Second?"

"Fine. How often does it happen that anyone manages to keep something from you?"

Fear flashed in his eyes.

I blinked. Not often at all.

And there was only one place he would've taken an order like that from.

"Beau!" Like I'd summoned him up with the thought, Martin Rickers stuck his head in the door, stopping short when he saw me. "Faith McClellan! To what do we owe the honor?"

"Just catching up with an old friend, Senator."

Rickers had been around Texas politics since before I was born. He was widely regarded as the only person at the capitol who was a bigger asshole than Chuck McClellan, and he'd managed to hold power for nearly three times as long.

"Beau, come in when you're free," he said.

I stood, and Rickers waved a hand. "Don't leave on my account." His eyes said he didn't mean a word of that.

He left, and I put a hand on Beau's shoulder.

"The cars and the drivers will be back?"

"Thursday. I swear."

"I'll be back if they're not. And I'll bring Skye."

"They'll kill me, Faith. They might kill you, too."

"Not if I find them first."

I paused in the doorway and watched him sit up straight and shake off the fear, the mask of the best-connected political operative in Austin settling back over him.

Waving goodbye to Mike and stepping into the sun, I couldn't help but wonder how much good someone like Beau would've done by this point in his life if my sister hadn't died.

———————

Erma had one of those smiles that lit up her whole face. She was a handsome woman all the time, petite and strong with an angular jaw, wide eyes framed by thick lashes, and enviably high cheekbones. But the smile made her glow. Made her gorgeous, because in it, you could see her heart.

She beamed when I waved from the back of the coffeehouse, rushing through the morning crowd with her arms out and pulling me into a hug. "You are more beautiful now than you ever were in any crown, *mija*." She sat in the chair opposite mine. "You look happy."

"I am." I smiled.

"You always did enjoy getting under their skin." Her dark eyes sparkled mischievously. "But you are doing what you always wanted to do. Living the dream, as Javi would say."

"I get to help people not have to wonder like we did."

Pain flashed in her eyes and she touched her forehead, chest, and shoulders in the sign of the cross. "My sweet angel. Never forgotten."

"I know."

"She would have been forty last year. I wonder sometimes what she would have done."

"Something great." I heard the wistful tone in my own words and blinked hard to head off emotion. "How have you been?"

"The same. A little slower, a little more gray, a little more tired. But getting older is a privilege denied to some."

"You'll never be slow, Erma."

I swallowed hard. I had to do what I came here to do—but I didn't want to ask her. She'd tell me, eventually. I was confident in that. But digging information out of Erma felt...icky.

Rock, meet hard place. Best to rip the Band-Aid.

"Two Fridays ago, the Governor had a dinner party." I reached for my coffee mug, taking just half a beat to let the words settle. "Ruth said they had steak and lobster, so there weren't many people there. I need to know who they were. And if you heard anything they were talking about."

She tipped her chin toward her chest and slid her glasses down her nose, peering at me over the frames. The way she did when she found out I'd skipped chemistry for a month after Charity died. I squirmed just a little in the seat, but held her gaze.

"I can't tell you that, Faith." Ouch. Erma didn't use my name unless she was past angry and on to disappointed. "The Governor's affairs are private. You'll have to take it up with him."

I'd always been in awe of the way my father could leverage money and power to inspire loyalty in people he treated like afterthoughts, but to a person, everyone who worked in that house or on the grounds would close ranks against inquiries from outsiders. And I was an outsider. I had been all along in a lot of ways, but the look on her face made it clear. Erma loved me. But her loyalty was with the Governor and Ruth.

I knew that when I got here, though.

"Three nights ago, this man disappeared." I pulled up Avesta's photo on my phone. "The same night, two men were burned alive, the fire investigator believes with napalm. I believe he might've been one of them."

Her eyes popped wide when they lit on Avesta's face.

"I know he was at the ranch for dinner that night. I have video of the car dropping him off." I kept my voice soft. Concerned. Flicked the screen to the copied photograph of my father and his cabinet. "This morning investigators found this in a car at the scene of that fire. My mother snuck out in an Uber Saturday night to ask for my help, Erma, because you know the Governor wouldn't. Someone could very well be coming for him. Whoever this is, they are smart, methodical, pissed off, and harboring a massive grudge. Help me protect them."

She stared at the photo for thirty seconds that felt like thirty weeks.

"Ask him."

I leaned forward and reached for her hand. She pulled it away. "You're asking me to violate a trust I have spent my entire life building, Faith. And you have no concept of what you're asking me to forfeit in the process. I appreciate that you're good at your job. I hope you're good enough to be successful here without me, because I can't tell you anything."

"Erma, whatever he's promised you, you know Ruth runs the house. She will make good on it. She wouldn't have come to talk to me about whatever he's up to if she wasn't afraid." I put one hand on the photo. "I'm scared. I don't always get along with them, but they are my parents. And so far I haven't come up with a single lead on whoever might be doing this. Whoever killed the nephew of a powerful Iranian politician. Do you know how few damns you have to give for your own personal safety to risk the wrath of a family like that?" I pulled in a shuddering breath. Steady. I wanted to scare her, but only enough to make her talk to me.

"You always talk too fast when you're upset." She patted my hand. "I believe in you, *mija*. You'll catch him. I read in the paper you've never missed one yet." Her accent was soft after so many years working in a house where the Governor insisted that everyone speak the king's English, but emotion always intensified it.

"You know how closely he guards his secrets," I said. "He didn't even let Ruth in the room at that dinner. Erma, if you heard anything, you have to tell me. Everyone in the house could be in danger, not just him."

She slumped forward and rested her head in her hands, whispering a prayer.

"Money. They were talking about money. Quietly, for the most part, moving it or maybe hiding it—the one..." She waved a hand at my phone. "The one who was so angry stopped talking and hushed everyone else every time I walked into the dining room."

She sniffled and sat up straight. "That's all I know."

"Had you ever seen this man before that night?"

"Just once, last winter, he was meeting with the Governor and I heard him chatting with Miss Ruth about her gardens. He was interested in unusual plants that grow in the heat."

"Did you know any of the other men at the dinner that night?" I asked.

"They were there." She waved a hand at the photo on my phone.

I leaned forward. "Who they? Which ones?"

"All of them."

23

All statewide high offices in Texas are elected, but Chuck McClellan had some mighty wide coattails. I knew every face in that photo. They were the Governor's cabinet, his most trusted colleagues. Powerful men who'd been in and out of my house almost daily when I was young. I'd called half of them "Uncle" by the end of the Governor's second term.

I hugged Erma tightly and promised she wasn't the person who told me anything before I watched her climb into her little 1998 Honda Civic. She smiled at me, but it didn't reach her eyes.

Which made me feel like shit.

I slid behind the wheel of my truck and opened my texts. A new one waited from Archie.

I got dental records from the embassy. Jim is 98 percent that Avesta was the victim without the knee implant. So now we need to know who he was there to meet and why.

And we need to find that without anyone else knowing Avesta was there, I sent back.

I leaned my forehead on the steering wheel. Fan-goddamn-tastic.

Jim and the two of us are the only people who know.

And whoever sent you his dental records.

I got his whole medical history. They think he collapsed and is in a hospital here. We can make that hold for a few days, at least. Parliament is in session in Iran, Azari is tied up with that.

Thank God for small favors.

Okay. I know who was at the—

My phone started buzzing.

Graham.

I put it to my ear. "We don't need the rest of the car services," I said in place of hello. "I know who was there that night. And Avesta was officially killed in the Clay Street fire now, thanks to Archie's vast network. So. Tick tock, and happy Monday."

He spoke at the same time. "I caught a conversation in the detectives' bullpen on my way out of the office, and I think we have another victim," he said. "Dammit."

"Wait. What?" we both said.

I took a breath. "I'm sorry, start again?"

"You have a list from the Governor's dinner party?" he asked.

"You have a dead person, you go first. Why do you think we care about this one?"

"William Harold Haynesworth."

He didn't have to say more.

"Uncle Bill," I whispered.

"I figured you knew him. I'm sorry, honey."

"What happened to him?" I had to focus to keep the car on the road. He had the best laugh in the whole world, that man. Big and loud, it was a whole-body show. I memorized a joke book the summer after fifth grade so I could pounce when he was on his way in or out of the Governor's office and hear that laugh.

"He spent the weekend on a houseboat on the lake. It blew up late last night."

I swallowed hard and made a U-turn at the next intersection. He'd kept his boat at the North Marina when I was a kid.

"Faith? You okay?"

"No."

"What do you need from me?"

"I'm going to the lake. Can you call Archie and meet me out there? North Marina."

"On my way, baby. Drive safely."

The lake looked so much different than it had in April it was hard to believe it was the same body of water.

Waves lapped gently at sand and gravel, the swimming season over and the landscape under the wide blue sky quiet on a Monday morning in the off-season.

Except for the sheriff's patrol cars and medical examiner's vans. I stopped in the lot outside the marina and pulled my sunglasses down my nose as I stepped out of the truck, scanning for familiar faces.

Bolton's angular jaw and giant biceps would've stood out in a crowd of professional wrestlers.

"Hey there, Deputy." I hurried across the lot.

Bolton turned from a portly, balding man with a cigar clamped, unlit, between his teeth.

The other guy's red face said he'd already been mad when I walked up and didn't appreciate being interrupted.

Bolton adjusted his grip on a pair of awkwardly-large sifting screens. "Ranger, how the hell have you been? Still on the heels of every killer, I see."

"Ranger?" The cigar-chomper turned to me. "Does that mean you outrank this moron? Can you please tell him he's keeping me from accessing my private property?"

"Sir, the marina is an active crime scene this morning," I said. "I am sorry for the inconvenience, but I'm sure you understand."

"Why is your investigation a reason for you to impound my boat?"

"Nothing has been impounded," I said. "TCSO is simply limiting access to avoid contamination of evidence until we find out what happened here."

"What happened is that fucking idiot Haynesworth probably fell asleep with a Cuban in his hand and I need to know how much damage his stupidity did to my property. I'm not the press, I'm not some idiot layman you can push around, I'm an attorney. And I'm going to my boat." He moved to step past Bolton—balls of steel, this dude—and I stepped in his way, touching my shoulder to Bolton's and making kind of a V with my torso and his hulking form. "I'm afraid I'm going to have to ask you nicely once more to leave, sir," I said. "The marina owners will contact everyone when the scene has been cleared and it's safe for you to approach and inspect your property."

"Like hell," he muttered. "Get out of my way."

I kept my voice low, but removed every fiber of softness. "If I have to ask again, I'll be forced to forget my upbringing and be less kind about it."

"I've seen McClellan be rude." Bolton brushed three fingers over a jaw I'd bruised in a sparring match after he said he didn't need headgear to fight a girl. "I would go if I were you."

"McClellan." The red drained out of the guy's face like my name pulled a stopper. He stepped back, his cigar drooping, stuck to his bottom lip. "Like, uh, like Chuck McClellan?"

"Oh, do you know my father?"

His entire demeanor changed in a blink. "I meant no disrespect, ma'am."

"The owners will call you," I repeated.

He turned and ran as fast as his stubby legs would carry him to a sleek silver Jag.

"Damn," Bolton said. "I remember hearing your old man's name on the news when I was a kid, but I guess he's a badass in his own right? You had to have come by it somewhere."

"The Governor is...something else." I turned back to the dock. "What do you know?"

"It was a massive blast. Damage to boats in every direction." He pointed. "The back quarter of the dock blown off. But we don't know much past that. The fire department is sending an arson investigator as soon as he's free. And there's a guy from the Dallas ATF office here pissing the commander off."

Jenkins. Well, at least this was his wheelhouse. Maybe he would be of some help today.

"Arson is the likely cause?" I asked.

"The ATF guy said there was one part of the boat that burned with 'significant inconsistency' to the rest of it. He thinks the explosion was caused by fire getting to the fuel tanks. They're still trying to piece it together, but it seems like there's a good possibility of arson. Two suspicious fatal fires in a week's time is...weird."

I nodded, but didn't comment further.

"Not surprised to see you here." The words came from behind me, the smirk on her face evident before I turned around.

"You're in the middle of a crime scene, Skye," I said. "No comment."

"I didn't ask you for one. I already talked to your father's press representative," she said. "And I must've missed the part where I'm suddenly legally barred entry to a public place." She cast a glance up the hill to the entrance of the parking lot, where a young officer was keeping her colleagues at bay. "Just because they don't know their rights doesn't mean we're all stupid."

"You can't interfere with the investigation," I said. "And right now, you're keeping Deputy Bolton here from completing his task." I turned and waved for him to follow me. "Go dig somewhere else, Skye. There's nothing here but a tragic accident and everyone else will have it at noon. It's not worth your time."

I wanted her to believe me, but couldn't count on it.

"You're good at getting rid of her," Bolton said. "She's uh...she's kind of scary."

I chuckled. Skye was about five-six in her crazy stilettos, and I'd bet she didn't weigh 115 after a big meal.

"I think you could restrain her, rookie."

"If I couldn't I'm going to have a serious word with my trainer. Nah, I mean she's...she gives me the willies. Like a witch or something."

"You're only off by a letter there." I stopped talking as he handed the machine off to a pair of deputies waiting at the edge of the boat slip. "Skye is a lot of things, but magical isn't one of them. Her only superpower is being a pain in the ass."

Chunks of the hull of Haynesworth's boat lay in pieces on a retrieval barge, Jenkins barking orders at the officers examining them as an artist sketched out ideas for how the explosion went down based on the damage.

"They think they found about 90 percent of it," Bolton said. "Commander said that's good for recovery in a case like this."

I watched the deputies in wet suits moving, arms linked, through the water to search. "The water moves less this time of the year. That probably helped. Did you hear anyone mention a blast range?"

"The farthest piece they found was across the road behind the parking lot." He raised an arm to point. "There were a couple over yonder near the island, too. But most scattered right around here."

I looked at the charred edges of the dock, about five feet of the end of it blown off, judging by the length of the one next to it.

"His remains?"

"They took what they found to the ME's office. The ATF guy said it's hard to recover remains from a scene like this." He was kind enough to keep the reason he was carting the sifters out there to himself, but I knew it was so they could strain the debris floating in the water to look for more pieces of charred human.

Dammit.

Haynesworth was the one person in the Governor's inner circle that I respected. He was smart. Shrewd, I might even say. But he had a kind heart. He cared about something other than power and money.

He wasn't like the rest of them.

"What do you know so far, Bolton?" That was Graham. I turned and put my arms up as he scooped me into a hug.

"The perimeter search around the parking lot and road turned up diddly squat," Bolton said. "No tire tracks, nothing on the cameras. There's security footage of the parking lot and the dock up to there"—he pointed to a shiny white and black yacht two slips down—"that runs continuously from before sunset last night to this morning, and nobody came back here. The ATF guy seems pretty convinced of foul play, but the commander says from the immediate evidence, it seems that like McClellan told Ms. Morrow, it might've been a tragic accident."

I raised my head and Graham dropped his arms as I turned. "You guys already have the surveillance video?" I asked.

"The commander watched it himself," Bolton said. "Says the ATF agent is full of shit."

My eyes strayed past the barge to the opposite shore of the inlet. The road above it was gravel and sand. I looked back at the length of dock we'd walked, then at the missing section. Turned to the one opposite.

There was a ladder at the end.

I ran for the parking lot.

24

Lake Travis has 271 miles of shoreline. About ten percent of that is dotted with inlets and small, hidden caves. Charity and I spent a hundred child-hood summer afternoons exploring them.

The one directly across from the dock where Haynesworth's boat had blown up was deep. And had a sizable shelf inside. We called it Mermaid Cove.

"McClellan, it's dark in there. And the water has to be cold," Bolton complained from farther up on the sand. "It feels more like early December than October out here this morning."

I bent and rolled my Wranglers up to my knees, frowning at my ostrich Laredos. Leaving them safe on the sand meant risking a foot laceration on the rocks.

Whatever. I'd sacrificed more than a good pair of boots to an important case before. And right then, looking for answers was one of the only things keeping me sane.

"It's not that cold yet," I lied, gasping anyway when it hit my shins. "You stay there. I'll holler if I need anything."

"I sure as hell hope you don't," he muttered, but I heard it anyway.

I clicked on a waterproof flashlight and shone it into the dark void at the entrance to the cove.

All clear above the water. I wasn't thinking about what might lurk beneath.

The surface shelves were maybe a little wider than I remembered, the water reaching just below my waist instead of to my shoulders, the rock shiny and slick-looking from the high water after the rain.

Except in one spot.

Dry rock, the finish matte beige against the deeper color of the wet shelf, in the middle of the widest section.

I sucked in a deep breath, my skin getting used to the cold, and waded in.

Five or so feet long and three feet wide across the bowed-out center, tapering symmetrically at both ends.

I swept the surrounding rock and water with the light.

There.

A flash of yellow bobbed slightly in the water when I moved, drifting toward the back of the cove.

A bit of litter, maybe.

Maybe not.

Dammit. Charity and I had played in here for half a summer back when summer meant something besides oppressive heat and increasing case-loads. The last time I'd been in this space, my sister dove deeper into the cave than we ever had before.

"Archie said don't go way back there, Char." I could practically hear the nerves thrumming in my ten-year-old voice, the high pitch bouncing off the walls around me.

"Archie worries too much, and so do you," Charity laughed, moving to climb onto the rock shelf. "Watch this fli—"

She lost the end of the word to a scream when she put her foot into a water moccasin nest.

My skin crawled all over in a way that had nothing to do with the chilly water.

I had my boots on. And I wanted whatever that was floating in the water. It might matter.

"Charity, if you're there, just steer me around the snakes," I whispered.

Two more deep breaths, and calm settled around me like a warm blanket. I moved my feet in a zigzag pattern, dragging them on the bottom to avoid surprises. One step. Two. Four. I stretched my fingers.

Four and a half steps.

Got it.

I backpedaled fast, sweeping the flashlight side to side in the space as I moved, nothing else catching my eye.

I was back on the sand next to Bolton, gasping and shivering in the ordinarily pleasant October breeze, before I managed to uncurl my fingers.

"What's that?" he asked, fidgeting next to me.

"I-i-i-i-n-n-n the w-w-w-w-ater." My teeth chattered so hard around the words I was a little worried about cracking one.

"Can I?" Bolton extended an arm. Shuffled his feet. "I mean, we should've grabbed a blanket...I didn't know you were getting in...May I?"

I would've laughed if my facial muscles had been capable of anything but rattling my teeth together. I nodded, ducking under his heavy arm.

He closed the other one around me and moved toward the truck.

Lord, he was so warm I might worry he was running a fever.

"Let's get you out of the breeze."

And onto the seat heater.

Buckled into the passenger seat of my truck with the heat blasting and the seat warmer on high, it still took a good five minutes for me to stop shaking.

Bolton turned the little circle of yellow plastic over in his hand.

"It looks like a cap. But not from a bottle."

"It's a flare cap."

"Oh yeah." He dropped it into the cup holder and pulled the gearshift into drive. "I thought it looked familiar."

I'd lit about a thousand of them on Texas highways in my days as a DPS trooper.

"Maybe someone had an emergency? People on boats use flares for that, right?" he posited.

"Sometimes. Though the kind you shoot from a flare gun would be the more common ones for that."

"That's probably true. I don't know a whole lot about boating."

I did. And flare guns are helpful for signaling distress on the water, but damn near impossible to aim with accuracy.

Someone with a good arm could toss a road flare from a decent distance with confidence, though. Like from far enough back to get a head start before the fire reached a yacht's gas tanks. Time to row a kayak out of harm's way, even.

"Turn left," I said.

"The marina is…" Bolton turned his head and blinked when he saw the look on my face. "Yes, ma'am."

I pointed him to the side of the gravel and dirt road up the hill and told him to stop, steeling myself for the breeze when I opened the door.

It wasn't quite as bone-numbing as it had been down by the water.

I hopped down, waving for Bolton to follow. "Stay on the gravel. There was a kayak on the rocks under here until sometime before dawn. This would be the closest you could get a car without leaving tire tracks on damp sand."

"Oh shit," he said, raising up on tiptoe and directing his gaze to his feet.

I walked about thirty yards up the right shoulder with nothing to show for it. "Damn."

I turned back. Anyone who'd parked up here and gone to the cave would've had to walk up and down. But our murderer had shown himself to be smart already. Probably smart enough to stay on the gravel.

"Hey," Bolton said.

I turned. He was on the left edge of the narrow gravel road.

"Shoe prints." He pointed.

I double-timed it to his side, squatting, the cold entirely forgotten as I watched the fine grains of sand scatter about in the breeze. Another half day and this wouldn't be here anymore. I tapped Bolton's knee and held my hand out for his phone. "Photos."

There were five and a half prints spanning probably a seven-foot area, all of them large enough to make the odds heavily favor a man.

"What leaves a print like this?" Bolton asked. "The toe box is wide, but there aren't any treads like a sneaker."

I handed his phone back and crouched again, studying the half print and the whole one staggered behind it.

"Sandals, maybe? Like the ones you slip off and on? Baseball players wear them over their socks when they leave a field after taking their cleats off."

"Why just here?"

I looked around. "The road isn't wide enough for two cars. Our guy is smart. If he parked here, he left the car on the gravel so it wouldn't leave tracks. And he would've walked on the gravel, too. Here, I think a car came along and forced someone to step off the road. These were made walking up the hill." I stood and turned back for the top, mindful that he was still a rookie. "We can't say this was our guy. It could be anyone, and assumptions are never helpful in this job. But it's worth looking for whoever might have seen someone up here early this morning."

Thirty yards farther up the hill, tire tracks ran in an arc on the right side of the road. Just one set, but the arc went way closer to the edge of the cliff overlooking the water than I would've been comfortable with. I pointed back to the gravel path. "See? If there was a car up here in the middle of the road, whoever passed back there and forced the pedestrian into the dirt would've gone around the other vehicle here." I directed my gaze to the tire tracks.

He handed his camera back before I asked. I snapped photos, hovering my hand over the tracks for size scale. The tracks were wide, the tread deep. I brushed my fingers across the gravel of the main path. It was loose in the middle of the arc. I stood and snapped a shot of the whole pattern, crouching again to examine the gravel where the tires went off the road.

"Bolton." I waved him over. This was a good lesson in paying attention to the details. He squatted beside me. "See here where the gravel is smashed into the dirt more where the tires went onto the shoulder?"

"I wouldn't have noticed it if you hadn't pointed. Why does it do that? And why do we care?"

"The material at the edges of any path like this one is always less dense than what's in the middle of the road. That makes it more susceptible to outside forces like pressure. And makes the results easier to see. We care because we can learn a few things here. The tires are fat, with deep treads by the prints in the dirt up there."

"Sports car?"

"Good, Deputy. And this…" I pointed around the arc and back at the gravel. "Tells us the wheelbase is wider than the shoulder of the road, because even when these tires were out there by the edge, the other set didn't get close enough to smash this gravel into the dirt."

He nodded slowly, his face spreading into a grin. "You know, Commander Hardin is right. You're a good cop."

"I pay attention to details other people miss." I stood, putting my feet heel-to-toe across the shoulder outside the arc of the tire tracks. "So we're looking for a sports car with fancy tire treads and a wheelbase bigger than about six and a half feet."

"That's wide for a car, right?"

"My truck is just over six feet, so yeah. That should give us a short list." I tucked the phone in my pocket, shivering in a gust of wind. "Let's go see what Google can tell us."

25

"A Lamborghini Aventador SVJ." I looked over my laptop screen at Graham. "Wheelbase is eighty-two inches wide, and the tires are a specialty racing line with treads that leave a herringbone edged pattern." I held up my phone, the photo of the tire tracks on the screen. "It was the first thing to blow away, but you can see a little of it there at the edge if you zoom in."

I'd narrowed the list from three models to one in less than half an hour on Google, twenty minutes of it spent studying images of tires.

Now we just had to find the right car, and hope the driver had noticed whoever they almost ran over.

"Not exactly a Camry." Graham offered a low whistle as he peered at the sleek Italian race car on my screen. "Shouldn't be hard to spot. I'll hit anywhere with a surveillance camera on my way out."

"Bolton, you check registrations," Graham said. "It's a four hundred and twenty thousand dollar car. There can't be too many of them around here."

"As long as the driver noticed the person they almost mowed down, we might have a bona fide lead here," I said. "But with folks who drive around in half a million dollars, that can be a dicey proposition."

He brushed one knuckle across my chin. "Get warmed up. We're going to get this guy."

I closed the computer, letting my eyes stray to the dock and the rubble beyond.

They had done something that caused this. I had no proof of that and I'd just told Bolton not to make assumptions, but I could feel it in my bones. Someone was pissed off at my father and his colleagues in a vengeful, almost righteous way. Jenkins was hunting a terrorist, but I wasn't convinced he was right. Or, at least, that the word meant what he thought it did here. Maybe someone had been hired to carry this out. But it all felt too personal to me for that to be the case, and going with my gut usually didn't fail me.

Ruth...she had come to me in the first place. And from the photo and the victims, whatever they had done had to stretch back years past that dinner party. No way the Governor had kept it a secret from Ruth for that long. She knew everything. Eventually.

"You guys let me know if you get a hit on this car?"

"Sure," Graham said. "Where are you headed?"

"To see if my mother is scared enough to tell me everything she knows yet."

Your father means well, Faith, and one thing I can say with certainty is that everything he's ever done has been to help this family.

The Governor had just stormed out of the room that night, seething when I refused to back down after he forbade me to change my major to criminal psychology. I could hear my mother's excuses as clearly as if she were in the passenger seat.

I was supposed to be a lawyer. Well—I was supposed to get a law degree and then marry a lawyer from the "right kind" of family, and then have babies and plan dinner parties while he had a career—probably keeping people out of prison instead of putting them in. Not murderers, mind you. Too sordid. No, the kind of attorney the Governor wanted to see me marry would've been the type to exploit loopholes to keep greedy rich assholes out of prison when they got caught embezzling funds, or stealing from pensions, or making insider trades.

The kind of lawyer who would make the sort of powerful friends who wrote big campaign checks.

The kind of lawyer who might be President of the United States one day.

My parents had planned my whole life before they ever put me into my first pageant. Needless to say, the Governor didn't handle it well when I said I was going to be a cop. He'd threatened to cut me off without a penny. I'd told him I'd get a job and loans.

Ruth looked horrified at the thought and jumped in to try to calm everyone down. Not that she was excited about my choice, either. But her concern was at least a little for my safety. The Governor's was entirely tied up in his lost dreams of having the ear of the most powerful man in the world.

Ruth lied to me that night. The Governor's sole concern was always himself. If good things happened for other people incidentally because of something he did, fine, he was always happy to take the credit. But everything that happened in his orbit was viewed through a lens of how it would affect him and his career before anything else.

What I didn't know was if Ruth fully understood the man she had married. I'd spent my whole life thinking they were two peas in a pod, but a few things had happened in the past year that had me questioning that.

I turned off the narrow road into the wide drive and pressed the buzzer at the gate. "Faith McClellan here to see Mrs. McClellan."

The gate swung wide. It was almost noon on a Monday in October. The Governor was all but guaranteed to be off networking somewhere. Time to go find out who my mother really was—or at least, who she wanted to be.

I threw the truck into park in the driveway and shoved the door open, the sound of squealing brakes sending me scrambling to the ground. I spun as my boot heels met the concrete.

A black Lincoln Town Car, stench of hot rubber coming from the tires, sat about a gnat's ass from the side wall of the bed of my truck.

I peered through the windshield to see who was driving. And flinched when I realized Ruth was.

She hadn't driven herself anywhere since the Governor...well, since he was elected governor. She said her anxiety was too high to go out alone in Austin traffic.

She slammed both hands onto the steering wheel and glared at me, screaming something I couldn't make out. I shook my head and raised both hands in mock surrender.

The window in the driver's door lowered. "What are you doing? Get the hell out of my way!"

I almost choked on my own spit. Ruth McClellan didn't curse. She declared it a sign of lacking intelligence and poor breeding. I hustled around the front end of the truck and jerked open her passenger door. "What on Earth?"

"Get that monstrosity out of my way." Her voice broke as tears welled and spilled over, dragging gray-black watercolor lines of mascara down her face faster than she could flick them away. Hand to God, but for the steely set to her jaw and the trademark two-too-many sprays of Chanel, I'd have sworn in court I was looking at a pod person.

"Mother." It rolled off my tongue awkwardly, hanging in the air and drawing her icy blue eyes up to mine. "Get out of the car. I don't know what the hell is going on here, but I'll take you where you need to go."

She pressed a clenched fist to her perfectly-red lips and sobbed.

My mother.

Sobbed.

Squashing panic that I might be too late with my questions, I set my face in my best impartial police officer expression and swallowed the bitter tang of fear as I raced around the trunk of her Lincoln, pulling her door open and grabbing her hand as she stood. "It'll be okay."

I had no idea what I was promising or even why, but something—some womb-forged connection that years of animosity had long buried—wouldn't let me watch her break down and say nothing. I opened the back door of the car and put a hand on her soft chignon to keep her from bumping her head as I helped her into the seat.

Behind the wheel, I put it in gear and spun to the left, skirting my truck by driving on her prized St. Augustin lawn. And she didn't say a word.

Shit.

I slammed the gas so hard we lurched toward the road. "Which way?"

"University Medical Center," she choked out, hitching in a breath before she spoke again.

Oh.

God.

I kept my eyes on the road, trying to make my mouth work to ask how he was.

"Erma," Ruth sputtered. "Erma was in a car accident this morning. Jaime said the doctors aren't sure she'll make it."

Every drop of blood in my veins went cold.

It wasn't the Governor.

It was a thousand times worse.

26

I hate hospitals.

The vast majority of my experience with them involves saying goodbye to people I love.

"Not this time," I muttered.

"I beg your pardon?"

Ruth clung to me like my arm was the only vine over a pit of quicksand, fighting to slow her breathing. I didn't think she realized that the mascara tracks would give away that she'd been crying. She didn't do emotion often enough to understand the fallout.

We rode the elevator to the ninth-floor ICU in silence, both of us staring at the lighted panel over the door and willing the thing to go faster.

Ruth bolted when the doors finally opened, the *click-click-click* of her sharp heels on the linoleum floor echoing off the tile walls. I stayed right behind her. Intensive care units are usually family-only. But these people hadn't met Ruth McClellan.

She pulled up short at the nurse's station. "Erma Hidalgo." Her words were clipped, drawing the nurse's gaze from the computer screen.

"And you're related to Mrs. Hidalgo how, exactly?"

"I am her employer," Ruth said. "And while I am certain you have already ascertained that we don't share blood, she is family to my husband and me. I need to see that she's okay. Ask Jaime. He'll tell you."

"I'm sorry, ma'am, but hospital policy says family only on this floor."

Ruth stood up straighter, squaring her shoulders. "Perhaps you could tell your supervisor that Ruth McClellan would like to speak to them." The ice in the words would've frozen five rings of hell right over.

The nurse stood, leaning on the desk on both arms and sliding her glasses down her nose.

"It's your lucky day, Mrs. McClellan—I'm the nurse supervisor in this ward." She smiled. But not the kind sort. "I don't care who you are, or who your husband is. I haven't voted in twenty years, because politicians are a crooked, greedy bunch, and no matter who's in office, people still get sick. So as I said. Family only. Y'all have a nice day."

I slid from behind my mother to the edge of the counter. Was using my badge to get in there ethical?

Nope.

Did I give one damn right then, with Erma hooked to machines and poor Jaime watching it alone?

Nope.

I checked the woman's name tag. She was probably ten years older than me, with pink scrubs, dark hair threaded with silver at the roots, and tired, sunken eyes that showed the toll of beating back death with her bare hands on the daily.

One warrior to another, I could relate.

"Ms. Radigan, while my mother is telling the truth, what she's not saying is that I need to see Mrs. Hidalgo because we have reason to suspect foul play in her accident."

I had no such thing. But I wasn't leaving without seeing her.

"Mrs. Hidalgo is unconscious." She stood up straight and folded her arms across her chest, her eyes flicking to my badge.

"I can speak with her husband and assess her injuries," I said. "If you could arrange for me to speak to her physician, that would be helpful, as well." I held her gaze, not blinking. "She had a big hand in raising me, and time is a critical factor in any investigation. Please."

She narrowed her eyes. "I didn't hear any of the cops in the ER talking about foul play."

I tapped my badge. "Texas Rangers. I have a bit more experience than they do."

Nurse Radigan stared back for a five count before a machine started beeping in a room behind me. She rolled her eyes and waved a hand to her left. "Bed ten. Don't cause trouble."

I whirled and started that way, Ruth on my heels.

Erma looked tiny and frail in the bed, her head elevated and bandaged, a spiderweb of tubes and wires connecting her to the machines lining both sides of the small, glass-walled room. I caught a sharp breath and swallowed hard, pasting on a sad half smile when Jaime looked up from his prayerful posture. He rose and opened the door for us.

Ruth shocked the shit out of me for the third time in an hour when she pulled Erma's husband into a hug. "What have they told you?" She sobbed between the words. "Is she going to wake up?"

He patted her back and met my eyes over her shoulder.

"Her head hit the windshield and the window, and it shook her brain. Made it bleed." His chin quivered, and he pinched his lips together. "They said if she doesn't wake up in the first forty-eight hours, she might not. And she could have permanent damage even if she does."

Ruth sobbed again, and I swallowed a lump, trying to switch my brain into investigative mode.

"Did you go to the scene or meet them here?" I asked.

"Here."

"Did you talk to the police officer who responded to the scene?"

He pulled a card from his hip pocket. "This guy. He said her car was totaled and she was lucky to be alive."

I took the card, the name of an APD officer I didn't recognize stamped in blue across the front. Snapping a photo of it with my phone, I cleared my throat and handed it back. "Did they tell you where the accident occurred?"

"Manor Road, near the 183 overpass," he said. "They said she must've run full speed into the column."

"Witnesses?" There should've been. It was the middle of the day.

"No. A passerby called them when they saw the car bunched up under the bridge, but he got there after. He didn't see," he said.

The door opened behind us.

"Officer, I'm Dr. Harris."

I turned to a petite, raven-haired woman with kind eyes and a tablet in her hands. "Our nurse manager said you wanted to speak to me?"

I put out a hand to shake hers. "Thank you for coming in, I won't keep you. Mr. Hidalgo tells me Erma has two different head injuries?"

"Impact injuries. The damage to her cervical spine is consistent with it. Her head hit one glass surface first and then whipped back quickly to collide with another."

"Any other injuries?"

She tapped her screen. "Contusions consistent with the seat belts, a dislocation of her..." She trailed off, moving to the side of the bed and gently probing Erma's shoulder. I noticed a bump under the gown when the doctor called attention there.

"Is something wrong in her chart?" I asked.

She shook her head, her thin, dark brows furrowed when she looked back at me. "No. It's just odd. Her right shoulder is dislocated."

I kept a polite smile on my face, a wordless request for clarification.

"Well, sometimes when a front-end impact in a vehicle is severe, we see people with torn or partially torn rotator cuffs from the seat belt. But a dislocation of the shoulder suggests that the belt locked and then the body was thrown to one side with great force." She tapped her screen again. "The police said that the car hit the concrete support of the bridge head-on." She touched a finger to her chin. "Not that it's impossible. Forces and objects moving in crashes can get all kinds of things sideways. It is odd, though."

My stomach closed tight around itself and twisted.

I thought I was lying when I stepped in to handle Nurse Radigan. But what if I wasn't?

Erma had never been in a car accident. She was an almost impossibly careful driver. And she had been out having coffee with me. If whoever was taking out my father's cabinet members didn't want her to be able to tell me anything else, this was an easy way to make sure she stayed quiet.

What if it was entirely my fault Erma was lying there?

I almost couldn't breathe.

"Thank you," was all I managed to say to the doctor.

She glanced at Jaime. "I'll be back to check on her in a couple of hours."

At me. "If you need anything else, please let me know."

The door closed behind her and my mother shot me a measured glance before she moved to the side of the bed and cradled Erma's hand in both of hers. I took the same pose on the opposite side of the bed.

"The Governor and I won't make it without you, Erma," Ruth said. "You take all the time you need to heal and recover, but then you come back to us. It's not your time yet."

I crouched and pressed my lips gently to the back of the hand I held. "I'm so sorry," I whispered against her cool skin, too low for anyone else to hear. "Please wake up. We all love you. Your babies love you. And if someone did this to you, I will find them."

We were seated back in the car before Ruth said a word.

"You were amazing in there." The words were stilted. And was that... pride...I heard cloaking them? I'd forgotten the last time my mother sounded proud of me, but I'm pretty sure it involved a crown and a sash and a smiling walk down a runway with roses in my arms. "Truly. Thank you for getting us in there."

"You...you're welcome." I stammered around it a little. It was weird for her to compliment me on any level.

"Did you actually think someone was trying to hurt her?"

"I don't know. I lied to the charge nurse to get in to see her, but the two brain bleeds thing is weird. Coupled with the dislocated shoulder, it has me worried."

I was already trying to remember if there were cameras around that underpass.

"Jesus." The word hissed through her teeth, much more epithet than praise. "What the fuck has he gotten us into here?"

I almost ran the Town Car across the yellow line.

I'd never heard her say "fuck." Not once. In thirty-seven years.

Not that my mother's language should've been the focus of my attention at that moment.

"That's what I was coming to ask you." I flicked my eyes to meet hers in the rearview mirror. "Bill Haynesworth was killed last night. His boat blew up on the lake. And Benham Avesta was killed in a fire Thursday night. A fire where investigators recovered a photo of the Governor and Bill and other members of his cabinet from an expensive SUV parked near the scene. You said you weren't at the dinner party he threw a couple of weeks ago, but I knew Erma was. I met her for coffee this morning. She said all the men in this photo were there."

She shut her eyes, shaking her head. "Nothing is ever enough."

"Is someone trying to keep them from doing something they're getting into?" I swallowed hard. "Or am I trying to find someone who's pissed about something they already did?"

"Maybe you'd better drive a little faster," she said. "We need to talk."

27

I stopped Ruth's car outside the six-bay detached garage at the ranch in record time. Ruth opened her own door and got out without a word, going into the house through the kitchen door.

I followed her to her study, a smaller room off the hallway next to the main library.

She shut the door and punched a few buttons on a wall panel. Johnny Cash's voice poured from speakers embedded in the ceiling, and Ruth gestured to the polished cherry and silk settee, sitting closer to me than she would've normally been comfortable with.

She was afraid he had the house bugged.

In the middle of being horrified by that, I couldn't say it was impossible. Jesus. Was that how he always seemed to know everything? I'd spent half my childhood wondering if the servants were spying on me and Charity.

"Your father has always had the best interest of our family at heart." She leaned close. "I need to make sure you understand that."

I knew better than to argue. So I nodded.

"Does this go all the way back to his time in office?" I kept my voice low and even, impressing myself with the almost detached tone.

She put a tentative hand on my knee. "I think it might."

It would be unlike Chuck McClellan to hold an office as powerful as

Governor of Texas and not leave without significant personal gain. I had always figured some breed of political grift paid for the house I was sitting in. But I also figured the evidence was long burned and buried, and nobody would ever admit any of it ever existed.

"Insider trading?" I asked.

"If only."

My God.

I pinched my lips together. I needed her to keep talking. But I had taken an oath.

"Did they kill anyone? Because I can't hear that without opening an investigation." I watched her face carefully.

Two slow blinks. And then a twitch of her nose. "No."

Dammit.

Graham had called me his human lie detector since our second week as partners at the TCSO. Every liar has a tell. I just have a knack for spotting them. The nose, for Ruth, meant she wasn't sure.

She had said no. I could accept that. For now, anyway.

"I have to know where to start looking. We're out of time for needles and haystacks here." My tone was soft, an expression on my face I'd practiced in front of a mirror more often than any pageant smile. *Trust me with your secrets. I will keep you safe,* it said.

"I don't know," she said. "I thought maybe Lieutenant Baxter knew, that whatever your father did was the reason he finally left."

Archie left because he wanted to know why my sister was murdered. My father didn't want to know if the answer might hurt him politically. It was that simple. How did she not know that?

Whatever. Not the time.

"If Archie knew, I would know."

"We're going out tonight. We won't be home until midnight at least."

The house would be empty.

She was telling me to break in and look through his papers.

And I would. But damn I wished I didn't need to.

"Any luck?" I asked when Graham answered his phone. I drove back out through the gates of the ranch.

"Nothing yet, but I have two more places to check and then I'll head back to the office," he replied.

"See if Bolton found anything on the car registrations."

"Will do." He paused. "You okay?"

"Just anxious to get to the bottom of this one for about a thousand reasons." I paused. "Erma was in a car accident today."

"Oh my God. Is she okay?"

"She's in the ICU at UMC. The doctor seems on top of it."

"I'm so sorry," he said. "I'll see you at home in a little while?"

I turned the truck onto the highway, headed for a coffee shop. "I might be late tonight, but I'll let you know more in a bit."

"Okay. Holler if there's anything I can do."

"Thank you." I ended the call and parked. I opened a text to Archie.

I think I might be onto something, but it's too soon to tell. I'll call you later. Any luck with the medical device companies?

I ordered at the counter, then seated myself in a red velour armchair tucked into a corner, coffee steaming next to me and my laptop open, before I got a reply.

I added the names I was able to track down to your spreadsheet, but I only have about half of them. I got sidetracked by the explosion at the marina.

He sent another right behind it. *Did you agree to let that ATF jackass into our case?*

Damn. I didn't mention that to him, did I?

Yes? Sorry.

Well, since he thinks he's working with us and he thinks the same person blew the boat up, he's letting us into that one. So I guess I owe you a thanks. But Hardin was right, this guy is a douche.

Can you send me what you have on the knee implant and I'll take that over for now?

Sure. Give me ten minutes.

I tapped my fingers on the table and opened my email program. Then I opened a browser window and clicked the bookmark for the hacked traffic feed from the front gate at the ranch so I could see when my parents left.

I glanced around the shop, the sun drifting toward the horizon on the other side of the big picture window. Except for one guy with headphones on and the two young women working the counter, I was alone in the shop. A few quiet phone calls wouldn't hurt anything.

Archie sent me an updated file six minutes later. I opened it to see what I had left to find.

He had contacted all three device companies and gotten the names of the doctors for each listed device, and he had a dozen names in another column, each matched to a specific device. I went to the next doctor on the list and dialed. I picked my way through the automated menu to the records department, prepared to leave a message.

"Records, this is Angie, can I help you?"

"Angie, this is Faith McClellan with the Texas Rangers. I'm looking to identify a homicide victim, and hoping you might be able to help."

"Um." She paused for five beats. "Did you say homicide?"

"I'm afraid so. The medical examiner found a medical device—a knee implant, specifically. The manufacturer says it may have been sold to your office, and I need the name of the person it was implanted in."

"I'm not sure I can tell you that," she said. "Do you have a warrant or something?"

"I don't need one in a case like this. I do need your email address. The law says I have to submit the request in writing, and I'm sure if you read your office's standard privacy disclosure, you'll find that it provides permission for you to release the name to me in the incidence of a murder investigation."

"But can't you just get, you know, fingerprints? Or dental records?"

"In this particular case, we feel this is the easiest route to an ID."

"Can you hold on for a moment?" She still sounded wary.

"Of course."

Four minutes of muzak later, she was back. "I need the email to include your title and badge number and be from an official state address."

"Headed to you as soon as you tell me where to send it."

She reeled off her email.

My fingers flew across the keyboard. I copied the possible serial number and added all my qualification and contact information. Send.

"It should be there," I said.

Her keyboard and mouse clicked.

"Yes, ma'am," she said. "Here we go: Jeremiah Wexley."

I typed it in the right column and thanked her for her help before I hung up.

I had the number for the next doctor's office half-dialed before I realized where I knew the name.

"Oh no," I whispered, clicking open a new browser window and typing it to be sure.

The first return was a profile page from one of the largest, most influential law firms in the state.

The same law firm that owned the BMW we'd found behind the Clay Street house.

The second was from LinkedIn. Third was the state bar.

Fourth, his Facebook page, where his profile photo was a beach vacation shot of him and Caitlyn framed by blue water.

My sister's friend's husband wasn't gone on business. He was half-cremated in Jim's cold storage.

How in the hell was I going to tell her that?

Archie called every police and sheriff's department that might possibly have jurisdiction. Wexley hadn't been reported missing.

I ran credit card pings, and the last hit I found was Thursday at lunch. In downtown Austin.

"That's not conclusive," Archie said. "It's concerning, but without a definite serial number or a missing person's report, we don't have enough to say it's him."

"Archie. Are you serious? It's him."

"Keep going through the list and let me work this Wexley guy. Trust me when I say you don't want to tell his wife he's dead if he's not, and right now what he is, is one of more than two dozen possibilities."

"Yes. One who works at the law firm that owns the car we found in the alley, and may also be married to a woman who may or may not be connected to another murder. Involving fire."

Jesus, what if Caitlyn killed her husband *and* Bethany?

"Archie, what if we're looking at this all wrong? What if Avesta was a bystander who got caught in the flames when Wexley was the target?"

"Keep talking."

The words tripped out of my mouth as fast as my brain built the story.

"Something was bothering Caitlyn when Graham and I were at her house yesterday. I thought the husband was just an asshole, maybe the abusive variety...but what if he was screwing around with widowed former model Bethany from the garden club? Caitlyn follows him to the vacant house thinking he's with Bethany and finds him with Avesta, kills them both, then invites Bethany over and confronts her, killing her and hauling her body out to a trailer park with known drug trafficking ties to set it on fire in the middle of the night."

"It's not the craziest thing I've ever heard. But it doesn't explain Haynesworth."

"Or Erma," I murmured.

"Or what?" Archie's voice rose with alarm.

Damn. Nice, Faith. "She was in a car crash. She's in the ICU, she's stable, Jaime is with her."

"Why do we need an explanation for that?"

"She was on her way back from talking to me, and you know how careful she is when she drives. Plus the doctor said a couple of her injuries were weird for the type of collision."

"Who is on that? APD?"

"Yeah, I got the name of the detective, but I didn't call him yet."

"Do that. I'll get a warrant and send someone to pick up Caitlyn Wexley for questioning. You want to be here to talk to her, or no?"

She wouldn't talk in front of me. We had too much history, and I didn't scare her.

Besides, I had somewhere to be. He was right, my scenario only explained half of our victims. If Caitlyn wasn't the killer, we still needed to know who was. Which meant I needed to know what Chuck McClellan was hiding.

"Nah, you take it. You'll be much more effective at intimidating her."

He laughed. "Thanks. I think."

The sun disappeared, the last red-orange rays fading into an inky indigo twilight that crawled across the window.

I told Archie to keep me posted and hung up, dialing the traffic cop's cell phone from the photo of his business card.

Before he picked up, my father's white Cadillac Escalade pulled to the inside of the gate on my video feed. When the gates swung open, the monster SUV pulled out and turned toward the city.

I tucked the phone between my ear and shoulder, gathered my laptop and untouched coffee, and hurried for the truck.

It's not breaking and entering when you have a key.

I repeated it like a mantra to myself as I parked near a thicket of low, thorny mesquite trees and hopped the rail fence at the front of my parents' property.

The Austin officer was nice. He agreed with me about the doctor's comments and promised to keep looking for possible witnesses. I'd gotten everything I could've hoped for from him and hung up before I was halfway back to the ranch.

Which left plenty of time for the guilt surrounding this plan to seep in.

What if it was Caitlyn? What if the explosion on the lake was an accident, and Erma just wrecked her car?

Working homicide for a decade and a half has taught me that it's damned hard to see certain things clearly when you're so close to a case. I couldn't say for sure that I didn't want all this to be because of my father on some crazy level. He was a villain to me in many ways already. Having the world see his true colors wouldn't make me proud, but there was a lot of justice in it.

Was I actually going to go into their house when they weren't here?

"She told you to," I whispered to myself. "That counts as an invitation."

The memory of the look on Ruth's face was enough to carry me through the field to the kitchen porch, where I reached up to the short lip under the low edge of the porch roof, feeling for the key I knew Ruth kept there for Erma. She was notorious for forgetting her key if Jaime dropped her at work for the day, and she arrived way earlier than Ruth rose from bed.

I stepped inside soundlessly, scanning the perimeter of the room for motion sensors. Two small shuffles, and I spied the green light on the security panel. Ruth didn't set it, bless her.

Deep breath. Shoulders squared, I marched through the wide, wood-paneled hallways to the Governor's study and tugged the chain on the Tiffany desk lamp.

Whatever I was looking for was locked in the wide file drawers in the bottom center of the mahogany built-in wall unit. I opened his top desk drawer and poked through neat rows of Mont Blanc pens, ink, and paper-clips. No key.

I closed the drawer and stopped, closing my eyes. I knew Chuck McClellan. The key was in this room because he would see it as a waste of time to have to go elsewhere in the house to get it when he wanted something out of the files. But the top drawer was for amateurs. The Governor was an expert secret keeper.

I turned to the ornate shelving units lining the walls. A pen and ink sketch of Stephen F. Austin sat in the center of the highest shelf. I reached for the frame and flipped it over. Nope.

I worked systematically through books and keepsakes until I had checked everything across the top shelf the whole way around the room. I glanced at my watch. Nine thirty. Deep breath. Regroup. I still had time. I spun back to the desk, then to the shelves.

His ego would put something that important into an object he held as valuable.

An object he thought showed him as valuable.

Right in the smack center of the shelves. It even had its own little spotlight that never went off.

Folded into a triangle in a wood-framed box sat the American Flag that had flown over the state capitol on Chuck's last day as governor.

I lifted it carefully, turning it over. Nothing.

I had it halfway back to the shelf before I stopped, the puzzle boxes from the den flashing in my head.

I flipped it upside down. Almost invisible, a row of four circular cuts lay in the center of the thick wood frame.

I knew this one. Granddaddy had gotten me and Charity boxes of our own one Christmas, and mine had a code like this, but with more buttons.

What mattered to him that would work with only four?

I tried his birthday, always celebrated like the king's holiday in our house.

Nothing happened.

I knew it wasn't mine or Charity's, and definitely not Ruth's, hers was in September.

A framed photo of a young Chuck with President Reagan and Vice President Bush caught my eye from its spot on the desk where most people might keep a photo of their wife or family.

Surely not.

I tried it anyway. The first button wasn't a 1, it was a zero.

0-1-2-1-0-1. Would've been his first day in the Oval Office.

I clicked the last button in the sequence and a small door opened in the end of the frame.

I stuck a finger in and scooped out the key, laying the box on the desk blotter while I thumbed through his files.

I wasn't sure what I was looking for. What I found was enough to convene about a dozen different grand juries—campaign donors, dark money receipts, blackmail material on half the state senate, both former and current members.

Seemed Rickers had a thing for barely-of-age girls. A gross, violent thing that had put several in the hospital.

I swallowed hard and closed that file. Surely Beau couldn't—well. He wasn't the same person my sister had been ready to storm the political world with, for sure.

But I still didn't see anything here that would get Haynesworth killed. I drummed my fingers on the edge of the drawer, looking around. Hell, maybe I was wasting my time and Archie had the killer in interrogation as I snooped.

But my gut said I was underestimating the Governor once again.

I peered into the drawer, fat files skimming the bottom. Hidden in plain sight was his favorite game.

I crouched and examined the front.

Pulled a file out and held it up to the faceplate.

The damned thing had a false bottom. Checkmate, Governor.

I removed folders, stacking them in careful order.

Pressing every corner, I tried to figure out how to get it open. Nothing happened. I pressed the center. Knocked. It was hollow, for sure.

I turned on the flashlight on my phone, going around the perimeter of the panel. There. In the top right corner, I spotted an indentation. Hot damn. I turned to the desk and grabbed his letter opener, using the tip in the little groove to lift the drawer bottom. The puzzle king went low tech.

Only one folder lay in the compartment, small and plain and manila.

With a label written in Arabic.

Bingo.

I snatched it up before I replaced the bottom of the drawer, then re-hung the files in the exact order I'd found them.

Drawer locked, key and flag replaced, lights off—I could've sworn the file was burning my hands as I let myself out, tucked away the spare key after locking the kitchen door, and sprinted to my truck. Inside the cab with the doors locked, I opened the folder.

Every document was in some sort of code.

Damn him.

My gut said Uncle Bill died for whatever was in that folder. So my computer was about to let me in on the Governor's dirtiest, best-guarded secret.

I was half a mile down the road when Archie called.

I clicked the speaker button. "Hey. You find her?"

"Found her, questioned her twice. She's hiding something. Currently waiting for her lawyer."

"Uh. The husband is a lawyer."

"She insists he's out of town. In Chicago on business. Hotel says he never checked in."

"Because he's dead."

"That's looking likelier and likelier, yes."

"She's there for a while?" I asked.

"Yeah, the attorney wasn't pleased at the hour, but he's on his way."

"Do me a favor and text me if she leaves. Or, you know, confesses."

"Sure. You okay? How did the thing you said you had to do go?"

"Still going."

I turned south on the freeway instead of north, speeding toward Caitlyn's house.

Parking in her secluded driveway, I grabbed a plastic spatula and a handful of evidence bags from my glove compartment and strolled around the corner of the house like I belonged there, letting myself into the back gardens through a wrought iron gate.

In the back right corner, I lifted the tarp and took five samples from the center and sides of the area it covered.

I was in and out in less than five minutes, soil samples tucked into the console next to the Governor's file.

One of these roads had to lead to the killer.

Time to start shortening the route.

28

"You broke into your parents' house?" Graham folded his arms across his chest, a disapproving furrow deepening between his eyebrows.

"I did not. I used the spare key to let myself in. With Ruth's permission." I couldn't even look him in the eye as I said it.

"So you could steal a file from your father's study."

I already felt guilty enough, but it wasn't like I didn't have a good motive. "What else did the SO find out about Haynesworth's death today?" I cleared dishes off the kitchen table and opened both of our laptops and the file.

"The ATF is running the samples through their lab looking for accelerant, but so much of the evidence was compromised by the water, we don't know if anything useful will come of it." He shot me a grin. "But Bolton and I do have a lead on the Lambo: I spotted one with a Louisiana plate on a gas station camera. He tracked it down just a few minutes ago. The guy is registered at the Driskill. We can drop by in the morning. So why would your mother give you permission to steal from her house, exactly?"

"She thinks they were into something back then that's getting them killed now. Something that had all of them together with Avesta in my parents' home just a couple of weeks ago. I think it's likely whatever she's talking about is in this folder."

"Why would anyone keep a file with incriminating information like that in it? Why not just burn it?"

"Because if it incriminates him, it incriminates them, too. You should've seen the blackmail fodder in the regular locked drawer: Chuck makes J. Edgar Hoover look kind and cuddly."

"Damn." Graham jerked his chin to the folder. "What did you find, then?"

"It's all coded, and I'm not sure of the key." I pulled up an Arabic translator and snapped a photo of the label on the folder.

Armory 1995.

Huh. I read the result to Graham. "What kind of armory?"

"The National Guard has armories all over the state." He pulled his computer over. "Google says they opened forty-seven new ones while your father was governor. Biggest expansion in the history of the program."

I blew a deep breath out slowly. "That is definitely the kind of thing Chuck would find a way to work to his advantage."

"How?"

"However it could make him more rich or more powerful." I flipped pages in the folder. Not a syllable of plain English among them.

I found a codebreaking app for my laptop and carefully copied the first several lines of the first document into it. "This one looks like a letter. Let's see if the computer can tell us how to read it."

"How long will that take?"

"A few minutes if we get lucky," I said, eyeing the progress bar at the bottom of the screen. "A few hours if we don't."

"Can I have a look?" he asked.

I waved my hand. "Please."

He flipped pages, pulling one sheet out and holding it up. "This looks like an invoice."

I scanned the lines in the center column and the short collections of characters in the far right one. "I'd love to know what he bought that had such long descriptions."

"You sure about that?" he asked.

I sighed. "No. But yes."

"I got you."

I tapped my index finger on the edge of the keyboard. "I found the key in the study because I know him. He loves puzzles. There has to be a logic to this code."

Code.

The Governor loved puzzles. And political history.

"Son of a bitch, is it going to be that easy?" I reached for Graham's computer. "Can I borrow this?"

He pushed it across the table. I went to the Smithsonian's Museum of the American Indian site and searched for "code talkers."

Graham rounded the table and leaned over my shoulder.

"Aha. He's been telling people for decades he's part Comanche. My grandaddy swore no McClellan ever so much as set eyes on a Native American when our family came to Texas, but Chuck thinks it makes him sound like a badass warrior or something."

I opened a blank screen next to the code and went across the page carefully, typing the letters that corresponded to the Navajo words.

I sat back and stared at the screen. "Machine gun, M 249, by carton."

"Armories," Graham said.

"Oh my God."

My eyes went to the block at the top of the page where the recipient should have been. "Graham..."

He squeezed my shoulder. "I'm right here, baby."

My fingers felt heavy as I found and pecked out the letters and Googled the name.

"An Iranian general." I didn't even read the rest of the Wikipedia entry, the letters blurring together on the screen.

I moved to the next line item. Fatigues. Cases for the guns. Hundreds of thousands of rounds of ammunition.

At the bottom, in a space marked "authorization," I translated the name of Chuck's comptroller, Drake Collins.

"See? Dirt on other people." I pointed it out to Graham. "Collins isn't the kind of man who could mastermind this kind of bullshit, but the Governor made sure his name was on the paper trail."

I stopped the codebreaking app on my laptop and passed Graham's back across the table, pointing to the stack of papers and opening the code key page on my laptop, too.

"He didn't do something like this just for money. We need to know what he got out of it besides that. Whoever is killing these people is pissed in a way I'm not sure we've ever dealt with. The reason has to be in here."

"Are we looking for the wrong thing?" Graham asked an hour later, when we were halfway into the stack and no closer to an answer on why, other than several million dollars changing hands. "What else do we know? Who are the victims?"

"Avesta would've been in like junior high when all this was going on, but he has connections to power there now," I said. "Haynesworth was the Railroad Commissioner during my father's time in office. And contrary to logic, the Texas Railroad Commissioner has nothing to do with transportation or trains. He controls natural resource production—specifically, he controls oil and gas." I stared at another list of translated National Guard supplies that had been skimmed and sold off to the same general.

"Oil and gas." Graham tipped his head to one side. "What was Avesta's uncle doing when this was going on?"

Shit. The relation to a Middle Eastern government was pretty damned obvious when I thought about it that way.

I looked up the code talker word for H and started digging through the file.

The next to last page was a photocopy of a letter. I checked the rest of the name at the bottom.

"Haynesworth signed this," I said as I went to work breaking the code.

Five minutes later, I sat back in the chair and sniffled, wiping a tear from my lashes.

"They were fucking fixing global oil prices."

It made so much sense I was a little annoyed I hadn't thought of it earlier.

"My father coasted to a second term and ran for the White House on the economic expansion Texas experienced under his administration—it was the widest, longest ever."

"Because of an oil boom?"

"In large part, yes. West Texas Intermediate Crude went to $45 a barrel when Iraq invaded Kuwait—Chuck had nothing to do with that, but he rode the hell out of the economic numbers it produced. And it seems"—I waved a hand at the computers and papers—"he used other people's influence to make sure it stayed there."

I typed "Iran Contra," brushing up on my history before I looked up at Graham.

"So, after North got caught, the Iranian military had to get their weapons from somewhere."

I could practically hear Chuck in my head. He was a master at justifying his bad behavior, no matter how far he had to stretch reality to get there. Most narcissists are. "He would say someone was going to do it, and it didn't hurt anything, just like in the eighties."

"Except cost millions of taxpayer dollars to replace the shit he sold." Graham waved a coded copy of a letter from then-Texas Attorney General Shep Stevenson to the federal government, in response to a threat of a lawsuit over "excessive missing and damaged items."

I thumped my computer keyboard. "They made millions. The ranch. Haynesworth's yacht. My father's campaigns."

I couldn't breathe.

This wasn't a typical politician-led grifter white collar theft.

Iran was a hostile foreign power.

It was treason.

"How did they get them out of here?" I dove back into the stack.

Another half hour of searching and we still didn't know.

"Do we export oil?" Graham asked.

"No, even when the wells here are running around the clock, the United States has to import oil…" I stopped. Blew him a kiss. "You are a genius."

I opened a search window and found images dating back to my father's term in office of oil tankers leaving the port in Houston.

The thirteenth one showed what I needed. I followed the links and checked the source. "Right here. This ship is leaving to go back to Saudi

Arabia. But when the cargo hold is empty, the bow is high in the water; you can see a line."

Graham leaned over the screen. "No line."

"Because it was full of guns and military supplies."

"And the Saudis were just cool with that?"

"They might not have even known, if he had someone getting paid to pull the stuff off and get it out to the general on a near port stopover." I searched the name of the ship and the date of the photo.

"Yep. I bet that's exactly what he did. This one stopped at Oman, holding from a backup in the Strait of Hormuz. From there, it's a short trip to Iran across the water."

"He's a smart son of a..." Graham cleared his throat. "Gun. So how does all this relate to our dead people? Avesta is one of them, but he didn't have anything to do with this."

Erma's lilting voice rang in my ears. Business deal. Blackmail.

"But his uncle might have. Remember, Ruth said he left the dinner party early because he was angry. I bet you anything he figured them out and was trying to blackmail them."

"But then why would anyone kill him, too?"

I didn't know.

I checked my phone for the first time in two hours. Archie, an hour ago: *She's heading home. She was in Houston Thursday night, according to her American Express card. I'm waiting for the surveillance footage from the hotel to confirm, but we can't hold her. Hope you found what you wanted.*

Graham crossed to the fridge for a Diet Dr Pepper. "This is good," he said. "We have a road to follow now."

Yep. And it led to my father. Who was a fucking war criminal.

It didn't feel like a good thing to know. In all the cases I've ever worked, I've only come across a few things I wanted to erase from my memory. This went straight to the top of the list.

"We should alert his protection," Graham said just as I blurted, "We're going to have to arrest him."

"Who is we? Archie can arrest him. Whenever it's safe to."

Boy, there was so much poetic justice in that mental picture Whitman would weep.

"You think he's safer being hunted than he would be in jail?"

"Do you know how easy it is to get to someone in the county jail? We had an average of three inmate deaths every month last year. If someone smart and well connected wants him dead, putting him in jail is like putting a fish in a barrel at a shooting range."

The sheriff's office runs the jail, so I'd take his word for it. "Y'all should do something about that."

"With all the money we get from the state?" He rolled his eyes. "All anyone in government cares about the jail is how fast we can process people through trial so they can sell them to the private prisons."

I raised both hands at the anger in his voice. "You know I'm with you on that whole system. It's appalling."

He leaned on both hands on the back of my chair and kissed the top of my head. "Speaking of protection, who else was at that dinner party besides your father? We have to round these people up and warn them."

I reached for my phone. "Archie can arrange for protective details."

I touched his name in my favorites list.

Three rings. Shit. Was he asleep already?

"Faith?"

Yes.

"I'm so sorry to wake you," I said. "We have a situation here. We're going to need a handful of protective details set up, and we don't have time to waste."

"For who?"

"Everyone who was in my father's inner circle while he was in office. Who isn't already dead."

"What'd you find?"

"I'll fill you in tomorrow morning," I said, in place of *not over the phone*. "Haynesworth won't be the last one, Arch."

"How sure are you?"

"I'm sure."

"This is worse than I thought." He blew out a long, slow breath. "Avesta's uncle will land at DFW tomorrow afternoon. He wants to see his nephew."

I could feel the ticking clock hanging over us with every pore and nerve ending, but he'd taught me long ago that letting the clock be the focus almost guaranteed we'd never beat it.

"We're getting there. Just the next step."

"Yeah." He coughed. "Yeah. Send me a list. I'll get detail assigned now. See you in the morning."

"Sleep well, Arch. Sorry I woke you."

"I'll sleep a hell of a lot better when we get to the end of this one, anyway."

"Yeah." I agreed so much I felt it in my bones.

29

I couldn't see my hand in front of my face, but I could hear the phone.

"Who is it?" Graham sat up in bed behind me, knocking his clock off the night table.

That was my ringtone. I groped for my phone.

"McClellan," I said.

"Drake Collins is dead," Archie replied, his voice half-a-twist-from-snapping tight.

I knew the feeling.

"Shit. Is the fire department on scene? And how the fuck did someone get to him with armed guards outside his house?"

"From what the troopers I sent to guard him said, it sounds like he got to himself," Archie said. "Single GSW to the head, no fire engines necessary. I'll send you the address."

I squeezed Graham's hand and wriggled out from under his arm, moving to the closet. My eyes landed on the clock.

Three twenty-six.

"We'll be right there."

Graham stood and reached for the pants he'd just taken off a couple of hours earlier. "Jesus, what now?"

"I'm beginning to think Jesus is busy this week. My father's comptroller just blew his brains out with two state troopers outside his front door."

Collins was older even when I was a child. Back then, he was always in a hurry, he had little use for small humans, and he never could find his glasses. I never saw him without a briefcase, and he was in and out of my father's office at all hours of the day and night. I had a specific memory of him being there the morning they found Charity's body. It was barely light out. And it was the only time Collins ever spoke to me. He came out of the Governor's office as I stood in the hallway in my nightgown and bare feet, and he put a hand on my shoulder and said he was sorry for our loss.

Of all the people who came through our house that week, his condolences stood out. Maybe because he'd seen me first. Maybe because he seemed the most sincere.

I knew that the Governor thought Collins was smart, but he didn't like Collins on a personal level. He cracked nasty jokes about him to other people, sometimes even when Collins was in the room. I always kind of thought that must mean Collins was a better person than I gave him credit for being.

Sipping my coffee in the car while Graham sped through dark, empty streets toward the north Austin suburbs, I thought about what we'd learned —what could've driven Collins to shoot himself—and figured I might've been right about that.

We flashed our badges at the deputy guarding the perimeter at the end of Collins's wide, manicured-lawn-lined street.

"Ranger McClellan!"

I didn't turn my head, pretending Skye's voice had gotten lost in the sirens and crowd murmurs. I was not in the mood.

Graham stayed right in step with me, shortening his stride as we walked up the street, away from a growing crowd of neighbors and reporters.

"She's going to make a stink," I muttered. "She doesn't get up in the middle of the night to chase a story unless she's going to cause trouble."

"Let her. She doesn't know anything," Graham said.

"Oh, she knows plenty, I'm sure. I don't think you understand how many powerful people in this town—in your own department, even—that woman has her claws into."

"She's not our problem."

I tipped my head from side to side, but let the comment go by. She was our problem if her ratings-chasing nonsense complicated or compromised our case. But I also didn't have time to worry about trying to block her from being able to do that. Keeping Skye Morrow distracted was a full-time job, and I already had one of those.

But my mother didn't.

If Ruth could keep Skye busy without telling her anything, it would be helpful. And if anyone knows how to talk to a reporter for hours and say nothing at all, it's a politician's wife.

Coming up on the gaslight-topped brick pillars at the end of Collins's driveway, I spotted Archie's Stetson across the yard, cutting across the stamped concrete drive to a wide, emerald lawn so meticulous I wouldn't have been surprised to see someone cutting it with a pair of scissors.

"How do you get everywhere before we do?" I stopped at Archie's elbow as a local PD uniform tipped his hat and walked toward the front door.

"Sleeping in my clothes." Archie waved a hand at his wrinkled shirt. "It was an accident, but it came in handy tonight." He sighed, turning to look at the house. "What the ever-loving fuck?"

"Not here. But I do have an idea. I'm hoping it will get us somewhere."

"Before Azari Avesta gets here?"

I checked my watch. "We can hope. Have you been inside?"

Archie shook his head. "I just barely beat you here. I was making my way to the door when y'all walked up." He gestured for me to walk in front of him. "Lead the way."

"I'm going to take a look around out here," Graham said. "Just to make sure nothing is out of the ordinary."

Archie on my heels, I crossed the lawn and exchanged pleasantries with the officer at the door.

The large oak and marble foyer was packed with police officers and forensic investigators.

I weaved through the crowd, averting my eyes from the blood spatter marring the leather-bound books behind Collins's desk.

"Rhonda!" I smiled when I saw her graying head bent over a clipboard, her navy medical examiner's polo particularly dark against her pale skin.

"Faith McClellan." She smiled back. "I didn't think the Rangers cared much about suicides, but it's nice to see you."

"You're sure about that?" I asked. "The suicide part?"

"Local PD says it's his gun, powder marks on his hands and splatter pattern are consistent with that. I think they even—" She stopped when a petite Round Rock officer with red hair and a smattering of freckles over the bridge of her nose touched my elbow. "You're Faith McClellan?"

"I am."

She pressed an evidence bag into my palm. "Any idea what that means?"

Embossed, textured paper, Collins's initials center set in a monogram at the top.

Faith—

Some sins can't go unpunished. And some people don't deserve saving. Be careful.

His signature faltered and trailed off into a thin black line two letters in.

I swallowed the bitter tang as my coffee tried to come back up.

I handed Archie the bag, returning my attention to the officer. "I haven't spoken to Mr. Collins since my family moved out of the governor's mansion," I said. "I assume he knew I've been investigating the death of another of his colleagues."

"William Haynesworth, killed in an explosion yesterday," she said. "It was easy to link them because they worked together in your father's administration." She folded her arms across her chest. "Powerful families stick together, I guess." One corner of her lip curled as she snatched the bag back from Archie and sauntered away muttering about dead people not mattering to rich folks.

Archie's hand landed on my shoulder. "You're not your parents."

I knew that. I also thought I knew where the guilt dripping off Collins's letter came from, and it made my blood run cold to think my parents might not even have the capacity to feel such a thing. Hell, I was surprised Collins did. Which made me wonder if my opinion was jaded by too many years in law enforcement.

I watched Rhonda zip the heavy black body bag over Collins's face. I had failed him. The crowd began to thin as the initial scene examination and evidence collection wound down.

"It's going to be hard to convince me our guy isn't responsible for him, too," I said.

"Sure sounds like it," Archie said. "Collins always had a fear of fire, you know. I was assigned protection for him on an economic development jaunt once. He'd gotten a slew of death threats over a tax fraud investigation he was running, and he made the hotel manager bring up detailed floor plans and drew his own fire escape routes, one for each of four contingencies depending on where the fire started and which way the wind was blowing."

"I did not know that." So it wasn't just guilt that motivated this, it was fear, too.

Archie glanced at the window. "The sun will be up soon. Buy you a coffee?"

"Please."

I stopped to say goodbye to Rhonda on my way out.

"Don't be such a stranger," she said. "I might not get as many of the alarming ones as Prescott, but I'd still like to see your smile once in a while. That star looks good on you. I knew the first day I met you you'd get there. You'll find your truth someday, too."

I patted her arm. Once upon a time, Rhonda had spent hours with Deputy Faith, poring over every public record about my sister's death. Not that I'd gotten anything but a few geese to chase and a dozen dead ends out of the time we'd devoted, but it was nice to hear she still believed in me.

"One murderer at a time."

"That should be a company slogan for y'all. But there was no murderer here tonight. Try to go back to bed."

Yet. There was no murderer here tonight. Yet.

Archie and I were almost out the front door when Graham burst through it, his chest heaving from a run.

"We were closer than we thought, Faith. I think maybe we talked to this guy and didn't even know it."

30

Graham grabbed my arm and hauled me outside.

"We talked to who?" I asked. "What did you find?"

"A truck from that nursery. The one that specializes in the weird plants that victim in Goliad had in her hair?" He pointed to the corner just past Collins's house. "I saw a truck with the logo on the door parked just around there."

I turned toward the corner. "Was it Dan Fortwright? Could he have been making an early delivery for someone's landscapers?"

"I didn't see the driver. Truck revved up and took off when I started toward it."

"That's not exactly deliveryman bystander behavior," Archie said.

My brain struggled to make what we'd learned in the last six hours line up with that. Why would a plant guy be pissed at my father and his colleagues about an international oil price fixing scheme? "I need coffee."

"Amen to that."

I checked my watch. Not quite five. "Where is open 24 hours?"

"Doocy's in the north end of the city," Graham said. "We used to stop there when I was a rookie and I worked that part of the county on graveyard."

"Meet us there?" I asked Archie.

"Will do."

Graham and I picked up our pace as we neared the media corral at the corner, but Skye pounced as soon as we stepped through the barricade.

"I'm hearing that Drake Collins killed himself. Can you confirm that?"

I froze, my eyes going to her scarlet-tipped talons wrapping my forearm. "No. Comment." I put my best impression of my mother's ice queen voice into the words.

Skye uncurled her fingers one at a time.

"Two former members of your father's cabinet dead in two days, Ranger. There's more to this story. Your only decision point here is how you come off in the final edit." She kept her voice low, her eyes hard above the circles she hadn't had time to cover fully with makeup.

"She said no comment." Graham shook his head at Skye. "And she saved your life a few months ago. Short memory you have there, Ms. Morrow."

"Old news." She flashed a sickly-fake smile at Graham and stepped back, keeping her eyes on me. "Have it your way. I always get my story."

She was right about that, only because she didn't give one damn who she had to step on, bribe, or sell out in the process. I had no doubt she would figure this out, too. The question was whether she'd get it before I had a suspect in custody.

As soon as I closed the car door, I pulled out my phone and dialed my mother's cell.

"Faith?" Sleep thickened her voice. "Are you hurt?"

"Drake Collins is dead," I said flatly. "He shot himself in the head with two state troopers stationed outside his house. Left me a note I need to speak to the Governor about. And I need you to handle Skye Morrow."

The last words struggled up my throat. I didn't ask my parents for... much of anything, in years now. And I wasn't in the mood to suck up to them after reading the contents of the Governor's secret files. But no matter what my father had done, I couldn't stand by and let more people die. Skye's snooping might cause that.

Ruth wasn't sleepy anymore. "Of course."

"I'll be there in an hour."

"I'll put coffee on and get him up." She faltered on the last word. "Faith..."

Two beats. Four.

"Yes?"

"He's not an evil man." Her voice sounded broken.

She needed to believe that, and I understood just exactly how much.

We grabbed a booth in the back of Doocy's and ordered coffee and pancakes. Graham and Archie both asked for large sides of extra crispy bacon.

"So your father had a dinner party less than two weeks ago, and now three of the people who were there are dead."

"And they won't be the last. Stevenson is still breathing?"

"He is." Archie sipped his coffee. "I've been thinking about what you said earlier. About Erma talking to you."

I poked at my pancakes, guilt bubbling up my throat.

"What if her accident didn't have anything to do with you? She was there that night, too. Why would the killer spare her?"

"She wasn't burned, she was run off the road."

"Which looks like a random accident and at least has the potential to be a quick death instead of an excruciating one." Archie broke off a piece of bacon.

"Well then." Graham sipped his coffee. "Maybe this is a good thing."

Archie and I both turned wide eyes on him.

"That came out wrong. I mean, maybe if that's true, it'll help us. Whoever is doing this would have to know she was there. They'd have to know Avesta was there. The maid wasn't in your father's cabinet, and you said your father didn't seem to even want to tell you that Avesta was there."

"Because Avesta was blackmailing them and Chuck didn't want me to know why."

"What?" Archie has had a lot of practice keeping his voice down.

"What do you remember about oil prices when my father was in office?"

"Not exactly my area of expertise."

"The global market was volatile, because of instability in the Middle East. Iraq invading Kuwait, the Saudis feuding with Iran...That kept our wells running here. The Texas economy is never better than during an oil boom, even if it did diversify substantially when Chuck was in office." I spoke carefully.

Archie's eyes widened when he got it. "Cartwheeling Jesus on toast," he muttered.

Graham snorted.

"What did he have to give?" Archie asked.

"Weapons."

"From where?"

"It's not like they're hard to come by around here."

"You're sure?" he asked. "Someone told you this?"

"She figured it out." Pride dripped from Graham's words. "Because she's a damned fine detective."

"What'd you have to steal?" Archie's tone said he knew I was a damned fine detective who didn't regard rules when they got in the way of the truth.

"It's at least fuzzy on theft when it's a relative. And the person who told me when the house would be empty is on the deed to the property."

"She's got to be scared out of her mind." Archie's face darkened for such a split second I wasn't sure I hadn't imagined it.

"I'm not sure anything actually scares Ruth McClellan."

"So. Now all we need to know is who knew the guest list for the dinner party, who would have reason to be pissed at them over this scam they were all in together, how Avesta and a possible blackmail scheme figures into that, and why a gardener was hanging out near a crime scene in the wee hours of the morning," Archie said. "We should be done by lunchtime, right?"

"And whether the Lambo driver staying at the Driskill saw our suspect last night at the lake," I added.

"Excuse me?"

"It's a long story, but the end of it is there's a guy driving a half-million-dollar car in town from Louisiana, and he might've seen the person who blew up Haynesworth's boat."

Archie shook his head. "When it rains, it pours. Seems like the theme of this one."

"From the start." I checked my watch and gobbled a few more bites. "I'm due at my parents' house."

"I'll go to the nursery and feel out Fortwright on the oil industry and politics, see if he lets anything slip," Graham said. "And if that doesn't work I'll ask why he was at Collins's house this morning."

"I guess I'm going to the Driskill?" Archie said. "Do we have a room number for the sports car guy? How do we know he was at the lake?"

"Saw the plate on the video feed at a gas station near the marina," Graham explained.

"From the tracks I found, he almost ran over the possible suspect, and then almost drove into the lake trying to not hit a car. Hopefully he noticed something."

"I'll let you know." Archie put two twenties on the table and waved Graham off when he tried to object. "You two check in with me by phone in one hour. Until we know more about what we're dealing with here, everyone is a suspect. And this is the kind of secret folks kill indiscriminately for. Bloodlines and badges will not protect any of us." He stared hard at me, not blinking until I nodded.

I squirmed a little in the seat. International crimes notwithstanding, I knew Archie knew more about my father than I did. Probably a lot of things I didn't want to know.

I also knew I might be about to find some of them out, want be damned.

31

The Governor was unnerved.

Pacing the length of the living room double-time, he tossed back his second double scotch—at six a.m.—and refilled the glass, his shaking hand sloshing amber whiskey over the sleeve of his thousand-dollar suit jacket.

It was all I could do to keep my breathing even. While I wasn't sure what to expect when I rang the bell, I had never seen him like this.

Never.

Not when he lost the presidential primary. Not when my sister died. Not the night someone tried to shoot him as he left a fundraiser.

I knew better than most people how to handle Chuck McClellan.

But I didn't know how to handle his fear.

"They're sure Collins killed himself?" It was the third time he'd asked that question in twenty minutes.

"I know the ME who was on the scene. She's good. She agreed with that assessment. Archie said Collins was afraid of fire." I repeated the whole spiel for the third time.

I stepped closer. "He left a note. Addressed to me. 'We deserve no better,' was how it began. Who knows what you did? Someone who might want to make you pay for it?"

His head snapped around, his arm raising the Waterford highball glass to his lips. I met his eyes, trying to ignore the wobbly glass.

"I don't know what he's talking about."

Ruth sprang off the silk settee in the corner and left the room. I had forgotten she was even over there, to be honest.

"Gov—" I sucked in a deep breath. "Dad. I can't keep you safe if you won't talk to me. People are dying. If you know who's doing this, you have to tell me. If you know anything that might help me figure out who's doing this, I need you to tell me."

"Faith, I know I haven't—"

"What the fuck did you do with them?" The door slammed open, my mother as unkempt as I'd ever seen her, her shoulders heaving with heavy breaths. The anger radiating off her made her look bigger—her tall, solid frame filling the doorway almost ominously. "I have sat by and looked the other way and hidden your bullshit for almost forty years, but damned if I'm dying for your sins, you sonofabitch. Give her the file. Now."

She got louder with each word, probably egged on by the Governor's head shaking, which sped up as she talked.

I took an involuntary step back. Part of my job is to intrude on private moments, but this was a different dimension—it was private to me, too. I had never liked watching them fight, often hiding with pillows in my closet when I was a child, or in Charity's bed if she was home. Chuck McClellan was known in the capitol for his temper—it was part of why a whole host of party insiders thought he wouldn't make a good president. But his political colleagues never saw it the way his family did.

He'd never hit her that I knew of, but he screamed some things in his big, booming baritone that probably hurt worse and left deeper scars.

"I don't know what you're talking about."

He didn't shout. The opposite, actually—his voice was small, in a way I had never heard him sound. From the way Ruth flinched back and deflated, neither had she.

"I—" She faltered. "Chuck, so help me God, if you're lying to me..."

He wasn't. My father sweats when he lies, across his forehead and down the bridge of his nose. Watching him was how I learned to read signals so well.

His face was dry. And way too pale.

"If you're talking about the file concerning the shipments to Iran, I have it," I said, directing the words to my mother.

"How the hell did that happen?" Now he was yelling.

"I took them from your file cabinet while you two were gone last night," I said. "I had a feeling you knew something about the fire that killed Avesta, and I needed to know what. You weren't interested in talking. Now two more people are dead, both members of your cabinet, I know your dirty little secret, Azari Avesta will be here in about seven hours, and it's past time for you to talk."

The Governor drew himself up to his full six-five, looking down at me, the jaw clenching again.

"My own daughter walks into my house and tells me she's stolen from me, but I'm the asshole?"

"People. Are. Dying." I rocked up onto my tiptoes, tipping my chin up and moving closer to his face. "I am not afraid of you. I am afraid of losing another life because you're too stubborn to admit you did something wrong. I know what you did, but aside from the people at the dinner party, I have no idea who was involved. Did you screw someone over? Did someone die because of you?"

It was almost a rhetorical question, given the audience.

"Get the hell out of my house." His face was red, spit flinging from his lips and landing on his charcoal double-breasted lapel.

"Tell me what I need to know."

"You broke in here and stole private property, you figure it the fuck out on your own." He shook his head and finished his scotch. "I always knew those bastards who killed Charity took the wrong girl."

Ruth gasped so loud she probably scared the hell out of the neighbors, and the nearest ones were three quarters of a mile away.

I stood my ground, my face frozen in a blank mask I owed to hundreds of hours of practice, one that took over on autopilot when a suspect hurled some form of disgusting insult.

I held Chuck's gaze until he blinked, then took a small step back. "Tell your security detail you've put everyone in this house in danger." My eyes flicked to the whiskey decanter. "You're going to need more scotch."

I spun and walked in measured steps to the door. Damned if he was going to see me run. And tears were out of the question.

I was almost to my truck, my heart pounding twice as fast as I was walking, when Ruth grabbed my arm.

"I'm so sorry," she said. Damn, this was just a day of firsts all around for the McClellan family.

"You should go somewhere. Mexico, Jamaica, Paris. Get as far as you can away from him." And stay there. But I didn't add the last part. She wouldn't do it.

"You asked if they screwed anyone over," she said. "They did. I remember him talking about it. I don't know a name, but it was something to do with a land dispute and an armory. It was the biggest one, that would have the most inventory. The owner put up a fight and Chuck stepped in himself to take the land so he could get his guns."

There wasn't much more sacred to a lot of folks around here than land. But the people who lost theirs wouldn't have had any idea why Chuck really wanted their property, so that didn't fit.

"Thank you." I slid my arm from her grasp.

"Faith. He didn't mean that. He's scared."

I just shook my head. I had more urgent things to worry about.

My phone started ringing. I held it up and opened the truck door. "Call me if you think of anything. From somewhere that's not here."

She didn't answer.

"I'm serious."

She pointed to my screen. "Give Lieutenant Baxter my regards."

"Archie would tell you the same thing, Mother. Go."

"I know he would." She flashed a sad half smile. "Go do what you do."

I answered the call, looking at her reflection in the rearview from the end of the driveway. "I'm not sure this trip was worth it, Arch," I said. "Tell me you got something."

"Our guy was hurt. Limping."

"Yeah. Right leg. I had that from the footprints." I turned out of the drive, hoping it was for the last time.

"Oh. Well then. He has dark hair and drives a black four-door sedan. So no, I didn't get much."

"Dammit." I refrained from throwing the phone. Barely.

"You okay?"

"The Governor is in rare form today."

"He's a rare form of asshat. Whatever he did, I can assure you he's wrong."

"Thanks. I'll call Graham. Let's hope he had better luck. I'm going to drop in on Jim on my way back to the office."

32

Jim's truck was the only vehicle in the lot at the ME's office. With his wife feeling better, he was back to his old habits, coming in early and leaving late if there was something interesting for him to study, and there was almost always something interesting for Jim to study.

I walked in to find him standing over Bethany Marcil, closing up an autopsy incision running from her throat to her pelvic bone.

"Morning." He didn't look up. "JP down in Goliad said you already knew about this. I wanted to have a look for myself, given recent events around here."

"I'm interested to hear your thoughts. I tracked down some of the flowers Whitehead found on the remains. I might even have a suspect—I'd probably be surer about that if someone wasn't trying to kill my father."

He pulled the suture through the skin of her chest and up, keeping his eyes on his work. "You think he deserves saving?"

Leave it to Jim to cut straight to the heart of the matter.

"Doesn't matter what I think."

Jim grunted. "Complicated thing, families."

"Is this one related to the others?" I asked.

"It's the same accelerant," he said, pointing to a blue folder from the crime lab. "But the MO definitely isn't the same. Fuel is a mixture of kerosene and other fuels and additives widely known as aviation fuel. The few small chemical differences between this one and the one on the other victims weren't significant."

"Differences?"

"Chemical additives. Styrofoam components and alkali."

I knew those two from my Googling of napalm. "So she just got regular jet fuel, not the napalm kind."

"It seems so, yes. Do you know much about her?"

"She was the president of a fancy garden club down south of here in McMansionville. Had some enemies in the group," I said. "Including, because the six degrees of Kevin Bacon isn't weird enough with this case, my sister's best friend."

Jim looked up, studying me over the silver frames of his bifocals. "Damn."

"Yeah."

"But where did a rich ladies' garden club get jet fuel?"

I shrugged. "Not something they carry at Nordst—"

Oh, shit.

Jim watched my face for a few beats before he tipped his head to one side.

"You know something you didn't know you knew."

"You're good at seeing through bullshit," I said. "I had already figured we were dealing with jet fuel, because Agent Jenkins ended up here tracking a stolen fuel truck from DFW. But Caitlyn said something about using stuff they have on hand to improvise in the gardens when we were looking at hers. So I'm wondering: what if this was an accident?"

"You think someone accidentally strangled this woman and burned her remains? Do you need a vacation, McClellan?"

"Strangled? I thought her neck was broken?"

"Badly bruised, but after she fell because she was strangled. Hyoid is in three pieces. It was violent."

"So someone was pissed at her." I pivoted when I reached the doors, walking back slowly. "I'm not saying 'accident' like, they didn't mean to kill her, at least not in the moment. I'm saying, what if it was *all about* being in the moment, and then the killer panicked and tried to get rid of the body by burning it? Like, with whatever kind of accelerant happened to be handy?"

"So you think someone killed her"—he pointed at the table—"who knew the person who killed them." He waved a hand at the storage lockers.

"Given that there's a decent possibility that our knee implant came from someone this woman might have known? I do."

"No shit? I mean, I guess it wouldn't be the weirdest thing we've ever seen."

Dan Fortwright was in bed asleep at four twenty that morning.

At least, he had a woman at his house who swore to Graham he was.

"He says he has no idea how the truck got there or why the person in it would've driven off when I walked up," Graham said.

"Was the truck stolen?" Archie asked.

"It was in the drive when I got there, so if it was, whoever took it brought it back." Graham sighed. "The thing is, I didn't get the plate outside Collins's house, I was coming at it from the side. So all I can say is that a truck matching the description of his was there. I can't say it's the same vehicle."

"But there were no black sedans on his property?" I asked.

"Not that I saw."

I sipped my third coffee of the day and wiggled a black Expo marker between the fingers of my other hand.

"Lots of promising questions here this morning," Archie said.

I put the cup down and walked across the conference room to the white board.

- Known contacts of garden club members and their spouses
  - Black sedan
  - Limping suspect
  - Dinner guest list
  - Armory locations

. . .

"Your mother is leaving the ranch?" Archie asked when I turned back.

"I told her to. She'd be stupid to stay at this point, and she is many things, but stupid isn't one of them."

"I can't believe he wouldn't talk to you," Archie said. "He's going to get himself killed being stubborn."

"Wouldn't tell me what I wanted to know anyway."

"Shep Stevenson has been moved to an undisclosed location with four state troopers who have instructions to not so much as let him piss alone," Archie informed us.

I circled Stevenson in the photo and put a star over his face. He was covered.

The Governor was the only one left.

"Stevenson say anything?"

"Eh. For a lawyer, he didn't seem to know he couldn't plead the fifth with law enforcement." Archie shrugged. "As a cop, I know he's not going to say shit no matter what I do, so I chose to use my energy more productively."

"Graham, was Fortwright limping this morning?" I asked.

"Nope. I watched close enough to get some funny looks from him and his lady friend. But it's been more than 24 hours since Haynesworth's boat blew up, too. If you were hurt and trying to hide it from a cop, I bet you could fake it for as long as I could ask questions and make excuses to be there without a warrant."

True. I turned back and put his name on the board.

"Open your computer and find out where there were armories constructed in the state when my father was in office, would you?"

"Why?" Graham asked.

"My mother said something about a land dispute this morning. Fortwright said something..." I closed my eyes and let the words trail. It was tickling the back of my brain, but I couldn't bring it to the front. Too much caffeine, too much stress, and too little sleep. I opened my eyes. "Apparently even my memory has a breaking point. But I know he said something the first time we met him about that land being in his family for a long time."

"Yeah, he moved home to keep it, or something." Graham typed faster.

I snapped my fingers. "*So the state wouldn't take the whole thing.* That's what he said."

"How does that fit with the weapons trade angle?" Archie asked.

"I've been thinking about that, and I don't know that it does," I said. "Except, what if we found out about the weapons thing by accident? What if I was wrong and that's not the motive, it's just plain old-fashioned revenge, and the same people were involved because most of those guys have been up to their asses in every shady bullshit scheme the Governor has hatched since he was a state representative?"

"Huh. Normally I'd say lightning doesn't strike the same place twice. But this is Chuck McClellan we're talking about."

"He makes his own lightning," I said.

Graham scrolled down his screen. "Holy shit, Faith."

I crossed the room and leaned over his shoulder, already pretty sure what I was going to see.

"There's a National Guard armory just the other side of Fortwright's back forty."

"I'd bet my house the family didn't sell them that land."

Graham clicked a few more keys and hit search again.

"Nope. It was eminent domain."

"You said there was a woman there with this guy this morning," Archie said. "Did you get a name?"

"Candace," Graham said. "She insisted Fortwright was there all night. She still had a skimpy robe on. Sounded like Janis Joplin."

The overflowing ashtrays. "She lives there," I said. "Graham, can you—"

"On it." He typed.

I paced.

"She's his ex-wife. But her current address shows as his house."

"They split up and got back together," I said.

"But we still have no bead on whether she'd lie for him," Archie said.

"I mean, his truck was stolen, taken to a suicide scene, and then returned?" I asked. "We don't buy this. It's more logical that Collins saw him coming."

"It won't get us a warrant to bring Fortwright in," Archie said.

"And he isn't talking without a lawyer," Graham said. "He was polite this morning, but all he said was he was home all night."

"And she said she was, too?"

Graham started to nod. Stopped.

"No. She said he was there." He pulled out his notes. "Damn. Yeah. He was there. Not he was there with her. I was focused on him."

"So let's walk backward and see if we can put either of them at any of the other scenes," I said. "Graham, pull records for every vehicle registered to either of them or the business. Employees, too."

33

Two hours and two more coffees later, I had nothing that put either Fortwright at any of our earlier scenes, and we'd run out of places to look.

I thumped a fist on the table and closed my laptop. "We're missing something."

"Me, I assume?" I looked up when the door opened, Agent Jenkins pocketing his sunglasses as he shut it behind him, ignoring Graham's glare. "Apologies for my absence yesterday, there was an explosion nearby and I happened to be in the area. You all are up and at it early today."

"It's nine-thirty," Graham grumbled under his breath. "And we know there was an explosion."

"Just trying to beat the clock," I said, stepping closer to the board. "Any luck yet with the fuel truck?"

"My guess is someone has hidden it and is using it to carry out these crimes against your father's former cabinet." Jenkins kept his eyes carefully trained on my face. "You're sure you haven't thought of a reason why they might be targeted?"

I held his gaze, pinched my lips into a thin line, and shook my head.

"Faith was a child when her father was the governor." Archie layered a warning note into his voice.

"I'm aware. But I'm guessing she was always precocious."

As an ATF agent, the illegal transfer of firearms to a foreign government would definitely fall under Jenkins's purview. But Archie didn't want to talk to him about it, either. I knew better than to think it was that Archie wanted the collar for the Rangers; he had stopped giving a shit about things like that years ago.

He didn't trust this guy. Graham didn't trust this guy. And for a reason I hadn't been able to put my finger on, neither did I.

"Catch me up on what I missed?" Jenkins asked. "The one thing I hate about working for the federal government is all the fingers in the pot of every investigation. One crime scene followed by three meetings that could have been one email, and I've lost a day in an important case."

"We held the fort down while you were gone." I touched the tip of the marker to the bullet point next to the garden club. "Speaking of that fuel truck, I think we need to revisit this with different eyes—Bethany Marcil's remains made it onto Jim's table today, and her hyoid was busted all to hell."

"Someone was pissed at her, too," Archie said.

"Caitlyn Wexley is strong. She was a national champion on the bars," I said. "Were you able to confirm her alibi?"

"The restaurant she was at doesn't open until 11, so I don't have video," Archie said. "But there's a charge there Thursday night to her Amex card. I checked it myself with the credit card company this morning."

Shit.

"Okay." I wiggled the marker, thinking. "But the lab says the accelerant matched the bodies from the Clay Street house. Where I'm pretty damned sure Caitlyn's husband died. The M.O. was very different, all the other victims were men, and Bethany was dumped in a field...so Jim and I were thinking, why her? And we had an idea." I walked back to the table and picked up the case file on Haynesworth. "What if we were right and Bethany wasn't part of this case, but sort of accidentally adjacent to it? If someone got pissed at her and murdered her, but not the same person who's murdering my father's cabinet. Just someone they're close to— someone who would've found a stockpile of jet fuel in a panic with a dead socialite on their hands and used it to try to destroy the evidence?" I turned to Graham. "We assumed they put the body near that trailer park because they wanted someone to find it, but what if they didn't? What if they didn't even know the trailer park was there? It's pitch dark out there in the middle of the night. I mean, if you learn criminology from TV shows, a body cremates in a few minutes, not a few hours. So dumping Bethany and dousing her with the fuel before they dropped a match and hauled ass should've kept anyone from knowing she'd been murdered. Right?"

Graham laughed. So did Archie. Jenkins was still.

"You have a theory, Agent?" I asked.

"Where would this other victim have come into contact with whoever has the truck?"

"I don't have anything that will get us a warrant at the moment, but I do have a hunch. There's a garden club in her neighborhood that runs some pretty seriously competitive landscaping wars. The guy who runs the nearest exotic nursery said they get pretty intense. So I think that's a place to start looking."

"I'm looking for a fuel tanker that refills commercial aircraft," Jenkins said. "It would stick out in the suburbs."

"But if Caitlyn was in Houston, what if Bethany was in her garden?" I paused. The giant, prize pinky purple flower that had been cut. "What if she got caught, and there was a struggle? Given the accelerant match, it's worth it to look into the neighbors. Caitlyn's address was on the invoice for the one weird plant they found on Bethany, but I didn't see the other one."

Archie's phone rang—the one on his desk outside. He excused himself, closing the door.

"You're too fixated on this garden club nonsense," Jenkins said.

"I would agree if it weren't for the accelerant match," I pointed out.

Archie appeared in the doorway.

"I think maybe we let Charity's friend go home too soon," he said. "Her husband's secretary was on the phone—he did borrow that BMW last Monday, for a potential client, but it was a client he didn't want anyone to know he was courting until he had him signed, so it wasn't in the logbook."

"Avesta," Graham and I said.

"Who?" Jenkins looked between us.

"Never mind," I said. Oops.

"The APD forensic team tells me Avesta's fingerprints were on the steering wheel of that BMW, so yes, I think you're right," Archie said.

I held up one finger, turning back to the board. "So Wexley arrived in the hired car I saw on the restaurant's security feed, not Avesta?"

"It seems so."

That meant Avesta had the photo of my father and his cabinet.

"Could Wexley have been arranging a meeting for Avesta?" I asked, a little dizzy as the whole case flipped on its head for about the twelfth time.

"What if Caitlyn or Caitlyn's neighbors knew the killer because Jeremiah knew the killer?" I turned to Graham. "You started off saying 'professional hit.' What if Avesta was looking for a hired gun to take out the Governor and his colleagues, and things went sideways? They got double-crossed? Something?"

"So I'm still hearing that you think my truck is in the suburbs," Jenkins said.

"It's possible, Faith." Archie ignored him. "But so are ten other things we've said in the past couple of days. None of which we know with enough certainty to get a warrant."

Just the next thing.

"Is she under guard at home?" I asked.

"I put the troopers who were at Collins's house on her place," Archie said. "It's been quiet there all morning."

"Good. Now let's see what we can find out about Caitlyn and Jeremiah Wexley."

34

Caitlyn and Jeremiah counted some of Texas's most influential power players among their neighbors.

"Damn, no wonder these people are killing each other over landscaping." Archie scrolled down his computer screen. "The neighborhood tax records read like a who's who of cutthroat lawyers and businessmen."

"But isn't the garden club the wives?" Jenkins asked. "I agree that the accelerant match is odd, but I'm afraid we are chasing wild geese here, and there are still lives in danger."

"Men like that marry women who like to win," I said. "And about half of murder cases that end with an arrest come down to a lucky break. I think this might be ours on this one. But you're free to go look into whatever you please."

I scribbled down the names Archie called out, opening the *Statesman*'s website to the society page.

Graham strolled back in from the break room and put a cold Dr Pepper on the table in front of me, leaning over the back of my chair. "Uh. What'cha doing?"

"Finding out who Caitlyn's neighbors like having their pictures taken with," I said.

"Looking for a link, she means." Archie smiled. "That's my girl."

"I don't follow." Jenkins walked up behind Graham. "Is that the society page? Jesus, who still prints one of those?"

"It's an old truth in Texas power circles that nothing counts if you don't see it in these photo collages. Sort of the great-grandfather of 'pics or it didn't happen,' Agent. So if there was someone important these kind of folks wanted to be seen with, we will find it here."

I typed the first name on my list into the bar at the top of the screen. "Caitlyn said her husband is a lawyer. Lawyers often turn into politicians. So let's start with who Jeremiah wanted his picture taken with lately."

Thirty-nine hits in six months. Damn, did they do anything but attend galas and charity events?

I clicked the images link.

From the headshot on the law firm's site, I knew Jeremiah was good-looking. But in a tux, rubbing elbows with power players and celebrities, he looked every inch the superstar in his own right. Chestnut hair, straight, slim nose, dark eyes, almost too-symmetrical face. His wide smile showed a bright set of bonded white teeth.

I zoomed out of the first photo, looking from Jeremiah to the people around him. They were at the museum, tall marble pillars and walls of priceless art rising high around them. I saw two talented prosecutors I knew had political aspirations, a judge, and the Travis County Sheriff. "If this guy wasn't planning a run for office, I've never met a politician."

I clicked through photos. He'd win, too—great smile, good resume, excellent networking skills. I saw Caitlyn, in a crystal-encrusted blue gown that hugged her figure, one hand on her hip, bright smile directed just artfully enough away from the camera to make it look like she didn't know it was there. She had paid good attention to my mother growing up.

"That would explain him wanting to get in Avesta's good graces," Graham said. "I'm sure a guy like that could help win an election."

"Or rig one," I said.

A dozen more images flashed by before one stopped me.

That was Caitlyn and Jeremiah with my parents. Different dress, different suit—this was a garden gala in late July. But she told me she hadn't seen my mother in years.

I saved that photo and kept going.

Three weeks later, at a gallery opening, a shot of Jeremiah with Haynesworth.

Two pictures behind that, looking at one from the same event, I inhaled a mouthful of Dr Pepper.

I grabbed Graham's wrist and pointed to the screen. "Is that who I think it is?"

He leaned over my shoulder.

Scrawny. Sunglasses inside. And I was pretty sure I'd seen those particular gold Gucci sneakers in person.

"Jimmy Sewell. Holy shit." Graham leaned one hand on my shoulder. "What the hell is happening here?"

"Jeremiah Wexley was a private practice securities and tax attorney at one of the wealthiest firms in the state," I said.

"Jimmy Sewell has a lot of money," Graham offered.

"Certainly wouldn't be the first time a lawyer got in bed with someone into some shady shit in the name of money," Archie added.

Jenkins stood and crossed to the head of the table. "Now we've moved from a dead socialite that's a local police matter to a con man," he said. "Not to bring the party down here, but there's still a couple of victims left alive on your list, and I still have a truck to find. We're changing focus to the wrong thing."

I stood, leaning on the table. "You invited yourself into our case, Agent Jenkins. And I disagree with your assessment. It's possible we're finally looking in the right place, and I'd like to see where this path takes us. We've done this a time or two. We'll find your missing truck. And I have no intention of letting anyone else die."

"I hear that Shep Stevenson has gone into hiding. Did you have something to do with that?"

"We did," Archie said.

"Where'd you stash him?"

Archie's eyebrows went up. "I'm sure you understand that the fewer people who are privy to that information, the safer Mr. Stevenson will be for now."

Jenkins whirled for the door. "You people are going to let someone else die because you're stubborn, and I'm not going to sit here and watch. So much for the legendary investigative prowess of the Texas Rangers. I'll figure it out myself, but I can't sit through any more distraction here."

He slammed the door on his way out.

"I hope it hit him in the ass," Graham said.

I stood and started pacing again. "Arch. Something's off there."

Archie pursed his lips. "I wish I had a finger on what, exactly, but I don't like him."

"He's a control freak," Graham said. "He's wanted to run the show since the first time I met him."

"The first time we met him." I drummed a pen on the edge of the table. "He showed up the day after the Clay Street fire uninvited, and introduced himself to us. He was interested in what the fire captain had been able to figure out, and he said he wanted to work with us."

"With you," Graham corrected. "He barely looked at me, but he walked up to you and called you by name, remember?"

"That's right, he did, didn't he?"

"He knew who you were?" Archie asked.

"I didn't think anything of it; people do that sometimes," I said. "But stacked in with the way he's been so weird, it's...disconcerting. Like he came there that day to talk to me. But why would he do that?"

"Maybe the fuel truck isn't all he's looking for?" Graham asked. "Friday evening when you were inside the building, he was asking me a lot of questions. I just thought he was interested in the history of the Rangers, you know, because a lot of cops are. But...now I'm wondering. He wanted to know what Faith had worked on lately, if the rumors about her perfect homicide record were true...and he had a lot of questions about you, Archie, and your days in the governor's detail."

Archie stood. Started for the door. Paused.

"I'm not sure what I make of that."

I wasn't either, but I was sure every hair on my arms was standing at attention. So whatever it was, it wasn't good.

"I don't suppose your network of old buddies extends to the Dallas ATF office?"

Archie shook his head. "Not anymore. There was a kid I worked one case with up there a few years back, but he was transferred somewhere back east. Miller was his name. Smart kid. But this guy might not have been here long enough for them to have crossed paths."

"Can't hurt to call him and ask, right?" The words left my lips as my phone started buzzing.

Erma.

Please God, good news. I slid the bar to answer the call.

"It's Jaime." His voice was too high. Tight. A boulder settled between my throat and my chest. "She's awake."

"That's wonderful!" I sputtered. "Please give her my love and keep me posted."

"She begged me not to call you," he said. "She said talk to the local police. But the doctor was right about her shoulder—a car followed her and ran her off the road when she got away from the freeway, chased her until she was going way too fast, and then clipped her back bumper and sent her off the road."

I gripped the back of the chair. I fucking hate being right sometimes. But I didn't have time to focus on that right now. The next thing now. Guilt later.

"What does she remember about the car?"

"It was a black sedan. Nothing special. The driver had a hat and big, dark sunglasses. She saw them in the rearview."

"Them, like two people?" I asked.

"No, like she says she can't swear if it was a man or a woman. She couldn't see clearly enough with the hat and glasses and trying to watch the road."

"But they were white?"

"*Si.* Do you know who did this?" The words were coated in anger so thick they landed like rocks.

"I'm getting closer, Jaime. I will, I promise. You take care of her." I paused. "And please tell her I'm sorry. I would've never put her in danger intentionally."

"She knows. She says tell you go do your job."

"On it. Y'all call me if you need me."

I ended the call and looked at Archie. "See if you can find your guy at the ATF. A black sedan was spotted near Haynesworth's boat at the lake. A black sedan ran Erma off the road and almost killed her. And what do government agents usually drive?"

"Black sedans." Graham answered the rhetorical question. "Surely this asshole isn't using his government issued vehicle to run around murdering people?"

"Not taking anything here for granted at this point. Just because we wouldn't be dumb enough to do that doesn't mean he's not." I reached for my computer. "It's time to see what the internet can tell us about Agent Jenkins."

35

Jenkins made his way to the ATF via the El Paso PD with a short stint in Dallas before he jumped to Federal training. Dual degrees in computer forensics and criminal psychology from UT, three commendations, two of them for valor under fire.

"His record is unblemished," I said. "So either we're on the wrong track, or he's both good at hiding things and motivated by something massively personal here."

Graham put his phone on the table and stood. "I have to run to my office," he said. "I shouldn't be long."

"Now?"

"It's the Haynesworth thing." He waved a hand. "Forensics has a preliminary report ready. I'm just going to grab it and listen to their spiel. See if they found anything that might help us narrow this down."

"Drive safely. Hey—there are five bags with soil samples in my truck. Could you grab them and drop them at the lab for me? Maybe with a charming smile and a plea for a rush?"

He stopped on his way out of the room to drop a kiss on top of my head. "Of course. We will get this guy. Even if it turns out it's one of our own."

"Just the next thing," I said. "One of them has to be Archie's magic rock, right?"

"Always is. I'll be right back."

"I'll keep digging here."

I turned to the photo on the board, the Governor's less-lined face smiling from under a shock of darker hair.

"He's a narcissistic, difficult, stubborn bastard," I said.

"But he's your father." Graham squeezed my hand. "We're not going to let him get hurt."

He was such a good man. The kind of man people like my father hated because that sort of intrinsic goodness forces them to face their own short-comings.

"I love you." It was out of my mouth before I realized it.

His face flickered with a smile, a deep breath lifting his shoulders as he leaned down for a much more serious sort of kiss.

Archie cleared his throat from the doorway before we came up for air.

"I love you," Graham whispered as he pulled away. "We've got this."

He brushed past Archie in a rush out the door.

"TCSO has a prelim on the explosion that killed Haynesworth," I told Archie.

"I left Kyle Miller a voicemail," Archie replied. "He's their CO up in Richmond these days, so hopefully if he doesn't know our guy, he'll be able to find someone who does."

I tapped a pen on the table, getting up to cross to my board.

"The fuel truck," I said.

"What about it?"

"It's been the centerpiece of his case the whole time he's been here. At least, according to him."

"Sure. That's their wheelhouse."

"But why haven't we heard anything about it from anyone else?" I asked.

Archie shrugged. "I don't follow."

"He's the only person who's mentioned it. At all. No news reports, no Skye Morrow asking about it in relation to all these fires. Anyone at the scene Thursday could see the AFD had to use foam they requested from the airport to put out that fire. So if a whole tanker truck of jet fuel went missing two days before the fire, why isn't anyone else talking about it? Wouldn't the airport police have some jurisdiction there?"

"Not if the feds took over the case."

I pulled my phone from my pocket. "I talked to the chief there last summer when I was looking for Lindsey Decker."

Archie backed out of the room. "*I'll be at my desk,*" he mouthed.

"Chief Greene, Faith McClellan, Texas Rangers," I said when he picked up. "I have a quick question about a stolen truck if you have just a moment this morning."

"Ranger McClellan," his voice boomed. "Anything I can do for you, ma'am."

"I appreciate that. Y'all had a fuel truck go missing there last week?"

"Damndest thing I've ever seen; we still haven't figured out how this asshole circumvented our security cameras," he said. "That system was just installed nine months ago and it cost half a million dollars, supposed to be hacker proof. I told the board they need to get their money back."

"Whoever took the truck disabled the cameras?" I grabbed a pen and pad from the credenza in the corner of the room and jotted that down.

"Between me and you? I can't have this getting into the press until we get the damned thing back. Or ever, if I can help it."

"Of course," I said. "I am the last person you generally have to worry about blabbing to reporters."

"The feed that should've been the overnight hours Tuesday was replaced with film of terror attacks. From 9-11 to soldiers being blown up in jeeps. Nasty, graphic stuff, running on a loop."

I scribbled so fast my fingers cramped.

"How many hours?" I asked.

"Six. From when the last flights were clear to the maintenance crews arriving Wednesday morning."

"So you don't know what time the truck was taken?"

"Right. And there are more than 100 traffic cams around this airport. We're working our way through the footage, but my staff isn't large and we still have an airport to secure. We'll figure it out, but I'm worried about where that fuel is going in the meantime." He paused. "You find some of it?"

"Yes, sir. And I may have an idea about who took it."

Someone who would know how every safeguard worked. Who could sabotage the camera feeds and cover his tracks. Who had been trained in the use of explosives and accelerants. Dammit, had he been walking slowly this morning? I couldn't say for sure. And we'd let him walk right out the fucking door. "What are the security protocols for the area of the airport where those trucks are stored? Do people have to sign in somehow?"

"Anyone who has reason to be on the tarmac could get to those garages, in theory. But any non-employee would have to present ID and a valid reason for being there, and employees clock in and out."

"Signs of forced entry?"

"Two gates, one at the north end of the property and one at the south end, were forced, but they were forced out, not in."

So nobody would know which cameras to check for the truck. Smart.

"Can you check the logbook of non-employees for that afternoon and let me know what you find?"

"Don't have to check. Two people checked in that afternoon. ATF agent by the name of Jenkins, inspecting cargo holds, and a DOT beancounter named Mark Calendula."

"Son of a bitch," I muttered.

"Pardon?"

"Thank you for your help, sir," I said. "I'm going to go find your truck."

"Much obliged, ma'am."

I clicked off the call and whirled for the door, sprinting to Archie's desk. He was on the phone.

"Uh huh. I see." Archie jotted something down. "Anything else recent?"

More scribbling. I rocked up on the balls of my feet, swiping a mint from his candy dish and trying to pick one of the thousand theories flooding my brain to follow.

Jenkins was damned smart. Looking back over the past three days through a lens of suspicion, everything he'd done made perfect sense—for an entirely different reason than he'd like us to believe.

But jumping to conclusions rarely gets a cop anywhere good. So while Archie listened and grunted one-word observations into his phone, I picked apart my theory in my head.

To be behind something like this, Jenkins would have to be both a sociopath and a man with a personal mission. Getting caught would surely end his career, and field agent positions in federal law enforcement aren't easy to come by—they take hard work, dedication, and sacrifice. They also necessitate hours of psych evaluations that don't stop the day they hand you a badge.

Could the ATF have a psychologist on staff who couldn't spot a murderer sitting three feet from them?

I couldn't believe it of them any more than I wanted to believe it of myself. Had I sat with this guy several times the past few days, sharing details of our investigation with him, and not realized he was playing us all? Had Archie? Had Graham?

And what did he have against Chuck?

"Appreciate your help here, Miller. Congratulations on the promotion. You take care now." Archie put the phone down and looked up at me. "Agent Jenkins is on a leave of absence. Prior to being placed there, he was working an investigation of a weapons distribution ring that stretches across nine states. And probably overseas. Miller says his agent on that case suspects inside involvement. I think we have enough to proceed with caution."

"He signed in to the tarmac at DFW the day that truck went missing. And their camera feed was hacked. Guess who has a forensic computing degree from UT?"

Archie stood. "You know where he's staying?"

I pulled my keys from my pocket. "Courtyard off Main."

He pulled out his cell. "I'm calling Hardin. We might need backup."

36

"How much longer?" My voice sounded tight even to me, my breath going in on a sharp *whoosh* as Connally's cold fingers brushed my rib cage.

"Four minutes, and we'll have officers in a full perimeter," Graham said from the central chair in the TCSO mobile command trailer, touching keys on a panel and calling up body cam videos from the armed special teams deputies making their way into strategic positions around Jenkins's hotel, hopefully without being noticed–always more of a challenge when the suspect is law enforcement.

Connally finished affixing a wire to my rib cage and I pulled my shirt back into place. We didn't have the evidence—or time—for a warrant against a federal officer. They were ten times as hard to get a judge to approve. So plan B was to send me in to try to get him talking. He liked talking to me, but someone who'd been as smart as he'd been all this time probably wasn't going to blurt out a confession.

The trick was to lead him into a lie he didn't know I had the information to contradict. Get him on tape, then confront him and try to catch him off guard. If I could knock a hole in his careful wall of lies, he might bring the whole thing down around himself.

A girl could hope, at least.

Graham had officers sliding into position on rooftops and street corners for a two-block radius around the hotel. I checked my mic.

My phone buzzed.

Manny Gonzalez.

Huh. I clicked the green circle. "McClellan."

"I can't find anything in your files on Sewell about his connections in Iran," he said by way of hello. "Checking to see if I'm missing a file, or if you might know something you didn't put in a report."

"Kind of busy right now, Gonzalez," I said, half listening, my eyes on Graham's monitors.

Wait.

"Did you say Iran?"

Graham and Archie both turned to me.

"Yeah. So far there's been a shit ton of activity on about 200 of these cards, all of it crossing between the US and Iran. Some for small orders of things that aren't embargoed, but make no sense for someone to order from us, and some for tens of thousands of dollars in merchandise or materials."

I froze, closing my eyes and trying to tune out not only everything around me, but all the noise leaking in from every corner of my brain.

Coming up on a hundred and thirty murder collars, my perfect record had taught me to never ignore a coincidence. Sometimes they're just that— but more often, they're clues masquerading in something that shouldn't fit if you look beyond the surface.

My father's trade way back in the day involved Iran. I had a dead Iranian diplomat in Jim's morgue. A dead diplomat whose powerful uncle was due in town in less than four hours. Who was likely blackmailing my father and his cabinet.

And now Jimmy Sewell's cards were buying and selling between the US and Iran.

"Online transactions?" I asked.

"Every single one."

"Did you check the sites they're using for merchant certificates?"

"The American ones have them. We're working on the Iranian ones."

I tapped a finger on the side of my thigh. "The certificates don't mean it's not a shell company," I said. "It's a small back stop, but they're not hard to get if you know how to fake paperwork."

"Right, and we know Sewell excels at that."

I snapped my fingers. "You said tens of thousands. The limits on those cards were fifty each," I said. "Check with the bank and find out if they're paying them."

"On it," he said. "Stand by."

"Find out and call me back in half an hour," I said. "Or call Baxter."

"Whatever you're into, watch your back, McClellan."

"Always. And Gonzalez? Get this weaselly little son of a bitch. Whatever he's up to, I'm beginning to think it's bigger than I thought he was capable of."

I clicked off the call just as the last SWAT officer gave Graham a high sign through the camera.

"Why would Sewell fake a card and then pay it?" Graham asked.

"Money laundering," I said. "They call it transaction laundering when it happens online, and it's the single most untraceable area of bank fraud. We do such a shit job of controlling it from a law enforcement perspective that there are private data companies who sell banks a service to try to catch it, but it's hard when someone is good at it."

"You worked in fraud for like a month and a half. How do you know that?"

"I read seven books and about seven thousand journal articles. These guys will buy something small with a card and then send a massive over-payment to the bank, which gets them a refund check they then cash..."

"And the money is clean without them losing a dime of it." Graham let out a low whistle.

"Yep."

"And this is your guy Sewell?" Archie asked.

"Yeah. Two hundred cards in use so far, every transaction crossing between the US and Iran."

"That's...uh. That's interesting."

"Gonzalez is checking on the payments. If he calls you, pick up. Sewell was in that photo with Caitlyn's husband. If they've been washing money, I want to know where it's coming in dirty from. And what it has to do with Iran."

"This just keeps getting more incestuous the further we wade in," Archie said. "It's giving me a headache."

"Still looking for where Jenkins fits in with them." I checked my weapon and squared my shoulders.

Graham stood, putting his arms around my waist. "I know you want this guy, but do not go in there and underestimate him. I expect you to come out of there in one piece, and signal if you need help."

I leaned my forehead against his chest as the four other cops in the trailer turned away to give us some privacy.

"Yeah yeah. Blackbird. I know the safe word. Er..." My cheeks heated as everyone around me snickered.

"I could've happily lived all my days without hearing you say that." Archie's shoulders shook with laughter.

"You know what I meant," I snapped.

"I do. Doesn't mean that wasn't funny. You ready?"

"Let's go get him."

"I figured you'd be wasting your time on the society pages still." Jenkins smirked when he swung open the door of room 347 and stood aside. "Come to apologize?"

So much for small talk. We'd just get right after it, then.

"I had a talk with Chief Greene at the DFW PD, actually," I said. "I assume you know him well?" I perched on the arm of the chair in the corner, my feet still firmly on the floor, my posture relaxed—at least that's the way I wanted it to look to him.

"He's a good guy. Maybe in a little over his head with the amount of contraband that can move through his facility." He leaned against the wall opposite me, folding his arms across his chest.

"When was the last time you saw him?" I asked.

"If you're asking why I was on the tarmac the day the truck went missing, I'm sorry, but I cannot answer that."

I raised one eyebrow. "Not exactly the answer I expected. But I'm interested to see the video from the hangar."

"The video was dubbed out," he said. "Nice try, though."

I shifted on the arm of the chair. "I'm sorry?"

He shook his head. "This is the best you have? I must admit, I'm disappointed." He jerked his chin toward me. "Let's see the wire, then."

"I'm not sure what you're talking about." He was trying to call my bluff, but I wasn't giving in yet. "I came by to ask your opinion on my theory after I spoke with the chief."

"No, you called him to check up on me. And I'm sure you think you have this whole thing figured out."

"Not yet," I said. "But I'm getting closer. You know they had a separate video circuit in the cargo area they think might show which way the truck went and what time, right?" I tipped my head to one side. "They're sending it to our cyber guys for enhancement."

He didn't move. Not even to breathe.

"I just assumed you knew, but it doesn't sound like he'd told you that one was on the old system still," I said. "Maybe he just didn't know that before you left Dallas."

He studied my face, unblinking, for ten fast heartbeats. I kept it blank, my breathing even. This was it. I was all in on this bet.

I didn't dare so much as flicker an eyelid.

He had to fold first.

My father's life might depend on it.

Jenkins's nostrils flared, a fine sheen of sweat materializing on his stubbly upper lip.

I counted twelve more beats. My eyes felt like they were going to crack right open.

"Goddammit," he muttered, crossing the room and grabbing my arm, his free hand going for the buttons on my shirt.

37

In half a blink, I planted both feet at an angle as my right fist came up and straightened, connecting with his eye socket.

I honestly couldn't say if the crack I heard came from his face or my hand, but his grip loosened. I wrenched my arm away and backed up, trying to shuffle crab-style toward the door without getting too close to him.

"That's a wicked right hook you've got there." He raised both hands. "I'm not going to hurt you. I need the mic off. I see now that wasn't the best way to go about it."

I kept my fists up, moving slowly toward the door. "I have zero reasons to trust you." I spoke clearly so Graham would know I was okay. I didn't need the cavalry. I needed to figure out what the hell was going on here.

"Dammit, McClellan. I came looking for you on purpose. Your record speaks for itself, and I knew you wouldn't want to let your father die, whether you like him or not. Pull the fucking wire. I will tell you the whole story. As soon as I get some ice for my face." He pulled his gun from its holster and flipped it, offering me the butt end. "I'm not the bad guy here. But people are still in real danger, and I'm tired of this agency family feud bullshit. Let's talk. Cop to cop."

I didn't look away as I took the gun, keeping it in one hand.

I still didn't like him.

But his eyes weren't lying. Neither was his upper lip, which had stopped sweating.

I put the gun on the dresser. "I passed an ice machine in the hallway," I said.

"I'll be right back."

I lifted my shirt and pulled the wire off when the door closed. "I think there's something else entirely going on here, y'all," I whispered into the mic. "I'm fine. But if I'm not back in thirty minutes, send your team in, Graham."

I clicked it off and laid it next to Jenkins's gun, re-tucking my shirt as he walked back in with a plastic baggie of ice on his eye.

"I'd apologize, but you ought to know better," I said.

"Point taken." He gestured to the mic. "That's off?"

"Don't make me regret it."

He sighed, sitting heavily on the edge of the bed. "How much do you know about your father's illegal activities when he was in office, and where your family's money came from?"

"Less than I should," I said. "Enough to know he ought to be in prison. Which we are working on."

"Join the club. He's a slippery old bastard, I'll give him that."

"I know probably better than you do that just because he deserves to go to prison doesn't mean he will. Which is what I think our vigilante knows, too. I just can't pin down a motive. I didn't have one for you, either. That's why I came up here."

"You ever hear of a computer geek fraud ring run by a guy named Jimmy Sewell?" he asked.

"I'm familiar, yes."

"So. Sewell has much more big-time aspirations than anyone would ever give him credit for. With the new trade embargoes against Iran, he took up where your father left off. He's been playing modern day blockade runner, structuring a carefully concealed system for trading metals and supplies to them, selling to the highest bidder."

"How is he getting the stuff there?"

"The same way your father did. The oil tankers go back to the Middle East empty. Well. Not when he has anything to do with it. But they just offload the materials to mercenary pilots who drop them outside Tehran. The blueprint for it was all laid out for him by the Mexican drug cartels that gave him his start. Smart kid—he paid attention. But now he's moved on to the big time. Defrauding banks and creating fake accounts to move millions through for a cartel is no longer a challenge.

"Now, he's stealing guns that are being seized by our agents and selling them. To Iran. Has been for probably ten months, best I can tell. He's extremely thorough about covering his tracks."

"Why not just tell us this from day one?"

"The animosity between the Rangers and the ATF runs both ways," he explained. "I was put on leave to come here—that's how much some people in my office don't want to work with you all. I was supposed to get access to your information without sharing ours—my CO claimed you would compromise our case to protect your father. I thought that was bullshit a week ago, and I'm even more convinced now. I'm done with games. Let's get this fucker."

"I still don't understand how my father figures into what you were talking about with Sewell."

Jenkins put the ice down. "I'm not quite sure he does. I think there are players that cross between Sewell's operation today and your father's operation twenty-five years ago. And I think someone is set on punishing them all for your father's sins."

"But why? We haven't been able to find any possible motive that covers every victim." I watched him carefully. "Your lip sweats when you lie. What are you still not telling me? I thought we were done with the games."

He wiped at his upper lip and grimaced. "I'll try to work on that. And I'm not playing a game. I'm just not sure you want to know."

"I promise this would've all been much easier if you'd just walked up to me Friday and told me the truth."

"Right. If I'd walked up and told you I happened across information that said American soldiers died as a direct result of your father's actions, you would have been inclined to talk to me?"

I sucked in a sharp breath. "We didn't have soldiers in Iran during my father's term, nor were we at war with them. He is a bastard, I'm the first to admit that, but he wouldn't put American soldiers in danger, not for money or power. My grandfather was a veteran." I had to avert my eyes halfway through my words. I wished I felt as sure about that as I sounded. What kind of monster was Chuck McClellan?

"We didn't officially, no."

Oh. My God.

Jenkins was calm. Assured. "I'm sure you know not all American military operations are documented and publicized," he said. "And your father's illegal weapons trade involved a high-ranking general who was close with Avesta's uncle."

I sat back on the arm of the chair. Heavily. "I didn't know the general was connected to Avesta's family. So that's how he knew to blackmail my father and his co-conspirators?"

"Probably. Do you have leads on anyone else who could've possibly known what they did? I thought it was someone in his cabinet who'd finally had enough of the guilt eating at them for all these years, but since they're being picked off, probably not."

"Sewell? It seems he's in this up to his Ray-Bans. He's a hell of a computer hacker."

"I tracked Sewell and every henchman on his payroll for weeks before the first fire."

My eyebrows went up.

"Yes, even through your credit card meetup, Miss Richardson." Jenkins winked. "When Avesta was confirmed as a victim at the Clay Street house fire, I thought their deal had gone sour, but Sewell was nowhere near that building when the fire was set. And neither were any of his associates."

Their deal. Because this whole web of people we'd been dealing with had their fingers in this case.

Fucking hell. We got played, but not by Jenkins.

By Sewell.

38

He stayed low crossing the lawn, coming to the kitchen porch from the side, out of reach of the lights blazing from the front of the house. On tiptoe, he reached to the small shelf at the low edge of the boxed ceiling, just as the Ranger had done. Dust and grime slid softly under his fingertips until they found metal.

Plucking the key from the shelf, he opened the door silently and slipped inside. The large, inviting kitchen was dark and silent, the smell of bleach lingering in the air from an after-dinner cleaning.

He crept to the staircase at the opposite end. He could hear his target shouting from the upper reaches of the house.

He could favor speed over stealth—nobody would notice a creaky stair riser or two over that racket. On the landing, he peeked around the corner.

No one in sight, the hallways dark. The voice louder.

Up another flight. He followed the voice to a set of double doors in the middle of the long hallway. Sliding a hand into his pocket, he found the syringe.

"What do you mean, there are no first-class seats available?" Panic oozed from every syllable, permeating the thick oak doors, settling around him.

Just in time, it seemed.

He turned the knob, light spilling across his worn leather and mesh Army issue boots, the tan laces speckled with rust-colored stains.

The target stuffed expensive clothing into a large leather suitcase. "Fine, put me in coach. I don't care how much it costs. I'll be there within the hour."

He crossed the plush rug in five steps, sinking the hypodermic into the side of Ruth McClellan's neck just as she tossed her phone onto the bed.

His eyes skated the perimeter of the room, looking for something to go wrong.

All clear.

He didn't even get the plunger all the way down before her eyes rolled back and she collapsed into his arms.

She was tall and strong, not easy to lift, but he had practice, and his muscles had a long memory.

He tucked her phone into his pocket with one hand and balanced her against his torso with the other arm before he scooped her up, sweat beading on his forehead before he made it to the door.

Before he stepped back into the darkness, he looked down at her slack face. Her skin was pale, her cheeks flushed from stress, her skin as unlined and youthful as her daughter's.

The Ranger didn't seem to like her mother.

But that didn't mean she wouldn't come to save her.

39

I swung my arm, erasing the white board in the conference room at Rangers HQ before pulling the photo of my father and his cabinet off. Between Jenkins's hotel and our office, I had managed to do this exceedingly complicated math—and the answer wasn't at all what I'd thought. "Sewell's system was set up to work flawlessly, moving goods and laundering money—keeping plenty of it for himself, mind you.

"But Avesta got greedy. He didn't want just the cut he got for helping distribute the guns in Iran, he wanted more. And since his uncle's old friend the general told him how to set up the accounts and route the boats, he knew my father and his colleagues had been in the arms trade back in their day. So he set up the dinner party to blackmail them."

"Blackmail?" Jenkins asked.

I glanced at Graham. "That's what they were fighting about when Avesta stormed out. Two weeks later, he wound up burned alive at the Clay Street house with Jeremiah Wexley, who wanted to be Avesta's attorney."

Archie raised a pointer finger. "And who was also Sewell's attorney, by the way. I talked to a partner at his firm while you were in with Jenkins."

"So are we looking at this wrong? Was it...Collins? Is that why he shot himself?" Graham asked. "Nobody else has died today."

I shook my head. "No, Jenkins said he thought it was one of the cabinet members, too, but I don't think so. We just didn't have the whole equation until now. We've been looking for one killer and trying to make all the victims fit because it's all so close. But that's where we got tripped up." I held up my notes from my call with Chief Greene. "The other person who checked into the tarmac at DFW that day did it with DOT credentials."

"So?" Jenkins furrowed his brow.

"Before he crossed to the private sector, Jeremiah Wexley did legal work for the DOT," I explained. "Which is where Caitlyn comes in. I think she killed her neighbor over something to do with their garden club." I pointed to Graham. "The soil samples I sent to the lab with you this morning are from under the tarp in the back of her garden near the shed. I was looking for jet fuel residue, but I bet they're going to show that Bethany Marcil spent a few days there after Caitlyn strangled her—her hands are definitely strong enough to do the damage Jim saw to Bethany's hyoid. Charity wasn't even that good on the bars, and she could crush a soup can like it was a wad of paper.

"So once Caitlyn calmed down and got rid of the body, she had Sewell engineer a ping for her credit card in Houston, which he would do with no problem for his lawyer's wife, because it gave her an alibi for the night Bethany was found. But I bet Bethany was dead before that."

"Wait." Jenkins held up a hand. "Back up. Why would she leave a body in her backyard?"

"She never was terribly good with making decisions, if I recall correctly," Archie said.

"Right. So she didn't know what to do. She asks the husband, who does Sewell's taxes, did work for the DOT, and…" I pointed to Graham, following my last hunch. "See if he was the lawyer for the Fortwright family, as well."

Graham opened a laptop and typed, raising his head to smile and nod. "Taxes. And real estate."

"I thought you were the lynchpin here," I said to Jenkins. "Then I thought it might be Sewell. But it's Jeremiah. There are three different equations moving here, and he's the common variable that links them all together."

"But Jeremiah is dead, right? It was his knee implant you found? So who's the killer?" Jenkins leaned forward, finally enthralled by my story.

"Dan Fortwright. But he didn't take your fuel truck. Caitlyn did. And she lent him the firm's black Lincoln, too. There was a photo on the society page when I was 'wasting my time' earlier of them getting out of it at an event, and I remembered Archie saying the person he asked about the BMW at the Clay Street house told him they had a couple of Town Cars. Fortwright knew the vehicle couldn't be traced to him, and he had Caitlyn over a few barrels, which gave him the accomplice he needed to put his plan in motion." I looked at Graham. "Remember, he told us he learned about plants overseas? And he came home when his father died so they didn't lose the whole farm?"

"Yeah. So?"

"So, he wasn't off on a vacation. He was in the military." That was the key to the whole damned thing. "That whole story he told us, every generation of his family, they were all soldiers. So was he."

Graham shook his head. "I would've found records when I ran his background."

"Not if the government didn't want us to." I pointed to Jenkins. "This morning, he told me that my father's scheme might have hurt American soldiers—soldiers who might've been sent somewhere they weren't officially supposed to be. And that would mean the records were classified, and—"

"Classified military service files don't appear in background searches," Jenkins interrupted.

Archie and Graham stood. "Are you sure?" Archie asked.

"I am."

"Then tell me the rest of how you figured it out later," Archie said. "Let's go put a stop to this right now."

He strode from the room barking orders at other officers between us and the doors.

Graham pulled out his phone to call for TCSO backup.

I reached for mine because it was ringing.

Ruth McClellan. I ought to change that photo from Maleficent to... something not Maleficent.

Later.

"You left the ranch like I asked, didn't you?" I said by way of hello.

"Afternoon, Ranger McClellan. The first lady cannot come to the phone right now. But I'm willing to make a trade. To make sure your father and Mr. Stevenson get what's coming to them. You will come alone. And I'll know if you don't."

I stopped dead in the doorway.

Graham ran smack into me and I didn't even notice, staring at my phone after Fortwright hung up.

"What?" Graham asked.

"He has my mother. He must've figured we were onto him when you went over there this morning, but he's not ready to give up. Graham, I have to..."

I stopped talking.

Every drop of blood had drained from Archie's face.

"Oh, no," I whispered.

He leaned on the doorway, and I ran to him. "Are you okay?"

He nodded. "My heart might break, but it's still pumping." His voice was hoarse. "We'll find Chuck. You go on to your mother. Please."

Damn, humans are messy.

I whirled back to Graham.

"Do you love me?" I asked.

Jenkins blinked, confused eyes darting around the room.

"More than my life." Graham didn't skip a beat.

"Stay with him. I will get her back. But y'all can't go with me. Fortwright knows that land, and he's paranoid about finishing his mission."

"What are you going to do?" Jenkins asked.

"I'm going to bluff better than he can."

40

The light in the barn was on.

I put the truck in neutral and let it idle down the hill, my eyes sweeping the landscape as I descended. I didn't see anyone else, but I didn't want to become an extra piece of bait if I could help it, either.

After days of these people milling around my thoughts, the combination of the society page photos and Jenkins's revelations had put the variables in the right order, and it all made sense: Caitlyn had always loved dropping that she knew my family into any conversation. So she'd told Fortwright. Then Avesta came to Texas in the winter, and while he was at the ranch, he'd asked my mother about specialty plants. Avesta met with Jeremiah Wexley to discuss legal representation—at Jeremiah's home, to avoid questions about why Avesta needed an American finance attorney— and Caitlyn recommended Fortwright when Avesta asked about her gardens. And that was the last link. Somehow, Avesta must have let something slip about my father's scheme where Fortwright could hear. And somehow, my father had something to do with why Fortwright's military files were classified.

That was the part I still couldn't figure out—that and why Avesta would spill a secret he was using for blackmail to a perfect stranger? But it was the only link I could see, and my answer was obviously right. Whatever Avesta had said, Fortwright, whose service record Jenkins had a contact at the Pentagon trying to unclassify, lost his mind, quite literally.

All of which meant I had to get my mother out of this alive so my father could go to prison, and Archie's heart wouldn't be shattered.

Archie. And Ruth. I couldn't even try to unpack that right now.

The truck rolled to a stop in front of the open barn doors.

The jet fuel truck was inside, Ruth McClellan handcuffed to the steering wheel in the cab.

Dan Fortwright, outfitted in a fire suit with the hood and helmet hanging down his back, was running a stand mixer in the front corner. A huge one, like the one Erma had at the governor's mansion.

I stepped through the door with my hands out and visible, the sharp stab of fuel and something I couldn't place right away practically singeing my nose hairs.

"I'm sorry it had to come to this," Fortwright said, not looking up. "My issue isn't with you ladies. But that cowardly bastard Stevenson has more armed guards today than the president, and your father is missing." He shut the mixer off and turned to face me. "My mission isn't complete until they pay for what they did."

"Believe me when I say there's nobody walking the Earth who knows more what a horrible human being Chuck McClellan can be than me," I said. "But...letting anyone push you to take another life, Mr. Fortwright, is giving up far too big a piece of yourself. That's what the justice system is for."

"The justice system is going to work for me, when there's no record anywhere in Washington of what happened to my brother? To our friends? When they trained us to be murderers and then sent us somewhere we had no business being, and covered it up when people died? My brother didn't even get a goddamn military funeral! We left him, we left all of them, in Tehran. And if it hadn't been for him..." His eyes went to the windshield of the truck, and to Ruth behind it, her blue eyes wide and dark with terror, tears streaming down her cheeks. "We wouldn't have ever ended up there."

"We didn't know, Faith. Nobody knew. Even Chuck couldn't do that." Ruth's voice was high with panic, muffled behind the glass.

Clearly she'd heard more of the story than I had.

Fortwright turned back to me.

"My father had no authority over the movement of US troops, even when he was the governor," I said gently.

"They were wearing American gear. Uniforms. Helmets. Guns. It was dark out. We thought they were US National Guard. We were near the Ukrainian embassy." He opened a tall silver canister and started scooping a foul-smelling, jelly-looking substance into it. Homemade napalm. Supercharged with jet fuel. In a fucking flamethrower.

Jim and I had been right about how much he hated the people he was after, it seemed. "It was an easy run. We were supposed to bring papers to drop off, along with a bug, of course, but we were out of the battle zone. The tallest guy, he spoke perfect English. Said they'd show us a back door."

His voice wasn't angry anymore. It was detached. Like he was disconnecting from the memory on purpose, for self-protection.

"They were fucking terrorists. Called us filthy American pigs." He screwed the base back onto the canister.

"Terrorists?" My eyes went back to my mother as he started filling a second container. "Surely not even the Governor would..."

She shook her head, her shoulders heaving with sobs.

"The people your father needed to keep the goddamn oil prices down didn't have honor," he said. "They didn't have a side. They just wanted guns. And money. The terrorists there are like the mafia here. They have the money to pay. And we were the perfect sitting ducks."

Christ. "I can't—Oh my God. I'm so sorry," I said.

"Thirteen days. They kept the four of us in a concrete and metal warehouse in a hundred-and-ten-degree heat. We ate bugs. Drank our own piss. And got the shit kicked out of us every day for refusing to give up our company's location. The US government refused to admit we were there. So on the fourteenth day, they brought a camera in. Had us give our names. Then went down the line. Smitty. Johnson. My baby brother. They cut their heads off. I felt the blade touch my neck before the door blew open." He sniffled, closing the second canister. "Two weeks it took those motherfuckers to get there to pick us up, and they were twenty minutes too late.

"They took out the whole cell and scooped up the tape, so nobody ever found out we were there. They sent me home, injured honorable discharge." He patted his leg. "Nineteen broken bones, including my hip socket. It still gives me trouble when I have to climb a long hill or swim any kind of distance. I got here to find the state had taken a third of my family's land to build an armory. I've wondered for months now if your father took the equipment that caused my brother's death from the armory they built on our land. Wouldn't that be some kind of bullshit? But I didn't put up too much fuss because someone had also mysteriously lifted every lien on the property my family had accumulated in fifty years of shit business decisions. Farm was mine, free and clear. And the world had changed while I was gone. Rich people wanted to build big houses on big lots just north of here. I'd learned a lot about exotic plants that love the heat while I was in the Middle East. I got a computer and a modem and ordered a few." He attached a hose to the tanks. "I bred them. Cross-bred them to new varieties. Went around and knocked doors. Before long, those broads in the garden club were offering me blowjobs to create something for them I wouldn't sell to their neighbors." He chuckled. "Fucking nuts, right? Anything to win."

I slid my foot backward.

"Mr. Fortwright, I'm so sorry for your loss. For your pain. I promise, if you'll give me that hose, I will make them pay."

"You know as well as I do there's not a judge in this state who will send Chuck McClellan and Shep Stevenson to prison." He waved an arm in a "back up" gesture. I jumped back about four feet. A stream of goo hit the dirt floor when he squeezed the trigger, erupting immediately into flames and burning hot enough for me to feel it ten feet away. My eyes went to the truck.

"There's a bomb attached to it," he said, his eyes going to the clock on the wall. "You have four minutes and change to get her out of there and get both of you far enough away from here to avoid the blast. I have a mission to complete, and either I'll die in the process or everyone will think I died in this explosion."

I opened my mouth to argue, and he raised one hand. "Save it," he barked, showing emotion for the first time since I'd walked in. "Even if you could get them convicted, prison is too good for them. They'll get the kind with a golf course and chef-prepared meals. Not the kind we did." He waved the hose like a wand. "They deserve an introduction to hell as they're on their way there."

My eyes skipped between him and my mother, weighing options. On one hand, his argument was perfectly logical. I hunt murderers for a living, and one thing it's taught me is that death is intimate. It's almost always a personal crime on some level. Most often the reasoning is either twisted or selfish, or maybe a little of both. But his was not. He was risking lethal injection to right a wrong that was so clear and egregious, I had trouble finding words to argue with him.

In the darkest parts of my soul, the ones that lived quietly under my sense of justice and need to do right, there was a Faith who would take that hose from him and turn it full blast on whoever was responsible for butchering my sister, and not bat a single eyelash or lose a millisecond of sleep. But part of what helped me keep her at bay was seeing what that kind of hatred could do to people. People like Dan Fortwright. This wasn't the evil monster I'd envisioned standing at those crime scenes the past few days—he was just a man, a good one in many ways, who had lived through an extraordinarily horrifying thing.

And that was how I could talk my way out of this.

"Mr. Fortwright, why did you call me here tonight?"

He didn't want to kill us—the bomb on the tanker truck was a simple distraction so I couldn't call anyone or follow him, not because he intended for anyone to die. He knew I'd save Ruth. Which meant he got no real benefit from having her here, either. Unless he thought we knew where Chuck was, I couldn't figure out why we were here at all. And thinking briefly about my mother and Archie, I had no trouble believing she'd give Chuck up to save her own skin. I wondered if their marriage had ever been about anything more than mutual convenience.

"I looked you up, after the first day you came here," he said. "You have honor, Miss McClellan. I'm well aware of the fact that one of the guards at Stevenson's place might get off a clean shot before I see them. If that happens..." He paused. Turned to a cabinet on the wall and pulled out a framed photo and an envelope. "You make sure my brother and our friends are honored. Your family owes it to mine."

Jesus. My fingers closed around the envelope and the frame automatically. They were all in desert camo fatigues, arms around one another, smiling. Fortwright shared the middle with a younger man who looked a lot like him.

I'd heard stories about suicide bombers, and I'd heard my grandfather tell his father's tales of Normandy on D-Day. But I'd never met anyone so calm about giving their life for something they believed was right.

"Mr. Fortwright, I'm begging you." I reached out my free hand. "Don't do this. Please. Your brother and his friends will have their heroes' burials. My father will pay for this. But you don't need to die for it. I know three dozen judges, half of them veterans. Throw yourself and this story on the mercy of the state. Arrangements can be made."

I was pulling words out of my ass, with no idea if any of them were true. What I knew for sure was that my father had made more backroom deals in his lifetime than he'd signed bills in front of TV cameras, and this situation was impossible. Our system only works when people don't decide to take the law into their own hands.

But the government was responsible for Dan Fortwright's ability to take another human life. And my father and his friends were at least partly responsible for the loss of his brother. Somewhere, there had to be a solution that wasn't simply the death chamber in Huntsville or taking a bullet from a bodyguard.

Didn't there?

He stared at me, his hand going slack on the hose. Pinched his lips. Took the photo back.

"They died for their country. And we were just dropping off papers."

I made it half a step forward, my eyes on the hose and the canisters, when the engine in the fuel truck roared to life, shaking the dirt floor of the barn and rattling the soaring wood walls.

The truck rolled forward, knocking Dan Fortwright to the dirt and crushing his left leg.

I screamed, throwing my hands up as strong, wiry arms looped around my waist from behind, pulling me to the ground.

"Ruth, stop!" I couldn't even tell if it came from me or from Candace Fortwright, who struggled out from under me and crawled across the dirt floor of the barn. "Dammit, Danny, what have you done?"

"We have to go." I moved to the door of the truck, pulling my keys to uncuff my mother from the steering wheel. "There's a bomb."

"No," Fortwright croaked. "Made that up."

Tears streaming, Candace stroked his head. "He kept sending me away to shopping and spa stuff, and then this morning, my coffee tasted funny. I woke up about five minutes ago." She turned her eyes to Ruth and me, then back to Dan. "Why?"

He looked at us in turn, then at his pancake-squashed leg, and fainted.

41

It took an actual act of Congress to have Lance Corporal Caleb Fortwright, Sergeant Alex Diaz, and Corporal Dale Givens recognized as casualties of the Iraq war.

But there were more than a few congressmen among the people who owed Chuck McClellan favors.

Archie and I turned the files on the weapons trade I'd stolen from my father's office over to Jenkins, since technically the items traded were US government property entrusted to the state of Texas.

Jenkins served an arrest warrant during Sunday breakfast.

Chuck was back home by lunch with an ankle monitor, but Archie and Lieutenant Boone know people in high places, too. An old golfing buddy of Boone's who served in Iraq and sits on the state bench in Waco pulled a few strings with the trial. The current Texas Attorney General is a purple heart recipient. He took special purview of the case and the investigation in a press conference on the steps of the capitol, telling just enough of the story to spark outrage all over the internet and calls for investigation from Austin and Washington alike.

Gonzalez and I picked Jimmy Sewell up on money laundering and theft of a firearm charges after Sergei's drivers brought him and his top lieu-tenants back from Cancun—he'd asked Rickers to hide him when Avesta disappeared, and Beau was smart enough to send the driver Avesta had used along for the vacation so the police couldn't interview him. Jenkins met us at the Travis County jail with a federal warrant to stack on top of the state one.

And Shep Stevenson turned state's evidence against Chuck in exchange for the promise of house arrest on his farm outside San Antonio. Jenkins hadn't been able to prove Stevenson did much but look the other way, and while I couldn't excuse ignoring what my father had done, I was glad Fortwright hadn't gotten to him before I got to Fortwright.

Dan's leg took five hours of reconstructive surgery, and then three more two days later when he developed compartment syndrome. But he was recuperating at a rehabilitation hospital for veterans, and I'd heard from Candace that a private psychiatric facility would be his home for a while until an evaluation of his mental state at the time of the murders could be determined.

She had taken the truck to Collins's home the morning he died, because she'd found a blueprint of his house in the study with the routes to the bedroom marked, and thought Dan was sending her away on pampering trips because he was cheating on her.

"Here's to long days doing good work." Archie raised a Lone Star bottle to Graham's Tecate, my margarita, and Ruth's dirty martini. "The messy ones are always the hardest."

"But somehow they often feel like the ones where we make a real differ-ence in the world." I clinked my glass to Graham's a second time, reaching for his hand across the table.

Ruth reached for Archie's about the same time, and I kept myself from flinching by watching his face soften into the sappiest smile I'd ever seen on it.

I didn't get it. I wasn't sure I'd ever get used to it.

But I loved seeing him happy, and Lord knew I wasn't in a position to judge.

"I'd like to say something else." Before I lost my nerve. I sucked in a deep breath and squared my shoulders, turning to face Graham in the booth and taking both of his hands in mine.

"I only ever had one good example of what a marriage should be in my life, and my grandparents both passed on before I was out of school," I said. "For the most part, I've never believed there was a good reason to saddle yourself to someone legally."

Graham's eyes widened, and his Adam's apple bobbed with a hard swallow.

"More than that, though, I've never thought for one second that there could be a good reason to stick anyone I loved with my family. I've fought to keep my personal life, such that it's been, far away from my parents. Not just to protect you, but me, too. My..." I paused for breath. "My father would never accept you as my husband, Graham. And I'm ashamed to admit that I didn't know how to tell you that, so I've been cutting you off and avoiding this topic for a while now."

There went the Adam's apple again.

"Because I'm black?" He didn't look at anyone but me.

"Partly." I flinched as the word slid between my teeth. "But also because you aren't rich, your mother was single, and you don't belong to the right country club. There are a lot of ways he would spend the rest of his life trying to make you feel like you were something he needed the help to scrape off the bottom of his thousand-dollar wingtips every chance he could wrangle. I didn't want that for you. Because, as usual, he is wrong. It's me that's not good enough for you."

This was difficult enough to say to Graham without thinking about the fact that we had an audience. But it needed to be said. Liquid courage, and all that.

"Don't I get a say in that?" Graham asked.

"No." I smiled and squeezed his hand.

His mossy eyes narrowed, his mouth twisting to one side. "I beg to differ." He pulled in a deep breath. Sighed it back out. "Look, do you not understand that I've thought about this?" he asked. "I knew what I was getting into the first time I set eyes on you and tried to lock my heart down so many years ago. A white girl. And not just any white girl, either. The Governor's daughter. No matter what people say about progress, I know just how shitty some folks are going to be about us."

"But it's not just some people, Graham, it's me," I blurted. "Or at least, it was me. For part of my life—a part of my life I was old enough at the time to remember, sitting here today, I thought like those people." My voice hitched on the last word and I paused for a breath, blinking. "I had been told since I could talk, by everyone I was supposed to respect, that we were better. Superior to other humans because of our name, because of the Governor's power, because of money. And because we were white." A tear slipped off my lashes despite my best efforts. "I couldn't let you ask me because I don't deserve for you to love me, Graham. I certainly don't deserve to be your wife."

He started shaking his head before I stopped talking. "Whoa. I can sort of believe you when you say you remember thinking that before, but not for a second will I believe you think it today."

"Of course I don't. But that doesn't fix the fact that I did once."

His eyes softened. "Is that what this is all about? Baby, as we learn better, we do better. Hell, I grew up being taught that my only real value was on a ball field because I was black. That my fastball was what made me worthy, not my brain. And that's just as wrong as the way you felt, isn't it?"

"That's not the same." I could tell looking at him that he knew that. I could also see a love purer than any I'd ever known so plain on his face I wanted to cry. I wanted to fall into his arms and bask in that for the rest of my days.

It felt selfish.

But the pull was so strong I couldn't move away.

"I'm realizing that life is too short to walk away from people you love when you know they love you back." My eyes flicked to Ruth and Archie for half a blink. "So I will spend the rest of my days trying to make you feel as special and cherished as you make me feel every time you look at me. I will stand beside you, behind you, or in front of you, as you need, and we will face every horrifying and beautiful thing this world has to offer—together. If you'll have me." I pulled in a shuddering breath, ignoring the squeak my mother let out across from me and Archie's quick shushing.

"I'll always love having you for a partner, McClellan. In everything," Graham said. "Always."

The kind of free, unconditional love pouring from Graham's gaze was foreign to me. It wasn't predicated on anything. He knew everything—every shameful, ridiculous thing—about me and my dysfunctional family baggage, and he was still looking at me like that. Still wanted me for exactly who I was. I gripped his fingers tighter.

"Graham Thomas Hardin, will you marry me?"

He pulled his hands free and folded me into a crushing kiss that was all the answer I needed.

Nowhere to Hide: Faith McClellan #4

A series of brutal pig slaughters brings Faith McClellan to a small town where a ruthless serial killer prepares to butcher their first human victim...

When Texas Ranger Faith McClellan is called to investigate a series of gruesome small-town murders, she doesn't expect to find a slaughtered pig—but she agrees to take the case, suspecting the latest murder was targeted at Kelsey Marie, the teenage handler of the victim.

Kelsey Marie is smart, pretty, and successful, supporting her family's lavish lifestyle with her highly lucrative YouTube channel. She's also the target of massive online hate, with dozens of threatening messages sent to her channel each day.

When the killer carves up their first human victim, Faith knows she's running out of time—but with little evidence, too many suspects, and a serial killer who outsmarts her at every turn, the odds are stacked up against her.

And when the killer uploads the filmed murders to Kelsey Marie's YouTube channel, Faith will risk everything to save the teenager's reputation...and her life.

ACKNOWLEDGMENTS

I'm not sure this is actually the most difficult book I've ever written, but it was definitely written during the most turbulent time, which makes it feel that way. There were many points this past year at which I struggled to remember why what I do matters in a world where so many were facing danger, illness, and hardships every day.

Cue my incredible readers, who wrote me more often than in any year prior to tell me that my stories were giving them escape, my characters taking the place of distant friends, the mysteries providing distraction. Thank you—every single one of you—for your kind words that meant more to me than you will ever know. It is entirely possible that without them, you wouldn't be holding this book. I hope it's your favorite yet.

Fire scenes and arson investigations are tricky, y'all, and while I'm thankful to Google for providing information and case files on demand, my thanks go out to my Uncle Marcus, who taught me more than I realized by sharing his fire service war stories throughout my childhood, and to my friend Shawn A. Cosby, who was wonderfully patient and helpful in sharing his expertise when I needed help with cremation details.

Thanks also to Samantha Glass for lending her sharp eyes and forensic expertise to an early advance copy and confirming that I had all the science down, as well as offering kind words that let me know I got this one right.

Thanks to my agent, John Talbot, for talking me off a couple of ledges during this crazy year—I am so glad I have you in my corner, John.

Randall Klein, thank you again for making this a book I'm proud to share with readers. You have a true gift, and I am so lucky to get to work with you.

Andrew, Amber, Keris, and the rest of the Severn River Publishing team:

thank you for your patience and understanding as I battled illness that made me miss deadlines this year, and for caring more about the quality of the work than the timeline. Y'all make the sometimes challenging parts of the publishing industry so much easier and more fun.

Brian Shea and Tara Laskowski, writer friends whose talent inspires me and whose encouragement helped me get this one across the finish line—thank you for being there.

Last but never least: Justin and my littles. We made it, Walker family! Thank you for picking up the slack with everything from grocery shopping to laundry when I was sick and then again when I was frantically trying to meet my already-extended deadlines. I love you to the moon and back, and am looking forward to all our next adventures.

As always, any mistakes are mine alone.

ABOUT THE AUTHOR

LynDee Walker is the national bestselling author of two crime fiction series featuring strong heroines and "twisty, absorbing" mysteries. Her first Nichelle Clarke crime thriller, FRONT PAGE FATALITY, was nominated for the Agatha Award for best first novel and is an Amazon Charts Best-seller. In 2018, she introduced readers to Texas Ranger Faith McClellan in FEAR NO TRUTH. Reviews have praised her work as "well-crafted, compelling, and fast-paced," and "an edge-of-your-seat ride" with "a spider web of twists and turns that will keep you reading until the end."

Before she started writing fiction, LynDee was an award-winning jour-nalist who covered everything from ribbon cuttings to high level police corruption, and worked closely with the various law enforcement agencies that she reported on. Her work has appeared in newspapers and magazines across the U.S.

Aside from books, LynDee loves her family, her readers, travel, and coffee. She lives in Richmond, Virginia, where she is working on her next novel when she's not juggling laundry and children's sports schedules.

Sign up for LynDee Walker's reader list at
severnriverbooks.com/authors/lyndee-walker
lyndee@severnriverbooks.com